I0725173

WORKS BY J. W. JUDGE

Fiction

Watch Party

Casual Business with Fairies

Vulcan Rising (The Zauberi Chronicles, Book 1)

Seeking Sanctuary (The Zauberi Chronicles, Book 2)

Forging Bonds (The Zauberi Chronicles, Book 3)

The Murder Tree (A Short Story)

Non-Fiction

Write Your Novel One Day at a Time: How to Write a Novel While Having a Career, a Family, and a Life

A GOOD WAY TO WIND UP DEAD

J. W. JUDGE

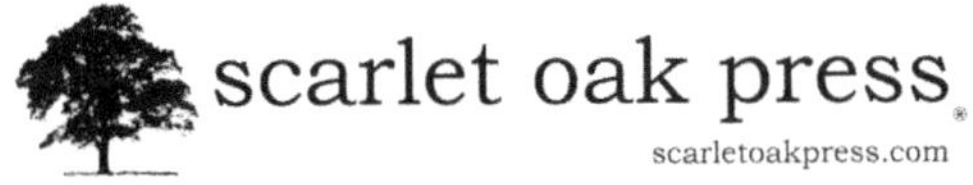

scarlet oak press

scarletoakpress.com

ISBN: 978-1-954974-25-8 (Paperback)

ISBN: 978-1-954974-26-5 (eBook)

Library of Congress Control Number: 2025905876

Published by Scarlet Oak Press (scarletoakpress.com)

A GOOD WAY TO WIND UP DEAD

Every man must do two things alone;
he must do his own believing
and his own dying.

Martin Luther

CHAPTER 1

IRREVERENT ABOUT THE DEAD

SAM

Sam took a last drag of her cigarette, held her breath an extra beat, and exhaled slowly. As Sheriff Tompkin's Suburban ground to a stop in the gravel driveway, she waited for him on the front porch. When the sheriff opened his door, Sam crouched down to put the butt out on one of the dusty boards and dropped it into the brass spittoon that had adorned that porch for several generations of Colemans who smoked and dipped.

Tompkins was already mopping his forehead by the time his boots scuffed the bottom step. "It's hotter than hell's pepper patch out here."

Sam nodded. "You know what I like about you, Sheriff?"

He waited to let her answer the rhetorical question. And he didn't come further than the steps because he hadn't been invited yet. Vampires and polite Southern folk had that in common.

"When all the other law enforcement officers have gone to rubber-soled shoes, you still wear those ropers every day. And even though all your deputies have baseball caps now, you've still got that Stetson. I bet it's sitting on the passenger seat right now, ain't it?"

"You really gonna play games with me while your daddy's laying in there dead as a doornail, Samantha Ray?"

"He ain't going nowhere."

Tompkins looked down at his feet and shook his head. "It's not right for you to be irreverent about the dead like that."

"A lot of things that weren't right happened under this roof. That's a big part of why the old man is dead right now."

"I thought when you called me, you said he killed his self."

Sam squinted, deciding how to answer. She met the sheriff's eyes as she kept him standing out in the blistering sun. "In one sense, he did. But in another, very real sense, I killed him."

He frowned. "You just gonna come right out like that and say it?"

"I think it's important that we be honest with each other."

He chewed on that for a minute, clearly unaccustomed to people being forthright with him. And to be fair, Sam didn't intend to be totally straight with him about everything either, but she could at least set a positive tone for their business relationship.

"Where's Desiree?" he asked.

"She lit out for the territories."

"You didn't kill her?" The sheriff showed his concern by dropping his friendly tone.

"She'll be fine as long as she does what she was told and makes herself scarce."

"Your brothers?"

"Dunno. Haven't seen them today."

"They know about this yet?" He gestured past her into the house.

Sam shook her head. "We gonna stand here playing 'Twenty Questions,' or should we get to it?"

"After you."

She led the way into the house. Daddy was lying exactly where she'd left him, which was to be expected since she'd put three holes in him not that long ago. Two in the chest and one in the nether regions. He had shot first, but it hardly mattered. She'd accepted the contract on him, so that first shot had been the last desperate act of an already dead man.

Tompkins surveyed the room with one hand on his hip and the other resting on the grip of his handgun. "Geez Louise, girl." After getting the lay of the room, he took a pen and nudged open the bag of money sitting on top of Daddy's lunch plate. He turned his head and raised an eyebrow at Sam.

"Business transaction. We didn't see eye-to-eye on it."

"Uh-huh. Where'd you get that cash?"

"At the gettin' place."

He set his jaw, not caring for her tone. "If my eyes don't deceive me, I saw your daddy's name written down on a piece of paper in that bag."

"You might ought to be more careful about letting your eyes stray into things they don't need to see."

"Now, listen here, Samantha Ray. If you go to threate—"

She waved him off. "I ain't threatening you. Threats are for folks who don't intend on actually doing anything." That second part wasn't strictly true. Threats had their place, but she'd made her point, anyway.

Sheriff Tompkins looked willing to move on to other things for now. "That bullet hole in the table been there long? Looks like it came from under the table."

"He took a shot at me. The first shot, if you want to know."

He nodded and took on the posture of a much-relieved man. "I can write this up as self-defense. That's gonna be a lot easier to sell than suicide."

Sam shrugged. "You do whatever you need to do. Don't much matter to me." When her phone rang, she pulled it out of her back pocket and saw Buddy was calling. As she swiped to answer, she stepped out onto the front porch, pulling the door closed behind herself. "What?"

"Well, good morning to you too, Sunshine."

"It's afternoon, Buddy. What do you want? I'm in the middle of something."

"I got a problem."

She sighed. "How bad?"

"I might have killed somebody last night."

"You either did or you didn't."

"It's not that simple," he whined.

There was a part of her that begrudged being her older brothers' keeper. But there was a much larger part that knew she was better off running the show. They'd both fall in line, though Jeb might take more convincing than Buddy.

"Why don't you quit talking in riddles and tell me what happened?"

"You might find it hard to believe."

She considered saying, *I don't believe most of what comes out of your mouth anyway*. Instead, she answered, "Try me."

"So I was on I-22 driving the tractor-trailer. Patrick was with me."

"Buddy, we don't do deliveries ourselves. That's what we hire the help for and why we pay them really well."

"We wasn't delivering anything. Just out riding around. Anyway, this lady steps right out in front of us. Something was super weird about her. Like she was see-through or something. I jerked the wheel to the right, but I dunno if I missed her or not."

"Did you stop and check?"

"Huh-uh."

"Did you call anybody?"

"I'm calling you now."

"Well, now is like twelve hours later. Why did it take you so long?"

It took him a long time to answer, and she knew the truth even as he started telling the story.

"I ... uhh ... we was kinda messed up. We'd been partying, so I didn't really have a clear recollection of things until we watched the dashcam video this morning. And Sam... ?"

"Yes?" Her voice was clipped with impatience.

He whispered, "I think she was a ghost."

"Great! That's the best news you've given me."

"Why's that?"

'Cause you can't kill a ghost, dummy. "Think about it. We'll talk later. Also, you need to come home." She hung up the phone.

"Everything alright?" Sheriff Tompkins asked.

"You've met my brothers before."

He nodded. "How are they gonna take this?"

That wasn't something she had put much thought into yet. "Buddy'll most likely disappear into a cloud of his drug of choice for a couple of weeks." There was no doubt about that. It took her a bit longer to figure on her oldest brother. "Jeb might try to assert himself as what he thinks of as his rightful place as the head of the family, mostly on account of he has a penis. I will disabuse him of that notion."

Tompkins frowned and rubbed the stubble on his cheek. "We can't go having a civil war over this. I'll have to intervene if bodies start piling up."

Sam scoffed. "War? There won't be no war, Sheriff. A kerfuffle, maybe. A commotion, at worst."

He didn't hide his skepticism.

Tires skittered across the gravel drive. The sheriff looked out the front window. "Coroner. I'll go meet with him before he comes in. Make sure he understands what happened. And speaking of, you and I have the same understanding I had with your daddy?"

She looked him directly in the eyes. It was important that she had his support so she could start lining up everyone else. "Nothing's changed, Sheriff."

He looked down at the bullet-punctured body on the floor and grunted. "We'll see."

As he stepped out of the house, Sam pulled her phone back out, scrolled down to her last text to Jeb and typed, "Come to Daddy's house. ASAP."

CHAPTER 2

PAY THEIR RESPECTS

SAM

BUDDY WAS A SOBBING MESS BY THE TIME JEB DROVE up. Not wanting to hear a grown man cry any more, Sam sat in a weather-worn rocking chair on the front porch, smoking the last cigarette in her pack.

Jeb said, "You got to be pretty dedicated to smoking to be doing it in this heat."

Sweat trickled down her back in agreement. "You smoke."

He grinned and pulled a blue and chrome device out of his pocket. "Nah. I vape. And I can do that most anywhere, inside or out."

"You know people hate you vapers for that, right?"

"You know what they say, 'Haters gonna hate.'" Jeb shrugged and immediately segued into another topic. "Is Desiree cooking tonight?"

"Probably not. I need to tell you something." *Wish I had another smoke handy.*

He jerked his head toward the front door. "What's that noise?"

"Buddy's upset. Sit down. I need to tell you something."

"Is he crying?"

"Yes."

"I don't think he's cried since that dog of his got run over. You remember that? Kind of looked like a paint horse." He was still looking at the door, like he sensed the danger looming over the conversation, but was afraid to take it head-on.

"Jeb. Sit down."

"Just tell me what it is." His tone was flat.

There wasn't any sugarcoating it. "Daddy's dead."

He blinked at her a couple of times as if waiting for a punchline, then choked out the word, "How?"

"It's complicated." Sam's throat constricted as she said it. The emotions that finally tugged at her didn't find their roots in what she'd done, but in the effect it would have on her brothers. They didn't have the same reasons to hate Daddy that she did. He hadn't done to them what he did to her. Presumably. And it's not like she could ask, *Hey, did Daddy diddle you, too?*

Finally, he looked at her, waiting for her to elaborate on her answer.

"He shot at me first and missed. I got the best of him."

"How's that complicated?"

"He had sent me to the Murder Tree to check it. I found a bag of money with his name on it. When I got back, I showed it to him, and he drew down on me. Thought I was going to kill him." *I was.* She didn't bother Jeb with that detail.

He walked over to the handrail at the edge of the porch and leaned against it with his back to her. "I reckon he had good reason to think that. If you took the money, you was obligated to do it."

Sam tried out a defense she had assembled. "I couldn't leave it there for someone else to pick up and try to take him out. I wanted to show him that someone was coming for him. He didn't give me a chance to explain."

The story might work as long as Desiree took Sam's threat to heart and didn't resurface.

Jeb nodded. "He *was* getting a little paranoid."

She didn't show her relief.

"Where is he now?"

"Funeral home," she said.

He turned around with a surprised expression. "Just like that? No autopsy or nothing?"

"Sheriff Tompkins came out. We have an understanding."

"You told him what happened?"

"More or less," she said.

Jeb's expression changed, like he'd come to a sudden realization. After he stood there clinching his jaw for a couple of minutes, Sam said, "What?"

"You ought not to have been handling all this without me."

"Why is that?" She stood up, getting ready for what she anticipated would be the second showdown of the day.

"Because I'm the oldest. That makes me in charge."

She smirked and said the next four words slowly, emphasizing each one on its own merits. "Like hell it does."

His eyes narrowed. "It's my turn now, Samantha Ray."

"We ain't the royal family. This here is a meritocracy. And the only thing you've ever been better at than me is getting high and getting arrested. That's why I was Daddy's right hand."

Anger flashed across Jeb's face. "Nah. You was his choice 'cause you let him stick his—"

Sam was on him with a knife to his throat before he knew what was happening. His eyes were as big as fish bowls. "Finish that sentence. If you think you can get it out before I paint this porch red. It needs some touching up anyway."

She felt something against her ribs.

The nose of Jeb's pistol.

The screen door burst open. "You two knock it off. You's always fighting." Buddy stumbled toward them as the words tumbled out of his mouth, a little sloppier than normal. He smelled like the whole liquor cabinet.

Sam pulled her knife away from her brother's neck and slipped it into its sheath on her hip. In exchange, he dislodged the gun from her ribs. She hadn't quite realized how hard he'd been pressing it against her. She winced at the sharp pain left in its wake.

Buddy flung his arms around their shoulders. "Family hug. Y'all make up now."

"We'll finish this later," she warned.

His curt nod told her he didn't have plans to let this go so easily. She slipped out of the unwanted hug and went in search of another pack of cigarettes. She needed to think.

If Jeb was going to create a rift over this, she'd better figure out who was on her side of the line. She had the distinct advantage of having been involved in all of Daddy's business for the last few years. Everyone who mattered knew and trusted her, which wasn't to say they liked her. Sam's blood ran a little hot, and she wasn't much to look at. She knew that. You couldn't hear "butter face" — as in, *nice body but her face* — whispered behind your back that many times without picking up on it. It shouldn't have mattered for business stuff, but it did. A pretty face would've made the medicine go down easier when she had to raise a heavy hand.

She wasn't nearly as likable as Jeb. He had a genuine *aw shucks* air about him that attracted people like a magnet. It didn't hurt that people remembered him helping Walker County High School get to the playoffs in football and baseball his last couple of years there. And more importantly, they'd beat Jasper. Never mind that it all happened a decade ago.

If you asked Jeb, he'd tell you those were the best years of his life. Sam thought that sentiment was fairly pathetic. She had ambitions, and not only because nothing in her past was worth wallowing around in. One thing was certain. None of her dreams had her being ground under the heel of Jeb or anyone else.

After Sam had shuffled through every drawer in her bedroom and moved every stray piece of paper and article of clothing without finding a pack of cigarettes, she snatched her waist bag — the one Daddy kept calling a fanny pack — and the keys to her truck and headed downstairs.

Buddy sat forward in the recliner, cradling his head in his hands and crying quietly.

Jeb paced like a panther. "Where are you going?" It was a demand, not an inquiry.

"Out," she said, brushing through the living room and letting the screen door slam behind her.

It popped back open as she skipped down the front porch steps.

"Hey, we got family business to attend to."

Sam whirled around. "No, *we* don't. I'll meet with Stan and Nick tomorrow and make sure everything is sorted."

A cloud of confusion passed over Jeb's face. "Who are Stan and Nick?"

"Exactly. That's why *we* don't have family business."

Confusion became blustery anger. Jeb wouldn't let his little sister show him up. She'd been smarter than him her whole life and had taken every opportunity to flaunt it. She'd paid dearly for it, too.

"You ain't said where you was going."

"I'm out of cigarettes."

Satisfied that he'd forced her into giving him an answer, he instructed, "Bring back some chicken with you."

Sam shook her head. "You act like you never been around when somebody died before. Half the county'll be by in the next couple hours. And every one of them will be bringing food. They gotta pay their respects. You can pretend like you're in charge for a bit. Keep track of who the casserole dishes belong to."

She smiled brashly and pulled herself up into her truck. Jeb had started hollering again, but she cranked the engine and the music to drown him out. It didn't take much to get his goat. It was hardly even fun anymore.

CHAPTER 3
DIFFERENT KIND OF TOURIST

SAM

SAM PULLED OPEN THE FRONT DOOR AT THE Warehouse and slipped in. She caught the bartender's eye right away. It was still early enough that the place's population was somewhat sparse. Someone Sam didn't recognize sat at the corner of the bar to her right, so she went to the other end.

"Naked Pig?" Jake asked.

"Might as well pour two of them. The first one won't be around long enough for its sibling to get warm."

When Jake brought back two frothy glasses whose contents were more malty than hoppy. That suited Sam. She flicked her chin toward the far end of the bar. "Who's that cat?" She didn't bother lowering her voice.

"Tourist."

"Tourist? He get lost on his way to the beach?"

The bartender shook his head. "Different kind of tourist. He's got questions about Valerie."

"Don't we all," Sam granted. She took her glasses of beer and headed to a booth.

Jake said to her back. "Sorry to hear about your daddy."

Without turning, she raised one of the glasses in acknowledgment. "No, you're not. Nobody is. He was a salty old bastard who ran this county with a heavy hand."

"You shouldn't speak ill of the dead, Sam."

She set her beers on the table and turned around. "I'll take my chances. He did enough ill in this life. I don't think he saved any for the next one."

"Not for him. It's for you."

Once she was in the booth, Sam dropped her waist bag on the table so she could feel the phone buzz if anyone texted or called. She slouched, closed her eyes, and leaned her head against the back of the seat. There were a thousand things that needed doing, and not one of them was going to be easy.

Something jostled the table, prompting her to open her eyes. The tourist was helping himself to a seat across from her.

"What the actual hell do you think you're doing?"

He plopped a handheld recorded onto the table. "Do you mind?" The tourist flashed a practiced grin at her with a sense of expectation.

That smile must have opened plenty of doors for him. And dropped some skirts too, for that matter.

"You're not from around here, are you?" Sam said.

"What gave me away?" Again with the smile.

Sam finally sat up. She looked at him for a long minute without changing her expression. "You lack propriety."

"Whoa! That's not a word I expected to hear."

She raised an eyebrow. "'Cause you thought we're a bunch of rednecks down here who don't know no big words." She gave the last half of the sentence of a heavy drawl.

The tourist at least had the decency to look abashed. "Right. Sorry."

"Whatever. Turn the recorder off or get up. I'm inclined to throw you out regardless. I've got some mulling things over to do."

He reached over to his recorder and clicked off the button with a red dot. "I'm Chase, by the way."

She nodded. "Well, Chase, now that we've established you're not from here, how about you tell me where you are from?"

"Philly."

"And why are you here?"

"I kind of thought I would be the one asking all the questions, seeing as I'm the reporter."

"Looks like you were mistaken. First impression says you're the kind of reporter who gets run all over by tough interviews. And since you're a reporter, I guess I need to say that nothing I say is on the record. Ever."

"So … I'm not a reporter exactly. I'm a podcaster. So it's kind of the same thing. Do you know …" His question trailed off.

"Yes, I know what a podcast is, you condescending carpetbagger."

He wandered through the silence for a minute before saying, "I usually have a better rapport with folks than this."

"To be fair, I'm probably a little more ornery than most folks."

Chase cleared his throat. "I'm not sure what protocol dictates here. Am I supposed to agree with you or not?"

Sam pushed her second beer across the table. "Peace offering."

Chase placed a hand on the glass, but Sam didn't let go quite yet. "I want you to know this is literally the nicest thing I've done for anyone all day, for whatever that says about me."

"Oh, you can't be all bad. What's the worst you could've done today?"

Shot Daddy in his chest and then in his balls and stood there watching the life bleed out of him. Sam deflected. "You never said what you're here for."

"Right. So, you know the missing woman?"

"Valerie Wilson."

He pointed at her. "Yes. Wait. Did you know her?"

"Do. Not did. Don't talk about her like she's dead. But, yeah. Walker County's a small place, and Jasper's smaller still." Despite her words, Sam had a pretty good idea that nobody was going to see Valerie alive again. People didn't go missing in Walker County and turn up fit as a fiddle a few weeks later. But saying it out loud seemed … too soon. "She was a few years ahead of me in school. Five-ish? Went off to college in Birmingham, then came back and married the doctor who used to be her pediatrician."

Chase's eyes bugged nearly out of his head.

Sam nodded. "It was pretty gross. He has kids about the same age as her. First wife couldn't have been happy about her replacement."

"How long ago was that?"

She made a noise that meant, *I don't know.* "A couple years, I guess. I don't really keep up with it all."

"Why are you telling me all this?"

"None of it's a secret. You're gonna hear it from somebody. At least, if I tell you, I know it ain't a hunting story."

Chase shook his head. "I don't know what that means."

Sam held her hands about shoulder width apart and slowly moved them outward. "Every time a hunter tells a story about some buck he killed, that buck seems to have more points and a bigger rack with each telling."

He nudged his recorder. "If you want to make sure I get the story right, why don't you let me record you?"

"Because I'm not going to be a part of whatever cloud of dust you stir up."

"I'm trying to get to the truth about what happened."

Sam's bark of laughter was sudden and cruel. "You're laying that on a little thick. You're trying to get a story and make some money off of it. Here's the problem." She leaned in and lowered her voice. "You being new in town, going around asking questions about a woman who's disappeared is a good way to wind up dead. Even the folks who've been running the *Daily Mountain Eagle* for a hundred and fifty years and know everybody in town are real careful about which hornets' nests they kick."

Chase stiffened. "Maybe that's why nobody has found her, because nobody's willing to ask to right questions. Maybe it'll take some new blood to get it done. Maybe you guys are all complicit in her disappearance because you won't do anything about it."

Sam pretended to take a hat off her head and hold it in front of her chest with both hands. "Thank you, Mr. Philadelphia man, for coming all the way down here to help us poor Southern folk to fix our problems. That's awful kindly of you."

He clenched his jaw and pushed himself out of the booth. "Whatever."

As Chase turned away, Sam said. "One more thing." He stopped and pivoted back to her. "Y'all."

"What?" he asked with a wrinkled forehead.

"*Y'all*, not *you guys*. Makes you stand out like ... a Yankee in a Southern bar."

He rolled his eyes and sauntered back to his spot at the bar, but not before snagging the beer she'd offered. It was just as well. Other people were starting to accumulate, and she was pretty sure she didn't want to be too closely associated with the true crime podcaster. She got some nods of mutual recognition from other patrons.

An old man she'd known all her life stopped by and patted her hand. She said, "Thanks, Mr. Tommy. But if you tell me he was a good man, I'll throw you out on your backside."

"You wouldn't hit an old geezer, would you?"

"The hell I wouldn't."

He laughed a deep belly laugh.

"Besides," she added, "I bet you still keep a .38 holstered at your back like you're some kind of outlaw."

Tommy put on as innocent a face as he could muster. "Sam, there's a sign on that door that says no guns in here. You know I'm a rule-abiding man." He gestured toward the bag on the table. "Should we do an inspection of that there fanny pack?"

"Not if you'd like to keep those bones intact."

He shook his head playfully. "You used to be such a sweet child, Samantha Ray. What happened?"

"I was never sweet. Y'all assumed I was because I'm a girl. Buddy has always been the sweet one in the family."

He patted her hand again and wandered back to his table of weathered miscreants. They all raised a beer to her. She returned the salute.

It was time to go. She hadn't done any of the thinking she'd come here to do, and her place in the booth was about to turn into a receiving line. She'd really rather not on account of she'd definitely make some regrettable quip if that happened. Not that she would regret it, but others would.

Sam cast an eye to the bar, where Chase sat people-watching. She sighed and grabbed a napkin and pen. She scratched some numbers down and gathered her stuff.

Avoiding the water rings, she put the napkin down on the bar in front of Chase. "If you get in a tight spot, call me."

He smiled a big, handsome smile. "I knew you'd come around to me."

"Hardly. To be clear, this isn't for social calls. This is in place of calling the police."

He looked surprised. "What would I hear if I asked around about you?"

"I think you'd find that folks are disinclined to answer a lot of questions about me and mine." With that, she headed out into the gathering darkness.

When her phone chirped at her, she reached into the bag

she'd secured around her waist. The text read, "Nice to meet you."

She shoved it back into her pack and strode toward her truck, where she was going to roll down the windows and blast some Charles Wesley Godwin loud enough to wake every hound between here and home.

CHAPTER 4
MAKING POLITE CONVERSATION

CHASE

CHASE STUCK AROUND FOR A WHILE MAKING POLITE conversation with anyone who sat near him. He got the sense that every interaction was like sticking his hand out to a strange dog to see if it would bite. Or perhaps he was the dog in this situation.

In the quiet intervals between chatting up locals, he pulled his Moleskin notebook out of his back pocket and jotted down notes. Names, descriptions, tidbits to remember people by. Aside from his conversation with the extraordinarily enigmatic woman he'd met first, he hadn't prodded anyone for information about his assignment. He'd realized only when he heard the old guy call her Samantha Ray that he hadn't even managed to get her name before she left. Tonight was about being a face that people started to recognize. Someone they became accustomed to at a minimum, comfortable with at best.

Tomorrow, the real work would begin. Official sources first: the police station, the sheriff's department, city hall, and even the local newspaper, though personal experience told him they'd be none too eager to cooperate. He would explain that they could collaborate, share information, that they served different audiences, so they had only things to gain by working together.

They would tell him to get lost, or whatever colorful colloquialism people in Alabama used in its place.

As he planned out his next day, Chase engaged in one of his favorite pastimes. Being a stranger in a strange town allowed him to indulge in people watching. It was harder to do uninterrupted in a place where people knew you and expected you to engage with them. Here, though, he was all but invisible.

"Who are you?" A gruff voice asked.

Not invisible after all.

He swiveled on his bar stool to discover a woolly mammoth behind him. It wasn't immediately clear whether the man was intentionally intruding on Chase's personal bubble or his gargantuan size lent itself to that reality.

"Chase. I'm new in town." He stuck out a hand to see whether the other man would shake it.

He did with a paw the size of a baseball mitt. "Oliver," he said with a smile that shifted to confusion. "I don't know why I said that. My mother doesn't even call me by that name. Or if she does, I know I done something and I'mma catch an earful."

"What do they call you then?"

"Shooter."

Between the live music and the dozens of patrons, it was hard to have a sustained conversation. Chase was nearly shouting to be heard, and he was watching Shooter's lips as much as listening for his words.

"Why do they call you that?"

Shooter shrugged. "That's what they been calling me since I was in Pampers. Nobody remembers why. My uncles say it's because I used to take my diaper off and piss on everything, but I don't know if that's true or not."

"You from here?"

"Nah." He used a thumb to point over his shoulder. Northish, if Chase had his bearings straight. "From the Free State of Winston County."

"The *what?*"

Shooter bellowed his response. "FREE. STATE. OF. WINSTON. COUNTY."

Beer breath poured over Chase.

"I heard you, but I don't know what means."

Realization dawned on Shooter's face, and he lowered his voice. "During the Civil War, Winston County was opposed to seceding and supported the Union. Even tried to secede from Alabama. Took to calling themselves the Free State of Winston County." He shrugged. "The name stuck."

A bar stool opened up beside Chase, and Shooter leaned against it.

"Huh," Chase said. "I thought you guys were all …"

"Racist?" Shooter supplied.

"That's not what I was going to say."

"No, but it's what you meant."

Chase was confused by Shooter's non-confrontational affect, which seemed like a peculiar contrast to the frankness of the conversation. But it felt like a conversation that should be quieter and not so open.

Not knowing what to say, Chase took a pull of his nearly room temperature beer.

Shooter continued where he'd left off. "I don't know whether they was racist or not. You can't never know another man's heart." While Chase registered that *can't* was pronounced *cain't*, Shooter kept talking. "There weren't many slaves in Winston County. Not much good farmland. Too rocky. But we got some beautiful sights up that way. I could show you sometime."

"What if I said, 'How about tomorrow?'"

Shooter tilted his head and looked down at Chase. "I'd ask what time."

"I'm a total stranger. Why would you do that?"

"You seem alright."

"You don't have work?"

"I'm not a nine-to-five kind of guy."

"What do you do?"

"Family business."

The answer was terse, unlike any other part of their conversation. Chase let it go, but he made a mental note.

Without any segue, the burly fellow asked, "Did you play ball? You're not a small dude. You must of played."

Chase looked Shooter up and down. "Compared to you, we're all little dudes."

"Truth," he acknowledged. "But for regular people, you're pretty good sized. I ain't regular people."

Chase said, "Outside linebacker in high school. Started a couple of years. But I wasn't anything special. You?"

"Played some college. Defensive tackle. But I wasn't much for school. Came back home and got to work. Been grinding ever since."

"I hear that. I went to school for journalism. Got out right as the world was changing. For better and worse, I guess. All the old media guys want to do things the way they always have — work the young folks like dogs and pay them hardly anything, like it's a privilege for us to work for them. So I gave that a middle finger pretty quick and joined a podcast outfit, trying to solve crimes. It doesn't pay all that well either, but at least I'm on the ground floor. If it takes off, I'll get a cut of it. If it busts …" Chase shrugged.

"Fight the powers that be," Shooter said matter-of-factly.

Chase did a double take. He definitely hadn't been expecting a Public Enemy reference. These folks were a constant reminder that he was going to have to reset his expectations.

"That what brings you to our fine little city?"

Chase nodded.

"The doctor's wife?"

Chase kept eye contact and nodded again.

"Best be careful. People don't usually disappear for no good reason, and the folks who disappear them don't take kindly to strangers snooping about."

"You're the second person to tell me that tonight."

Shooter didn't seem to be surprised. "Alright, then. I'm gonna go rejoin my people. Nice to meet you."

"Same."

Shooter turned to walk away, but swiveled back on the heel of his outsized work boot. Chase wondered briefly how many cows had to die to make a boot that would fit around this giant's calves. "You know the song 'You'll Never Leave Harlan Alive'?"

"Don't think I've heard it."

"Give it a listen tonight. Walker County ain't a far cry from Eastern Kentucky."

"Shooter, I've got to say, that sounds kind of like a threat." Even saying that out loud sent a flurry of butterflies through his belly.

Shooter smiled broadly, showing a mouthful of nearly perfect teeth. "I'm not the threatening kind. Just a big ole teddy bear. You'll want the Patty Lovelace version, by the way."

And that was that. He turned and weaved his way through the bustling throng, moving with a gentleness that belied his size. Chase looked at his watch. He ought to make his way back to the hotel. He had meetings to prepare for.

CHAPTER 5
VERY MUCH AN ACCIDENT

SAM

THE RECEPTIONIST SHOWED SAM INTO AN OFFICE that she always expected to be both nicer and tidier than it ever turned out to be. Accordion folders and stray papers littered every conceivable surface with an almost haphazard uniformity. The receptionist in her heels stepped through the room with practiced precision. Sam cringed with every step she made, hearing and feeling the crinkled carnage she narrowly avoided leaving in her wake.

The man Sam had always known as Mr. Davis rose from behind the desk. He stuck out a hand, which she gave an obligatory shake. "Sorry to hear about your daddy."

"I keep hearing that," she said dismissively and decided to test him. "How many cars and lake houses did his attorney fees buy you over the years?"

Mr. Davis eyed her warily. "At least one of each, I reckon." He came around the desk and gestured her to sit in one of two chairs. He took the other.

Sam took note of his ostrich-skin cowboy boots, and his *reckon* hadn't escaped her attention either. She wondered if he was from Texas or putting on a certain kind of airs. Cowboy boots weren't uncommon. She had a couple pairs. But when you wore ostrich, you were making a statement.

Mr. Davis cleared his throat. "I'm surprised to see you here without your brothers."

A fire kindled itself in Sam's belly. She had a pretty good idea of where this was going. "Why's that?"

"I assume you're here about the will and the businesses?"

"I am."

He nodded. "I figured Jeb and Buddy would be along for that."

Sam turned the chair so that it faced Mr. Davis more directly. She leaned forward, elbows on her knees. "I would've thought lawyers would be the ones to ditch their misogyny before everyone else. But I don't guess that's the case. I've been dealing with it from all Daddy's business associates, and I'll tolerate it from you … but only as long as I have to." A smirk crawled across Mr. Davis' face, further stoking her fire. "I don't need those no-account brothers to do what I have in mind to do. They don't know Daddy's business any better than they know the inside of a church. So for you to suggest that the men should be here to handle to the business dealings tells me that the Old Boys Club is still just that."

"Sam?"

"Yes, *Nick*."

"I thought the boys might take it better when I go over the contents of the will hearing things from me than you telling them. Same with the businesses."

He'd dumped a bucket of well water on her inferno. "Ah."

"So I'm in charge?"

"You are."

"Uh-huh." She sat back in the chair and scratched at her chin while she dialed back her temper. "Any way they could contest it?"

"There's not a lawyer in Jasper who would take that case.

And even if the boys found somebody in Birmingham, I expect Judge Pate and I could get on the same page pretty quickly."

"So my little temper tantrum was … ?"

"Entirely unnecessary," Nick said gently. "But understandable. Anger is a natural part of the grieving process, and it is very frequently misplaced. No skin off my back. I take worse scoldings from Tamera on a weekly basis."

From the desk outside his office, Tamera hollered, "I can hear everything y'all say. And I like her, so you better not let her go somewhere else."

"Even if she is super nosy," he said the last two words loudly, "Ms. Banks raises a good point. Once I administer the will, if you wish me to turn over your files to you or transfer them to someone else, I will do that. For that matter, you can have someone else administer the will."

Sam chewed on it for a minute. "What do you know about the family business?"

Nick took his time answering as well. "Your family settled these parts a long time ago. It's a pretty open secret what line of work the Colemans are in, aside from farming, of course. The term 'hillbilly hitmen' comes to mind."

Sam smirked at that nickname.

"But as for the specifics," he continued, "I know both as much and as little as necessary to keep from triggering any reporting requirements I have as an officer of the court. Does that satisfy you?"

"I think that's the most lawyer answer I've ever heard in my life."

"I thought it was somewhat more helpful than saying, 'It depends.'"

The conversation hit an uncomfortable lull until Nick said, "I hear no one has seen Marty Welker in a couple of days."

Sam was uncertain whether he was fishing for information or casually commenting on a matter of local interest, so she said,

"Wasn't he supporting some legislation that the coal companies weren't very enthusiastic about?"

"Indeed, he was." The lawyer nodded. Seemingly unrelated, he added, "Your daddy has some money left in my escrow account from his retainer. Eventually, that will be your retainer. But not yet. So if you'd like to keep having this conversation, I need something from you."

Sam tensed but tried not to show it. Although she hadn't yet lived a long life, past experience had taught her that when a man in a position of authority said he wanted something from you, the engagement of your fight-or-flight response wasn't far behind. And Sam didn't much care for flying.

"Do you have any cash on you?" he asked.

Sam wasn't going to walk very far down this road, but she would play along for now. She opened up the belt pack she had draped over her lap and pulled out a fistful of bills.

"Goodness! Have you never heard of a bank?"

She shrugged. "I've been preoccupied."

"Give me a couple of those."

"This is starting to feel like a shakedown," she complained.

"On the contrary, this is protection."

"Yeah, I've used that line too." Sam handed over a couple of bills.

"Good. Now I'm not only *a* lawyer, I'm *your* lawyer."

"Alright, then," she said noncommittally. "And that means what, exactly?"

"Have you seen the movie *Michael Clayton*?"

She shook her head.

"Well, never mind then. The point is, I'm the person you tell everything to — good, bad, or ugly. Don't lie to me and don't hide anything from me. Except, don't tell me what you're *going* to do. Only what you have done. Got it?"

"I think so."

"So ... back to our missing state representative. Know anything about that?"

Regardless of the last two minutes and that Daddy had managed to avoid any kind of legal trouble the entire time Mr. Davis had been his lawyer, she wasn't ready to fully trust him.

"I expect he'll wash up," she said coyly.

"And when he does, is that going to be a problem?"

"Not for me," she smirked. "What happened to him was very much an accident. Well ... the end result wasn't. But the way it happened was."

Nick tilted his head in curiosity. "Meaning?"

"He may have slipped and hit his head on a boulder while fly-fishing."

"Uh-huh. That sounds ... unfortunate." Nick stood up and shuffled back around to his desk. "Let's talk a little business. I need to meet with your brothers and go over the will and corporate documents with them so they understand how things come out."

"Which is what, exactly?"

"You own fifty-one percent of the companies; they split the other forty-nine percent evenly. So no matter what, you have control. Unless you sell any shares — don't do that. You get the house and the land. The bank accounts will be yours aside from distributions to be made to the boys and your step-mother."

"About her. She may not poke her head around any time soon."

"Did you ... please, tell me—"

"No. No. I just encouraged her to skedaddle after things ... uhh ... happened." It still wasn't altogether clear to Sam what she could and couldn't say. Not to mention that all of this was still pretty fresh. *Except Daddy. By now, he's cold as a cast-iron bra.*

"Do you want to be here when I meet with the boys?"

"You're damn right I do. This is like Jacob taking Esau's birthright and stealing his blessing, but better." Nick's dour expression indicated this was not the response he was looking for. She added glumly, "But if you think it's best, I could skip it."

He nodded.

"Could you at least video it for me so I can see their stupid faces?"

"I could, but I won't."

She grunted and pushed herself up out of her chair. "You're not a whole lot of fun."

"You're not paying me to be fun. You're paying me to keep you a free and unfettered woman."

CHAPTER 6
A PLUG OF COPENHAGEN

CHASE

A horn blared as Chase strode down the sidewalk that was nearly molten with heat. Summers in Philadelphia were bad enough. He had no idea what had led people to settle in here and stay. Beyond the heat, he'd almost been carried off by mosquitoes when he left the bar the night before. He looked at his watch for the date. *Almost Labor Day. Shouldn't summer have broken by now?*

The same horn screamed for his attention again. In his peripheral vision, Chase saw a red pickup truck keeping pace with him. He kept facing straight ahead. A primal section of his brain began evaluating exit strategies.

The sun's reflection bounced off the truck's window as it went down. A shrill cat-call came from within the cab.

In a heartbeat, Chase rolled his shoulders back, straightened his posture, and made a hard turn toward the truck. The driver braked and brought the truck to an immediate stop in the middle of the street.

"Feeling froggy?" Sam asked.

"What?" Chase felt like he could use a cartoonish shake of the head to clear his confusion.

"You look like you're ready to jump."

Chase smiled as the accumulated stress of the last minute bled off him.

"Hop in," she said. "I'll take you where you're going."

"It's only a couple of blocks."

"You're sweating like a madman. Get in the truck."

Chase didn't argue further. He edged around the nose and climbed in. The door made a thunk when he closed it, the way that only older vehicles do. "Nice ride."

"Thanks. Only ride I've ever owned — 1987 Chevy with a 454 big block."

Chase didn't know or care anything about trucks, but he knew enough about people to nod appreciatively.

"Cherry," Sam said.

"I'm sorry?"

"That's her name — Cherry."

"That seems appropriate," Chase said.

A car behind them honked impatiently. Sam showed them her middle finger but shifted the truck into first gear.

"One day in high school, a group of the baseball players were clustered around my truck after school. When I walked up, one of them stabbed an ice pick into the tire. Another one said, 'Hey, Samantha Ray, looks like somebody finally popped your cherry.' They got a pretty good laugh out of that."

"Oh, man. That sucks."

Sam shrugged. "They got the worst of it in the end."

"Oh?"

"The boy who said it, I kicked him in the nuts. He went down like a sack of concrete. Then I pulled the ice pick out of my tire, tripped the boy who'd done it. And while he was sprawled on the ground, I stood on his wrist while I stabbed the ice pick through his hand and pinned it to the asphalt."

Chase was dumbfounded and suddenly reconsidering his decision to get into a truck with someone who was all but a stranger. "No, you didn't," he said hoarsely, hoping she'd laugh and tell him it was a joke.

"I absolutely did." There was pride in her voice, too. Chase was confident he'd never met anyone like Sam before. "Got in a fair bit of trouble over it, though."

"Oh, I bet."

She laughed. "Not for the reason you think. By the time I changed my tire and got home, Daddy had already heard about it. He sent me to my Granny's house for her to deal with me. You know what she said?"

"I truly can't imagine."

"She sat me down on the porch, put in a plug of Copenhagen, and said, 'Samantha Ray, a truly dangerous woman don't lash out with a temper tantrum. No, ma'am. She bides her time and handles her business quietly. Ain't nobody needs to see you do it. Now these boys know there may be some pain involved if they mess with you, but they'll be entertained, too. I don't ever want to hear about anything like this again. You understand me?'"

"That's ... not what I expected."

"Right? She's kind of my hero."

Chase got the impression he might be going after the wrong story. Sure, the missing woman was interesting. But who were these people that were unfazed by an act of brutality, except to the degree that it undermined the real danger the girl might pose to her harassers? He engaged his journalist brain. "What happened to the boys?"

"Nobody gave much attention to the boy who got kicked. Besides, there weren't no lasting damage. He's got like eight kids now and is a minister at a church. Who knows? Maybe I helped set him straight."

"I was kind of more curious about the one who got a hole in his hand."

"Our daddies had a talk and reached the conclusion that my

tire and their health insurance co-pay cost about the same, so that made us square. Fortunately, I didn't hit any bones or tendons, or I suspect I'd have had to make some reparations."

I really have entered some alternate dimension. Chase thought about his own grandmother, who had spent most of the last couple of decades quilting and canning pears and was no more dangerous to another human than she was to an alligator.

"You got awfully quiet over there," Sam said.

"Yeah, I guess I did. I was thinking that we had very different upbringings."

"You have no idea," Sam laughed. "Real question though — how long are you going to let me drive you around the city square before you tell me where you're going?"

Chase looked down at his wristwatch. His cheeks flushed red. He hadn't paid any attention to the passage of time since he'd gotten in Sam's truck. It hadn't been all that long, but still. Back home, he never would've done this kind of thing.

"You can go to hell, my dear," crooned some country singer over the truck's speakers, further affirming Chase's notion that he was acting outside himself. *Everybody's too friendly. Nobody in Philly would have shown me anything more than passing indifference.*

"I was headed to the Sheriff's Department."

Sam went straight through an intersection when Chase thought they should have turned left. "Isn't it back there?" he asked.

"It is. But the sheriff isn't. Where were you coming from?"

"Police station, but—"

"But you were asking about Valerie Wilson, and they don't have jurisdiction."

Chase gave her a surprised look. "Yeah, how'd you know?"

"The Wilsons live outside the city limits. Not by much, but enough that the sheriff is stuck with it. Nobody wants that file — a missing doctor's wife who may never be seen again. Local news covered it for a bit. Folks came in from Birmingham and

Huntsville. Even a couple of national folks. They all lost interest, ut now you've popped into town. No one wants to deal with
you, especially when you remind them they don't have any
answers."

"I get that," Chase said as the buildings became more dilapi-
dated the further out they got from the city center. In a matter
of a couple of miles, the buildings gave way to trees and the
occasional residence. "How do you know the sheriff's not in his
office?"

"Because he caught hisself a dead body."

"Oh. Is that where you're taking me?"

"Yup."

When she didn't offer any additional information, Chase
said, "That's it. No more detail?"

"It's a doozy. I can tell you that."

CHAPTER 7
UPRIVER A WAYS

SAM

Sam drove east out of town, taking Highway 5 until she came to Sipsey Road, where the cows outnumbered the trailer homes and their residents by a wide margin. Chase took in the drive quietly. Sam wasn't used to folks who could sit quietly with their thoughts and not have to be blathering on about something. Most people felt real uncomfortable with the silence. Her brothers and step-mother — it's almost like they were allergic to the quiet. When they were all little, Daddy used to tell the boys they had "diarrhea of the mouth." It was a disgusting expression, and she prided herself on him never having said it about her.

She'd always been his favorite. It had only been after her boobs grew in that the favoritism took a darker turn. Her stomach knotted up and ached with the recollection of the dread that overwhelmed her with the ringing of the last school bell. Her brothers would be in sports practices. With any luck, Desiree would be home. Sam may have hated the woman, but her presence was the only hope she had of being left alone. Of course, that was all done with now. *Or is it? Maybe I'm a monster in a long line of monsters, capable of the same monstrosities.*

"You alright over there?"

"Hmm? Oh, yeah. Fine."

"I don't think you could have been any further away if you'd been on a different planet."

Sam tried to smile disarmingly, but all her lightness and affability seemed to have left itself inside the city limits. In addition to reliving years of trauma punctuated by her killing her father yesterday, she cursed her monumental stupidity. It was bad enough she'd be spectating at a murder scene of her own making like some deranged serial killer who got off on it without bringing a reporter along. But, Chase needed to see what he was getting himself into. She could warn him all day long, but until he saw it, her words wouldn't ring true.

A bridge came into view through the windshield. And on it were all manner of emergency vehicles. She slowed the truck and rolled to a stop on the side of the road, behind a line of cars that included both government vehicles with blue license plates and nosy residents checking out the commotion.

Sam opened her door and got out without explaining anything. Chase followed suit and joined her at the front of the truck. Together, they walked onto the bridge. She nodded her head at several folks whose faces displayed their surprise to see her at all, considering that she ought to be making funeral arrangements, but they were doubly surprised to be seeing her with a stranger. And not any ole stranger, this one was a total smokeshow. As soon as they got out their phones to start texting, she'd be the subject of new gossip and rumors. She could already hear the hens clucking.

The supervisory emergency personnel had set up camp on the single-lane bridge that ran parallel to the one traffic ran on now. The one they stood on ought to have been torn down decades earlier. But the folks doing the actual work were strung along the embankment down to the river. Several labored at disentangling a mud-stained bundle from a bramble of trees and brush that had piled up in the river.

Sam placed her palms flat on the concrete barricade on the side of the bridge and leaned forward. "You see that?" She indicated with her chin.

Chase took a half-step forward, but not too close to the edge. "Somebody drown?"

"Not just anybody. Somebody important. That there is Martin Welker. He was always Marty until he went off to college and came back a few years later married to an uppity girl from Mountain Brook. All of a sudden, he was Martin."

"You knew him?"

"Went to high school with my brothers. He was a golden child. The one all the parents of burnouts and screwups would say, 'Why can't you be more like Marty?'"

Chase looked around at the other folks on the bridge. "What's with all the suits?"

"Well, Marty was a state representative. I expect they're either GOP folks or congress people from other districts."

Chase gathered his courage and looked down again, but only briefly. "What's that he's wearing?"

"You haven't ever seen waders before?"

He settled in beside her again and shook his head.

"It's for fly-fishing. Upriver a ways is the only trout fishing in Alabama and the prettiest stretch of river in the state. There's the Smith Lake Dam up there, and several times a day they release water from the base of the dam. The lake is a couple hundred feet deep there, so when they release the water into the river, it keeps the temperature in that part of the Sipsey in the fifties all year round. You can't get in that for more than a few minutes without waders."

"Hmm. So he had a fishing accident and drowned?"

A chill flushed through Sam. *Something like that.* "That's what they're saying."

Chase turned his head toward her. "You don't believe it?"

She returned his gaze, surprised. "What makes you say that?"

Chase smirked. "I won't claim to know you all that well—"

"You're pretty safe there on account of I only met you yesterday."

"But," Chase continued, "I talk to enough people to know that when someone says, *That's what they're saying,* the unspoken part of that sentence is, *but I don't believe it.*"

Sam looked around to see if anyone was close enough to hear their conversation. "Are we still off the record?"

"Until you say otherwise."

"This is coal mining country. Has been for a hundred and fifty years. You can't count the fortunes that have been made and lost here. But coal is a dirty business. The coal is dirty. The men who dig it out of the ground and blow the tops of hills to strip mine it are dirty. But most of all, the money is dirty. Martin," she gestured to the body that first responders were now pulling ashore, "got cross-ways with coal. They used the carrot to encourage him to see things their way. But apparently Martin had got some conviction somewhere along the way about climate change and alternatives to fossil fuels. Or maybe somebody else offered more carrots. I don't know. So when that didn't work ..." Sam's voice trailed off as she visualized the fear in Martin's face when he realized his situation. Then he slipped and smacked his head. So she and Rodrigo had turned him face down and floated him off down river. Daddy negotiated a hefty pay day for that one, and it had turned out to be one of the cleanest hits she'd ever done, courtesy of some moss. *I guess we're gonna find out how clean it was.*

"They used the stick?" Chase said.

"Huh? Oh." She shrugged. "Who's to say? Could have been a fishing accident."

"So, how do you know all this?"

It was Sam's turn to smirk. "Bless your heart. The fact that you have to ask tells me you're in over your head here."

Chase pursed his lips for a moment and tilted his head. "I don't know exactly what *bless your heart* means in this context, but it sounds like one of the most patronizing things anyone has said to me."

Sam's smirk grew. "You've got the gist of it."

Another vehicle pulled up on the far side of the bridge. It had no sooner rumbled to a stop than a wailing woman burst out of it, screaming for her husband. Several sets of hands grabbed hold of her before she set off down the embankment, where a team was strapping Martin's body onto a gurney to carry him up.

"Time to go," Sam said abruptly and strode off toward the truck.

By the time they reached Jasper again, the music had drowned out the worst of the mourning that reverberated in her head.

Once the hotel's sign was within view, Chase asked, "You want to grab some dinner later?"

Sam's heart stumbled at a boy asking her out, if that's what that had been. It wasn't something she was accustomed to. "I've got a funeral to plan and brothers who are about to raise hell." She pulled into the hotel's semicircular drive. "Besides, you may want to ask around about me and my family before deciding how much you want to be seen in my company."

CHAPTER 8
A DELICATE BALANCE

CHASE

CHASE WALKED BACK INTO THE WAREHOUSE WHERE he'd spent most of the prior evening. The bartender was the same guy who'd been there the night before, Jake. Chase had made sure to check his notebook before coming in.

Remembering people's names was a tool of the trade, but not one they taught in journalism school. He'd picked it up from shadowing an old guy when he was an intern: "If you care enough to remember their name, they're more inclined to share things with you." He'd had to be intentional about it at first. Before, he discarded the names of random people he met like gum wrappers. Now he clung to them. You never knew who you'd need to remember. Or when. Or why.

"Hey, man," the bartender said.

Ole Jake definitely doesn't recall my name. Not that I blame him. There were a lot of people in here yesterday.

"Chase," he offered.

"Yeah, I remember. What are you having?"

Chase pulled up at a barstool and sat. "Dealer's choice."

Jake's eyebrows formed a question.

"I'm a simple man and easy to please."

Jake nodded and reached under the bar for a glass, which he filled with an amber ale and slid in front of Chase.

Smart move. Something middle of the road that anybody would have a hard time fussing about. I bet he has patrons that only come here on the nights that he's working.

"Can I ask you a question?" Chase said.

"Sure. Answering questions is about half the job. It's not in the description, but it should be."

"You know that woman I was talking to yesterday — Sam?" he pointed with his thumb at the booth she'd been sitting in.

"Uh-huh."

"What can you tell me about her?"

Jake stopped what he was doing and looked around the bar that was otherwise empty in the middle of a weekday afternoon. Even still, he lowered his voice. "What I *can* tell you, and what I *will* tell you, are very different things."

He looked spooked. Chase knew he needed to provide assurances. "I was with her this afternoon, and she said I might not want to be seen with her and I should ask about her and her family. So I'm asking."

"You're a reporter, right?"

Close enough. "Yeah."

"Not during this conversation, you're not. You're just a guy talking to his barkeep. You got that?"

Chase nodded. "I do."

"What do you know about Walker County?"

"Not much more than what I learned in a Google search or two before coming to town."

"That's what I figured." It clearly wasn't intended as a compliment. "White people started settling this area a couple hundred years ago. Most of them weren't particularly reputable, and many still aren't. The hill and hollers in this county particularly have housed their share of outlaws. Some have stuck around long enough that their family names are part and parcel of the place."

"Uh-huh," Chase gently nudged him to continue.

"The outlaw families carved out niches, especially after Prohibition ended. Whatever your particular sins—sex workers, dope, making somebody disappear — there'd be a different family you needed to see."

However this ties to Sam, it's taking a dark turn to get there.

Jake scratched his chin. Before continuing, he pulled his phone out of his pocket and typed into it for a few seconds. Chase took a pull of his beer while he waited. Jake's phone made a blooping noise.

On a hunch, Chase said, "What did she say?"

Jake smiled uncomfortably from one side of his mouth. "I told her you were asking about her people. She said to tell you whatever I had to say."

"You still don't look happy about it."

"Well ... yeah." He hesitated. "It's like how you can talk about your family to family, but not to anybody outside the family."

"And I'm not family."

Jake nodded in agreement and poured himself a shot of something clear, which he tossed down his throat before continuing. "You aren't family. And I've got more at stake than catching a beating from an angry cousin who heard what you said about them. Alright, here it is — the legend goes that in Walker County, if you want somebody killed, you take a bag of money and leave a name with it, and you put it in a certain tree. For obvious reasons, that tree took to being called the Murder Tree. If somebody takes the money, you have yourself a contract and sure as a goat's footing, that somebody is gonna wind up dead. Do a search for 'Walker County hit man.' You'll find all kinds of stories."

"How does this tie to Sam?"

"Do the math, son," the bartender said impatiently.

Chase looked skeptical, like he thought someone was telling him a tall tale to see if he'd buy it. "You're telling me that a twenty-something who doesn't weigh a hundred and twenty pounds is a hit man? Hit person? Assassin?"

Jake shrugged noncommittally. "I'm telling you what her people have been known for. I don't know what she has done or hasn't done. And frankly, I'm not going to be the one to judge. Besides, it's not their only source of income. They've got cattle and some other businesses too. They don't show it, but I think they've probably got some real money tucked away." The bartender lightly slapped himself on the cheek. "*Now,* I've gone to talking too much. That's the problem with telling secrets. Once you start, it's hard to tell just one."

That was something Chase relied on. "I was thinking the other day how one branch of my family has been on this continent nearly four hundred years, and until my grandfather became an engineer and made a good living, they were all flat broke. Every one of them for more than three centuries. How is that even possible? You'd think in all that time, somebody would have had a bit of luck. Bought a piece of land that became valuable. Married into a good family. Or something." Chase shook his head, looking down at his drink. He really had been thinking about this lately, and telling it now diverted Jake's attention from his regret at talking too much. In the early days, he felt bad about manipulating people this way, even if it was mostly harmless. But you couldn't leave them with a foul taste in their mouth or they'd never talk to you again.

Jake waved his hand, indicating things out beyond the bar. "I don't think the American Dream holds much water around here. Folks are trying to scrape by. Make things better for their kids if they can, but at the very least, not leave them worse off. But if you're a miner or a steelworker, and the mine closes or the plant shuts down, what are you supposed to do?"

It wasn't a question that called for an answer. As far as Chase knew, there wasn't a good answer. If his own family was any indicator, you got one of those lawyers who'd get you on disability, and you rode things out getting your disability checks and working odd jobs that paid cash and never said anything about income tax reporting.

Chase pulled his recorder out of his pocket and conspicuously set it on top of the bar. He didn't want any confusion. He pushed a button, and a red light illuminated on its face. "Can I ask you a couple of questions about Valerie Wilson?"

"Afraid not. I've done enough gabbing for one day."

After Chase turned off the recorder and slid it back into his pocket, Jake added, "It's like to be tough sledding getting folks to talk about that."

"That's sort of the impression I've been getting. Any ideas about where I should start?"

Jake waved at some folks who entered the bar and took a seat at a table near the front window. "There's no love lost between her and the doctor's kids — her step-children that she was nearly the same age as. They might have something to say."

Chase paid for his beer and left a generous tip, but not one so overly generous that it would make Jake feel like he'd talked for money. It was a delicate balance to strike.

The door had no sooner closed behind him and ushered him out onto the sidewalk than a thought punched him in the face. *The congressman! Did Sam kill the congressman who'd had the fishing accident?!* Dread and queasiness wracked him.

CHAPTER 9
THAT VINCE GILL SONG

SAM

Sam turned off the engine and pulled the key out of the ignition. She'd killed several hours at the lake fishing. Not particularly trying to catch anything, but working up the nerve to walk through the front door to deal with her brothers. Within a few long days, it would be her front door and her land that the house was sitting on, so long as she lived long enough to claim it.

She was a lion tamer, about to walk into a cage full of hungry cats, and if they sensed any fear or uncertainty, they'd crush her throat and fight over her remains. There was more at stake here than setting things straight with her brothers and getting them to fall in line. There were the other families who would happily take this moment to depose the Colemans. But Jeb and Buddy were first in line.

Every light in the house was on. She took three deep breaths, exhaling each slowly, then climbed out of the truck. On her way to the front door, Sam took out the compact .380 that she kept tucked in her belt bag. It wasn't her favorite gun, but it was small and light enough to go most everywhere she did.

Sam held the pistol down by her side as she pulled the screen door and then the front door open.

"In here, Sam," Jeb called from the living room.

She shut the door without turning her back to the interior of the house. She found both boys on the couch in the living room. There were some documents between them that she presumed to be copies of the papers Nick had shared with her this morning, which seemed like several eternities ago.

She strode across the room with her shoulders back and chest out and sat in Daddy's recliner. Neither of them had the gumption to do it, but this would help them understand how things stood. She set the .380 on the side table.

"Don't have that thing pointing at me," Jeb said.

"Sorry." *Not sorry.* She spun the gun ninety degrees.

Buddy said, "We went and saw Mr. Davis today. Thought we should have a family meeting."

"Alright. What else did you think?"

Buddy looked to his brother for affirmation, but Jeb wouldn't turn his attention away from Sam.

"Well ..." Buddy, always the peacemaker, was having trouble with the next bit.

"Get on with it," she pressed. "Say what's on your mind." She sat forward, elbows on her knees, giving him her undivided attention, which he absolutely did not want.

"We thought, all things considered, these papers was a little unfair."

Sam nodded. "What things are those?"

Confusion spread over Buddy's face. *Poor, dumb animal.* The weed he smelled like he'd been smoking since they got home probably wasn't helping provide any clarity for him.

"What do you mean?"

Sam patiently explained, "You said *all things considered —* what are the things you considered?"

"Don't be like that," Jeb said.

Still looking intently at Buddy, Sam replied, "You wanted him to be your mouthpiece, so I am making sure we're all clear on what we're talking about. Because what I suspect is that he means because y'all have a twig and berries and are older than me, but I don't want to put words in his mouth."

Buddy didn't know what to do. She was talking to Jeb but looking at him. Squirrels in the face of oncoming traffic are more decisive.

"Buddy. Say what you have to say."

"Okay," he said. "Well, like I was saying, it don't seem fair for you to get most of the money and the house and the business."

Sam nodded. "I can see how you'd think that. Let me ask you this — how do you think it should have been done?"

"Well ... I mean," Buddy stammered around like the drug-addled, mental invalid that he was. "That's not really for me to say."

"We agree on that." No further conversation with Buddy was going to bear any fruit. He may be unhappy, but he wouldn't do anything without his brother. In fact, she could probably turn him back to her side with enough coddling. Sam sat back in the chair, slouching into her most jellyfish-like posture, and raised an eyebrow at Jeb. "You have anything to say?"

"I got a whole lot to say."

"I'm all ears, brother."

"Nobody respects you. They all think you're Daddy's little puppet. And if you're gonna be in charge, they're gonna come for us. Hard. Just you watch. And that's why I ain't worried about what the lawyer said. You're gonna be dead soon anyway. 'Cause they're gonna kill you."

"You want a job?"

"What?"

"J-O-B. You want one? I'll hire you to work for me."

Jeb pushed himself to his feet in a fit of fury. "I ain't working for you. This ought to all be mine. Every bit of it."

Buddy took exception to that. "I thought you said it should be *ours*."

"You know what I mean."

Sam gave Buddy a look that meant Jeb had said exactly what he meant. Buddy might not be very bright, but he'd been crossed by a self-serving brother enough times in his life to know better than to trust him outright. There weren't only seeds of distrust; that plant had already born fruit. Sam had only to pluck it at the most opportune time.

"If y'all don't have anything else to say on that front, we have other business to attend to."

"What other business?" Buddy complained. He'd need some food or an upper soon so he didn't get fussy.

"Daddy's funeral."

"Don't seem right," Jeb mumbled.

Everything about his tone said he wanted someone to ask him what he meant. Sam knew if she waited long enough, Buddy would ask. He couldn't let it hang there, but it wouldn't be productive. What *don't seem right* was that she'd killed Daddy, and now she was set to profit the most from it. Fortunately for her, Nick had said Alabama required a conviction for you to be stripped of your inheritance. Not only would there be no conviction, Sheriff Tompkins would make sure there were no charges brought. All she had to do was keep the donations aimed at his future campaigns.

"The funeral's going to be at SouthSide," she said.

Buddy groaned. "That place is depressing."

Sam laughed unexpectedly. A nervous reaction that had gotten her in trouble more than once in her life.

"What are you laughing at?" Buddy asked with crossed arms.

"Bro," Jeb said, also grinning now, "it's a funeral home. They're all depressing."

"They said they can do it Saturday. Today is ..." Sam looked at her watch. "… Tuesday. That'll give us time to get word out to everybody."

"Don't forget," Buddy said. "We gotta get somebody to sing that Vince Gill song."

You can't throw a stone in the South without hitting a singer who wants to perform 'Go Rest High on That Mountain' at a funeral, so that wouldn't be a problem. "Can you handle that for us, Buddy?"

He nodded emphatically.

Jeb suggested. "Could they sing it at the graveside and not in the chapel?"

Sam shrugged. "Fine by me. Do y'all want to skip the chapel part and only do the graveside service?"

"Yes, please," Jeb said with a sense of relief. "Churches kind of freak me out."

"That's called conviction," Buddy said. "Jesus is trying to talk to you."

Sam laughed again. "Whoa, Buddy. Harsh!"

Jeb burst out laughing, too. If anybody else had said it, there would have been malice behind it. But not coming from Buddy. He was the only one of them with any tenderness in his heart. There may have been a connection between that and his drug use. He was for sure born into the wrong family.

The three of them hadn't laughed together in a long time. Probably since they were kids. And to think, all it took was Daddy's death. If only she'd known, she could have done it sooner.

"This may sound weird," Buddy said, "but this has been kind of nice."

Sam grinned. "You know what they say, you can't spell funeral without F-U-N."

"Oof." Jeb covered his face with a pillow to stifle his amusement. "That's dark, even coming from you."

CHAPTER 10

THE MANY FLAVORS WE OFFER

SAM

ORDERING A BLIZZARD FROM DAIRY QUEEN FIRST thing in the morning always felt peculiar, even if it was only an exercise in protocol. The moment her wheels came to a stop in front of the overly bright sign with a hundred ice cream treats and half as many chicken and burger options, a perky voice buzzed through the speaker. "Welcome to Dairy Queen. What can I get you this morning?"

How 'bout a warm cup of chill out? Geez. What must it be like to live inside a body that's this lively at 6:03 a.m.?

Rather than be grumpy though, Sam said what she was supposed to say. "I'll have a large Granny Smith Apple Blizzard."

"That's not one of the many flavors we offer. Can I interest you in a Snickers Blizzard instead?"

"That'll do."

"Thank you. Please drive around for your total. Have a blessed day!"

"Calm down, Teresa."

The speaker crackled. One corner of Sam's mouth turned up in anticipation of Teresa's reaction, but the speaker went quiet. She drove around to the window, where the woman wagged a finger at her. "Not nice, girl. You are not too old for me to come out there and give you a whoopin'."

"Yes, ma'am," Sam said, despite the temptation to further antagonize her.

"And if you call me by first name again without putting *Aunt* in front of it, I'll put in some extra prayers and get the haints after you that you done in."

Sam's eyes grew wide. Teresa shouldn't be talking like that so openly.

"Don't get all buggy eyed with me. Samaki and me is the only ones here, and he's got his ear buds turned up so loud that whole world could end around him, and he wouldn't notice. Watch." Teresa turned around and yelled. "Samaki, you want to step into the walk-in and go at it like rabbits?" She waited for a response before pivoting back to Sam, who cackled with even parts embarrassment and amusement.

"What if he'd have said yes?"

"You'd be waiting a few minutes longer for that ice cream, I guess."

Another fit of laughter came over Sam. When it died down, Teresa's demeanor changed. "Tell me what happened."

Sam collected herself and told her aunt the same account of things she'd given her older brother a couple of days earlier about finding Daddy's name in the Murder Tree and what happened after that. Teresa nodded along. "Couldn't have been a more fitting end." She leaned out and spit on the ground.

Finally, somebody else who understands.

"You best watch your back, though. If somebody was coming for him, they'll come for you, too."

"I know."

"How's your brothers taking it?"

Sam sighed. "Buddy's a mess, and Jeb is mad as hell."

Teresa pursed her lips. "Sounds about right. I'll call on them when I get off work. So, you want this phone number, or what?"

Sam got her burner phone out of the center console and powered it on. Once it was ready, she looked over at Teresa, who pulled the ten digits from her memory. Sam punched them in and set the phone beside her on the bench seat. "I still can't believe you memorize them like that. Aren't you worried you'll get the numbers mixed up?"

"Got no choice. It's not like I can go writing it down."

A horn blared behind Sam. She opened her door to get out, but Teresa pushed it closed as she leaned out of the drive-thru window and yelled, "Don't be rude! I'm the one who makes your food! Besides, I know your mama, Tracy."

Sam asked, "Do you really know her mama?"

"Of course I do. She's in here three times a week for tenders, fries, extra gravy, and a Diet Coke. Like that saccharin is some kind of medicine to offset the sludge she's turning her blood into." Teresa shook her head. "You go on now. You got business to attend to. I'll wrangle those boys and get them into line."

Sam nodded.

"Love you, baby girl."

A flush of heat spread through Sam's face as tears welled in her eyes at the affection. She didn't dare look at her aunt again. She touched her hand lightly and drove off. Sam cleared her throat and drove a couple of blocks to where Town Creek ran along the outskirts of the old baseball field. She parked on a bald patch by the water and rolled the windows down to hear it.

She always got a pit in her stomach before making these calls. Any phone calls really, but particularly these calls. Each one was like a blind date, but instead of having a miserable night and going home alone to watch a movie, you might end up dead or in prison if things went sideways. One of those options being preferable to the other.

When Daddy's voice reverberated in her head — "Ain't nothing for it but to do it, girl." — she punched the green call button. The phone on the other end rang three times before being answered with a clipped, "Yes?"

She immediately formed an opinion about the inflated sense of self-importance that a person must have to answer the phone like that. Not one to give any ground, Sam said, "You know who this is?"

"Yes."

"And how this works?"

"I do."

Ah, he does know other words. That came as something as a relief. The only other language she spoke was the swear words in Spanish that Rodrigo had taught her, and she suspected that wouldn't carry her very far into a conversation.

"Alright then, let's hear it."

"You will be delivering a package to Monroe, Louisiana. Do you know it?"

About the only thing she or anyone else knew about Monroe is that's where the guys from *Duck Dynasty* were from. There was a year or two where it seemed like that's the only show Daddy or Desiree ever had on TV at night. "Yeah."

"There's a package waiting on you to pick it up at the post office. General delivery. On the way to Monroe, you'll need to stop in Vicksburg."

"Okay."

"There's a fella you need to see."

"Uh-huh."

"He won't be expecting you."

"When?" Sam asked.

"Tomorrow. He'll be home alone between seven and nine. Wife'll be at some church thing."

"On a Thursday?"

The man sighed on the other end.

"Look, if somebody else is at the house on account of you had the wrong information, I'm out. So let's not act like I'm inconveniencing you by making sure that on a Thursday night, the wife really won't be home. Or would you rather roll the dice with your non-refundable deposit?"

"I'm sure. Church. Thursday. Something they call Visitation, per my client. I don't know what that means. Church wasn't my thing."

Sam nodded knowingly, even though no one could see her. "She's an evangelical. It's where they go … hang on. I gotta think of the word … proselytize people. You got the address?"

"I'll text it to you."

Sam bolted upright. "No, you won't. Nothing electronic in writing. I thought you said you'd done this before."

"You're right. You're right."

I know I'm right. I don't need you to tell me that.

He gave her the address. She repeated it in her head several times, committing it to memory. She wouldn't be writing it down on her end either. No paper.

"Does the method matter?"

"It'd be best if it looked accidental, but honestly, it doesn't make a huge difference. Nobody will be surprised, however he goes. Getting this done expeditiously is the highest priority. You with me?"

"Let me ask you something," Sam said timidly. *Don't do it. Let it go.* But she did ask. She couldn't not ask. "Does he deserve it?"

"What?"

She could easily have told him to forget it, but she didn't. "You heard me."

"Does it matter?"

"Look … humor me. I'm in a weird place right now."

There was a long silence on the other end. Sam pulled the phone away from her face to look at the screen and make sure she hadn't dropped the call. The seconds continued to tick upward.

"This is a little out of the ordinary," the man said.

"Yeah." She didn't offer any further excuses.

"What if I say he doesn't deserve it?"

"Dunno. Guess I'll have some reconciling to do."

There was another significant pause before the man said. "He's earned it. They'll be hard pressed to find anyone to give a proper eulogy for him."

"Alright then." Relief poured over Sam. She'd never asked that before. Never cared before. She didn't know why she did now. She would definitely prefer not to have some crisis of conscience. The timing couldn't be worse.

CHAPTER 11
SINS TO ACCOUNT FOR

SAM

Sam sat on the tailgate of her truck as Rodrigo came out of the post office cradling two boxes under one arm and carrying a letter envelope in the opposite hand. He set the box down beside her and handed her the envelope. "They give you any trouble?" she asked.

"No," Rodrigo said. "I never ask you before por que the delivery when you go out of town for ... business."

Sam tilted her head. "Are you asking now?" She trusted Rodrigo more than anybody else she knew, but him being inquisitive about the business was a departure from his usual manner.

He shrugged.

That's more like it. There was no harm in telling him. If he was going to turn on her, this detail wouldn't be the thing that did her in.

"It's a ruse. Do you know that word? Ruse?"

Rodrigo shook his head.

"Like a trick. I never want the place where the job is to be my final destination. It needs to be a waypoint on a longer trip. In case I ever need to account for my whereabouts. If I'm being a courier and delivering a package," she patted the box beside her,

"I have a reason for going through Vicksburg on my way to Monroe, for example."

Rodrigo contemplated this for a minute before tapping his temple. "Your papa teach you that?"

Her mouth turned down on one side. "Nah. Came up with that on my own. He was never deceptive like that."

"He was bull. You are fox."

That made Sam smile.

Rodrigo smirked. "But sometimes you are burro."

"A donkey?"

He waggled his hand from side to side. "Mas o menos."

"Watch yourself, hombre. I'm a trained killer."

"Not worried. I know where bodies are buried. Except ones the pigs ate."

The thought of that made Sam shiver, even though she was usually the one to leave them unburied so the wild hogs that ran rampant would dispose of them. "How about my brothers — what are they?"

Rodrigo flicked a hand dismissively and muttered something in Spanish. He took the box around to the passenger side of the truck and slid it into the floorboard. When he came back to the tailgate, Sam was fiddling with the envelope, tilting it from one corner to the next as the item inside tumbled around.

She shoved herself off the tailgate. "Alright, I gotta hit the road so I make my time window."

Rodrigo waved and sauntered over to his own truck. When Sam got situated inside the cab and the engine began loping gently, she turned off both her burner phone and her regular phone. It was kind of a hassle, but a whole lot less hassle than staring down the barrel of a murder conviction because GPS pinged her being at a murder scene. She glanced down to make sure her Rand McNally book of maps was still wedged under the seat, then pulled the gearshift into reverse.

Dusk painted the sky with pinks, oranges, and blues as Sam

parked her truck along the curb of a street first paved a couple of generations ago. Most of the houses in the neighborhood showed signs of having been updated since first being built. She appreciated the spacious lots. They gave her a little more buffer from the neighbors in case there was any unfortunate noisiness as she conducted her business.

She grabbed the envelope off the seat, flipped open her pocket knife, and sliced open one end of the envelope. Sam tilted it up, and a key slid into the palm of her other hand. *Bingo*. She slid out of the truck and strapped her heftier-than-normal belt pack around her waist, then checked its contents. Lighter. Syringe with the pop-top on — the last thing she needed was to accidentally prick her finger on a needle loaded to the brim with fentanyl. Pack of smokes. *Good to go*.

Sam walked around the truck with purpose, but not hurrying, giving herself the opportunity to scope out whether anyone was paying undue attention to her. This was always the part where all her spidey-senses tingled and the butterflies waged war in her belly. She pulled the .22 from the glove box and threaded the suppressor onto the muzzle before tucking it into her waistband behind the belt pack. It wasn't ideal, but it would only stay there long enough to get her across the lawn and out of eyesight of any neighbors.

The last thing she did at the truck was put on her yellow safety vest, slip her hands into a pair of black gloves, and grab the package labeled with this address. Now, she was nothing more than a delivery girl, making herself nearly invisible in the suburban Mississippi landscape.

At the back door, Sam shrugged off her vest, folded it, and tucked it into the waistband of her pack. She pulled the pistol out of the front of her pants. The front site snagged on the cloth, as they always did. That's why it was stupid to carry a gun in your pants without a holster and drew the biggest of eye rolls every time she saw some actor carry theirs that way in a show or movie.

She clicked the safety off, pulled the slide partway back, and saw the glint of brass from the chambered .22 round exactly where it was supposed to be. Reassuring, of course, but if it came to her needing to use it, things would have already gone sideways.

The key slid into the lock, and as she turned it, the deadbolt retracted back into the door like the completion of some weirdly metallic sexual act. Sam moved the key down to the handle and did the same thing. It turned, and she pushed the door inward slowly with her left hand, keeping the pistol ready.

A patter of toenails clicked on the kitchen tile. Several staccato woofs gave away the dog's excitement and location. Sam saw a flicker of tail in the crack. *No, no, no. Nobody said anything about a dog.* She wouldn't necessarily have turned the job down if she'd known, but it made a strategic difference. She could have brought tranqs or treats to distract the animal if she'd known. Furthermore, nothing made her feel worse than killing a dog. She had a lot of sins to account for at some point and expected some unavoidable dog murders to rate pretty high on the list when the time came.

Sam slipped into the kitchen and pressed the door closed behind her. Even though the golden retriever let out a couple of barks that it must have thought were ferocious, its wriggling tail and hind end belied its true feelings.

From the next room over, a man called in a thick, slurred voice, "Shut up, Waffles."

CHAPTER 12
A PRETTY GOOD SIGN

SAM

Sam froze, listening for footsteps. When none came, she squatted down and held out the back of her left hand. Waffles approached with cautious eagerness. After a burst of sniffs, she showed her approval of Sam by flopping on the ground and exposing her belly while her tail swept the tile like a haywire metronome.

Sam scratched the dog's belly a few times and whispered, "You want a treat?"

Waffles flung herself to her feet and skittered across the floor to an interior door. Sam followed, shuffling sideways to keep her eye on the cased opening that led in the direction of the man's voice. She flipped the switch beside the door, and light streamed out from under it. Waffles shifted to the side of the door, giving it room to open. Sam figured that automatically vaulted her into the top tier of the smartest dogs she'd known. All the mutts they'd ever owned had to be nudged out of the way with a knee as they tried to bull-rush the door the instant it cracked open.

When Sam had fully opened the door to the walk-in pantry, Waffles looked up at her expectantly. "Well, go on. Get your treat."

The dog walked into the pantry, and Sam shut the door

behind her. "Good girl," she whispered. It felt bad to trick a dog, like punching below your weight class, but it sure beat the alternative. But Sam couldn't let her run free and witness someone killing her owner. That would be messed up. No dog should see that.

Sam readied her handgun again, keeping it pointed toward the ground. No one else had responded to the dog's bark — a pretty good sign no one was here. She paused her advance toward the den to listen for the sound of running water. If a bath or shower were running, that person wouldn't have heard her or the dog either, but they might walk in on their dad/husband/significant other's demise. No one was supposed to be here, but she had gotten bad intel before.

Sam didn't hear anything.

Walking through the opening into the next room, Sam found her dumpy, past-his-prime target slumped in a recliner, chin resting on his chest, snoozing. A half dozen Bud Heavies littered the side table. The broadcast team for the Braves was commenting about the tepid attendance at the Marlin's game. *Things that are certain in life — death, taxes, and crappy Marlins fans. Even when they win the World Series once a decade or so.*

The side table on the other side of the recliner supported a lamp, an ashtray with a sizable collection of butts, and one of those tabletop air purifiers that smokers think masks their habit. Sam wasn't under that misconception and made no effort to hide her own vice.

Sam called, "Hello," to see how far into his drunk dozing he was. He didn't respond.

She was glad to see he was wearing short sleeves. This would have been harder to manage otherwise. She recalled a time when she was a girl that Daddy took her to the pharmacy for a flu shot and hadn't thought to change her out of her long-sleeve shirt. When the tech came out to give the shot and Daddy realized the problem, he was about to have her take the whole shirt off right there in the store. The tech, who did this a couple dozen times a day, took hold of the situation and had her shrug the collar down on one shoulder.

This situation was a little different. Sam couldn't make do with the meaty part of his shoulder. She needed that fat vein popping out of the crook of his arm.

She bent over him on his left side. This was the most dangerous part. If he roused now, her hands would be occupied and she would be exposed. *Either back out now or get to it. Don't dillydally.*

Sam pulled the latex band out of her back pocket and held it between her teeth as she cautiously took her mark's arm and placed it palm-up on the armrest of his recliner. It might have seemed almost tender if she weren't about to pump him so full of fentanyl that his body would forget how to function.

Sam wrapped the band around his arm and tied it right above the elbow. Several seconds later, the already-prominent blood vessel looked like a hose pipe trapped under his skin. Still, the man couldn't be troubled to awaken from his slumber. Without taking her eyes off of him, she unzipped her belt pack and pulled out the syringe.

"What did you do to earn this?" Sam whispered as she popped the cap off the syringe. In the movies, they always pushed the air out of the syringe, but it hardly mattered here. In a practiced motion, she secured his forearm, submerged the needle into the man's arm, and depressed the plunger.

"Hey!" the man yelled, grabbing Sam by the front of her shirt and pulling her toward him.

Sam slammed her other arm down on his wrist, trying to break his grip. The fabric of her shirt ripped as his hands held fast. Rage broke through the grogginess in his eyes.

She lost her balance in the tumult and fell onto him, noticing the band still wrapped around the man's arm and holding the opioids at bay. She used the confusion to swipe and tear at his arm. He shoved her off him.

Sam fell backward onto the carpeted floor. The man pushed himself to nearly standing before collapsing back into the recliner. When his eyes widened, Sam realized she had the latex band in her hand. As his breathing became erratic, Sam crab crawled away, keeping an eye on him in case he rallied again.

The fentanyl clawed its way through his heart and into his arteries. Sam didn't watch him die. Instead, she stood and stared emptily at the tchotchkes that adorned a hutch, mostly snow globes from various destination cities. The most absurd showed a snippet of Miami, which probably hadn't seen snow since the last ice age.

Several minutes after everything grew still behind her, Sam pivoted and returned to the man, putting two fingers to the hollow in his throat. She found no pulse.

Standing upright again, she scoured the floor for the syringe and cap that she'd lost in the tussle, and returned them to her pack, along with the latex band. She didn't see anything else on the floor that belonged to her. The .22 was still tucked into the small of her back. She hadn't even remembered it in the moments of chaos. *Not great, Bob. Time to wrap things up and get out of here.* It wouldn't do to have the wife come home while she was still here.

Sam pulled a cigarette out of the pack, laying on the side table. She slipped it into her mouth, the nicotine calling to her like a siren. She immediately regretted lighting it and expelled the air from her lungs with all the force she could muster. *Menthol. Gross. That alone makes you a worthy candidate for being killed.*

She flicked the lit cigarette onto the jumble of newspapers at the foot of the recliner. Layer after layer curled away from the glowing end of the cigarette. Still, enough heat accumulated to kindle a flame that reached out greedily as it grew. First magazines, next the carpet's synthetic fibers, and then the fabric of the chair.

Sam looked out the window. Darkness had enveloped the landscape. She dropped her safety vest onto the blaze, looked around once more to make sure she wasn't leaving behind any evidence of her presence, and slid out the back door.

When the truck rumbled to life, she decoupled the suppressor from her .22, put the gun into the glove box and dropped the suppressor into a bag of tools she kept under the seat. If she got pulled over, a gun in the glove box wouldn't raise any eyebrows, but one with extra hardware would draw unwanted attention and questions. Sam rested her head on the steering wheel. She had nearly screwed that one up. She didn't think she was being careless. *Just chalk it up to bad luck? Maybe.* She would have to evaluate later.

Sam was about to put the truck in drive when she shoved the door open and took off running across the yard. *Waffles.* Smoke was already escaping from the vents in the eaves. She had to stop herself from smashing into the back door. *Leave no trace,* she reminded herself, and began digging around for the key, which had slipped to the bottom of her pack.

When she opened the back door, smoke billowed out. The living room was an inferno. Waffles' muted yelp came from the pantry.

"Coming, girl." She ducked through the kitchen and yanked open the door to the pantry. Waffles cowered in the corner. Sam approached slowly with her arms out. A flick of a tail gave her permission to keep getting closer. "It's okay. You gotta come with me." She got a full wag this time. Then sixty pounds of joy bounded into her arms, nearly knocking her over. "I guess you're coming with me. Is that okay?" Waffles' tail pummeled her arm in answer.

CHAPTER 13
KIND OF A VIBE KILLER

CHASE

IF ANYONE HAD ASKED CHASE TO DESCRIBE WHAT HE thought a Southern sorority girl looked like, he would have given them a word picture of Ashleigh Wilson, down to the straightened blond hair and sun dress. He pulled the recorder out of his bag and set it on the side table between them. "Do you mind?"

She shook her head. "This is like so surreal."

"Sorry," Chase interrupted. "Will you say out loud whether it's okay for me to record?"

"Oh. Yeah. Sure. I consent and all that. Everybody wants verbal consent for everything now. It's kind of a vibe killer, right?"

Chase didn't engage. Some interviews were like this. The other person brought their own agenda to the table, and sometimes that agenda was to push buttons and derail things.

Rather than being discouraged, Ashleigh opted for a more overt approach.

"How about after you're done interrogating me, I can give you a tour of the place?"

"Sure," he said dismissively.

"We can either start with my room or end up there. Your choice."

Chase's cheeks flushed a deep crimson. He cleared his throat. "I ... uhh ... wanted to ask you some questions about Valerie Wilson."

Ashleigh sighed. "Oh, Val."

"How long have you known her?"

"She's kind of a B. Can I swear on this podcast? Whatever. You know that, right?" She covered her mouth with one hand. "I probably shouldn't say that. You think I'm a suspect now, don't you?"

Chase shrugged. "Suspects are for the police. I'm only gathering information. Besides, if we all killed everybody we didn't particularly like, the world would be a pretty empty place."

"You think she's dead?" Ashleigh showed actual interest in the subject of Valerie for the first time. "What do you know? Tell me."

"Oh. No. I misspoke. I meant in a general sense. Not like I have any reason to think that happened to her." *Well, this part is definitely getting edited out.*

"Okay, mister. If you're going to be all coy about it."

Chase clicked his tablet on and scrolled through his notes to give himself a minute to reset and formulate his next line of questions. He was fairly confident this was his worst start to an interview to date.

"Did you ever listen to that podcast *S-Town?*" Ashleigh asked.

Chase looked back up at her, taking a second to replay the question in his head. He'd only half heard it the first time. "Yeah, I remember that one. It took a pretty hard turn that I wasn't expecting."

"I know, right? When that guy d—"

"Can I ask you some questions about Valerie?"

"Bibb County's only like an hour from here. We should drive

down and see that crazy guy's property." Ashleigh's eyes brightened. "I bet we could find his gold."

"Probably not, though," Chase said. "How long have you known Valerie?"

Ashleigh sighed and pulled her legs up, folding them under her. "Like, my whole life. She used to babysit me when I was little?"

"Did—was—never mind."

"Was my dad boinking her when she was in high school babysitting me?" She came right out and asked the question he chickened out of asking a daughter of her father.

Chase shrugged.

"Maybe?" She shook her head slightly. "My mom had left by then. My dad and her dad were golf buddies, so it would have been weird. But he wouldn't have been the first guy to be doing the babysitter. She was pretty hot, and I don't think she dated anybody in high school. Whoa. I've never thought about that before. Or at least, not in that context anyway. Pretty weird."

Chase scribbled a note onto his tablet. *Doc groomed Valerie?*

"What about when you got old enough that you didn't need babysitting? Was she still around?"

Ashleigh looked out the window for a minute, tugging at old memories. "Not any more than any of my brother and sister's other friends, I don't guess. We were kind of the house where everybody gathered. Seems like there were always people here."

"Can I go back to something? Tell me about your mom leaving."

She sighed. "We came home from school one day and she was gone. All her stuff was gone. My dad was here waiting for us. He said she'd had some kind of mental break and left us."

"Was she having mental health problems before that?"

"I don't know, bro. I was a little kid. She was moody and cried a lot, but does that mean she was crazy?" Ashleigh crossed her arms over her chest. She was growing understandably disinterested in answering questions about her mom.

Chase pressed a little more. "When did you see her after that?" He was expecting to receive the standard 'Every other weekend and holiday' kind of answer.

"Didn't. She never came back." Her voice had fifteen years of pain behind it. She had finally, and probably inadvertently, allowed something real about herself to slip through.

Realization struck them both.

Two wives. Both disappeared. Coincidence? Not likely.

Ashleigh's hands blanketed her mouth and nose. Her voice was muffled when she asked, "You don't think ...?" She got no further before she began crying.

Chase was paralyzed, having no clue what the situation called for. Ashleigh decided for him. She pulled herself up out of her chair, walked over, and collapsed into a ball on the sofa, curled up against him. She buried her face in the crook of his shoulder, and he patted her on the back.

Chase watched out the windows, hoping no one else would come home now, because this would be tough to explain. *Everything's fine, folks. She just realized her mother is dead and her father might be complicit in two murders.* Another part of him wished someone would pull up. He'd never been more ill-equipped to deal with a situation in his life. He reached out his free arm toward the recorder, but anchored as he was, he couldn't get to it and the recorder continued to capture a woman's most vulnerable moments. So he kept patting as the crying quieted, evolved into hard breathing, and eventually stilled.

Ashleigh looked up at him with eyes made of sea glass. "Do you think Val left him, too?"

"What? No!" Chase said involuntarily as his brain inverted itself at her naivety.

She sat up and pulled back from him, leaving his arm suspended awkwardly until he reined it in. "What then?"

There was no way he was going to voice what he really thought happened. Not only was it not appropriate, but he had nothing to substantiate it other than one heck of a coincidence. His non-answer drew out, creating a divide between them that was almost concrete.

She stood up and loomed in front of him. *Loomed* wasn't the right word. It suggested some kind of intimidation. But in her bare feet, bright yellow dress, and standing a foot shorter than him, she lacked the necessary gravitas to affect that result. "Say it," she demanded.

"It's not my place." The answer felt impotent, but he had no idea what else to say.

"I think you need to leave," Ashleigh said. He stood up and gathered his things as she stood motionless with her hands on her hips. Her parting words to him were, "You're a real asshole, you know."

CHAPTER 14
SAFE UNTIL IT'S NOT

CHASE

CHASE WONDERED HOW MANY WEEKS OR MONTHS (OR years?) it would take of him coming to this place and sitting at this bar for him to be considered a regular. Or was Walker County the kind of place that no amount of time living here would make him *from here*? Folks were nice, but most regarded him at arm's length. In fact, he found it difficult to discern sometimes whether people down here were being genuinely kind or the surface-level politeness that was intrinsic to the place.

That people would be dubious of him was understandable considering the nature of his reason for being here, but what if he were doing something else or stuck around after the podcast gig was up? Not that he *wanted* to stay. It was more an exercise in curiosity than anything else.

Chase lurched forward, nearly toppling his beer, as a meaty forearm nudged him from behind. He whirled on his stool to find a mountain smiling down at him. "You keep showing up to the same place and people's liable to think you're part of the furniture."

"Howdy, Shooter."

"'Howdy' is it? I believe that's what we call cultural appropriation."

Chase laughed in surprise. "You don't think I can say howdy?"

"Not unless you've used a living critter for transportation or come from west of the Mississippi. I suppose you better stick with hi, hello, or even 'sup." Shooter did a quick head nod when he said '*sup*, which somehow the word required.

Chase had a fleeting memory of his sixth grade English teacher greeting everyone with head-nods as she passed them in the hallway. None of the other teachers could have gotten away with it, but she was young, and all the boys had a crush on her, and she was from somewhere out West, which seemed exotic to a bunch of kids from Philly who knew most everybody in their neighborhood for their whole lives. *Look at that — we've come full circle.*

"The Friday night crowd's like to be a bit rowdier than the Monday Night Football crowd that last time I seen you," Shooter said.

"What about when the Eagles play Sunday night?"

Shooter shook his head dismissively, then paused. "If Jalen Hurts is still their QB, there's plenty of Alabama fans that have a hard-on for him. They'll be watching. Other than that, the NFL is no more than passing interest for most folks."

"I take it you don't pull for Alabama?"

"Nah. I had dreams of playing for Ole Miss. Always fancied myself as a Rebel, I guess."

Chase asked, "Isn't that kind of ironic?"

Shooter furrowed his brow and tilted his head, looking very much like a confused German mastiff. "How's that?"

"You told me Monday that you're from the Free State of Winston County, but you're also saying you wanted to be a Rebel. That seems … incongruent."

"Hmm." It was more a grunt than a word. "That hadn't

occurred to me before." With no kind of segue, Shooter asked, "You ever been inside a coal mine before?"

Chase shook his head. The idea of being in a confined space where men had bored a hole into the earth's crust didn't particularly appeal to him.

"We oughta go some time. There's gobs of them around here. It's really something."

"Is it safe?"

"Until it's not." The giant shrugged, then smiled. "Nah, I'm messing with you. They're pretty safe.

Pretty safe was significantly less assuring than he preferred. He pictured himself trapped underground with a light whose battery was dying and air that was growing stale. No small amount of panic clawed at him.

Shooter looked over the bar's other patrons toward the front door, as a head of scrunchy hair made its way in their direction. "Looks like your friend is here. I'll be joining my people now. Have a good one."

Panic devolved into dread.

Chase raised his glass to Shooter as he departed.

"Samantha Ray," Shooter said in greeting to Sam, though it was less a greeting and more an observation.

"Oliver," she said in return.

Sam sat on the empty barstool beside Chase. Neither of them said anything for a couple of extraordinarily long minutes. She faced forward the whole time, as if she were counting the bottles on the wall. Chase didn't know whether to watch her or if he was supposed to look straight ahead, too, so he awkwardly alternated between the two. Finally, he tired of whatever this was. "I haven't seen you in a couple of days."

She swiveled to face him, her knees pressing into his hip. "I had to go out of town. What did you decide?"

"About?" It was absurd to play dumb about the question. It's not like she was asking him if he'd decided what to eat for dinner.

There was only one — gargantuan — question that lay unanswered between them, a chasm over which no bridge had yet been built.

She stared at him, not taking the bait.

Chase asked, "Did you kill the Congressman?"

The bartender, who'd been lurking nearby, dropped the glass he'd been cleaning. Sam slid off the side of her barstool and snatched Chase off his barstool by the front of his shirt. Before letting go, she said to Jake, "We're gonna step out back."

The bartender nodded slowly, then squatted to collect shards of glass.

"Outside," Sam demanded.

There was no question about his compliance. He followed her around the side of the bar, down a hallway that led past the bathrooms, and out the back door. The back lot could not have been more vacant. The gravel radiated the day's residual heat back up at them. With the door closed, all they heard from inside the bar was the rhythmic thump of the music.

Sam paced in front of him. "What makes you think you can ask me that in a roomful of people? Are you out of your gourd?"

Chase crossed his arms. "Did you?"

"Do you understand what's at stake? Certain people might turn a blind eye when a drug dealer or a kiddie diddler goes missing. They might not ask too many questions about that. But they can't do that when it comes to an elected official. So for you to even shine that light on me when other people could hear it …" She returned to pacing.

Chase could almost see the anger bristling in an aura around her, but he was unwilling to relent yet. "Well, did you do it?"

Sam stilled and stepped toward him. Chase took an involuntary step backward when she got within his personal bubble.

"Even if I did — I didn't — but even if I did, I couldn't and wouldn't tell you."

Chase tried a different tack. "I have journalist's privilege. If you let me use what you tell me for a story, they can't make me reveal my sources."

"The local cops can't. The state cops can't. But what about the feds? How long are you willing to rot in jail for contempt of court before you decide to roll over?"

"I wouldn't do that," he offered, though they both doubted the truth of it.

She laughed. It wasn't a pleasant sound. "Do you know how long a judge can hold you for contempt?"

Chase thought he knew the answer, but it didn't seem like she wanted any real contribution from him. He shrugged.

"As long as he wants. Until the jail crumbles around you. Until time itself calls it quits. You up for that? So pardon me if I'm not willing to stick my neck out and hand you a hatchet so you can have some answers."

Chase found himself getting riled up. She was treating him like he was somehow in the wrong. "How am I supposed to be friends with someone who goes around ..." He looked around for any passersby before whispering the next part of his question. "... killing people for a living?"

Sam waved a hand dismissively. "Rumors. Been plaguing this family for generations. Sure, we lean into it some, but nothing's ever been substantiated."

"But—Jake said—you—" She was messing with him. He needed to put his emotions in check and ask an intelligent question or two. "Fine. Let's say that's true. What exactly do you mean when you talk about the 'family business'?"

She grinned. "We own the biggest chain of laundromats and dry cleaners in the State of Alabama. Got places in Jasper, Cordova, Double Springs, Moulton, Dora, Carbon Hill, over in Cullman. I could keep going if you like."

"So that's it? That's the family business? Not ... the other thing?"

"Check the secretary of state website. You'll see the little empire I'm inheriting. I'm like the queen of Walker County."

They are literally laundering money. Chase tried his footing on some uncertain ground. "What happened to your dad? You never said."

Sam pursed her lips for a minute, but she didn't dismiss the question outright. "Self-inflicted wounds."

"You mean he committed suicide?"

She tilted her head back and forth, and said, "In a manner of speaking. He made some enemies, and somebody called his number."

Most of the fire had gone out of the conversation, so he prodded at it. "Because of the laundry business?"

"Exactly. Heavy lies the crown and all that. We good?"

"Sure." *What else am I going to say?*

"Good. I got a funeral to get through tomorrow. Can't have this weighing on me."

It didn't escape Chase's notice that in all of this, she hadn't threatened him. Hadn't even intimated a threat. Did it make a difference if she was principled about who and why she killed? Not something he'd ever had to contemplate before.

CHAPTER 15
IN THE COAL MINES OF HELL

SAM

As the last line of *Go Rest High on That Mountain* died on Aunt Candace's lips, Sam thought that if there was any justice in the next life, Daddy would find no rest anywhere but instead be slaving away in the coal mines of hell to atone for this life. She didn't expect much better for herself when the time came.

The problem with summers down South is that they're hotter than all hell. Now combine that with being all gussied up for a funeral and Sam was miserable. Sweat dripped down her back like there was a leaky faucet between her shoulder blades.

Her brothers, on either side of her, kept tugging on their collars and fiddling with their ties like it would give them some kind of relief. *Sorry, fellas. You're stuck, same as me.*

"In times like these," the ancient pastor said, "I find the words of the Apostle Paul to be a great encouragement. Now, you'll remember that Paul himself was no stranger to suffering. In the Book of Romans, he wrote, 'Who shall separate us from the love of Christ? Shall trouble or hardship or persecution or famine or nakedness or danger or sword?'"

He paused to allow the congregation to collectively say, "No."

"That's right. Paul goes on. 'No, in all these things we are more than conquerors through him who loved us. For I am convinced that neither death nor life, neither angels nor demons, neither the present nor the future, nor any powers, neither height nor depth, nor anything else in all creation, will be able to separate us from the love of God that is in Christ Jesus our Lord.'" The pastor closed his Bible that was nearly falling apart with wear. "Friends, there isn't anything in this life or the next that could keep our dear brother from the loving arms of his Savior."

A host of "Amens" made their way forward. Clearly not people who'd known Daddy well enough to know that if he had any kind of relationship with Jesus Christ, it was an adversarial one.

But maybe she was the only skeptical one. Her brothers' heads bobbed up and down as though they were buying it hook, line, and sinker.

"Let's close in a word of prayer. After that, the family will receive whoever would like to come by and say a word."

As soon as the pastor started with "Dear Heavenly Father …", Aunt Teresa made Sam and Buddy swap places and pulled Sam tight against her side. Teresa slipped her arm through Sam's and whispered, "I'm proud of you, girl."

Sam asked, "For what?"

"For not busting a gut when Pastor Ed was talking about your Daddy being with Jesus."

Now Sam laughed. A barking laugh she tried to convert to a cough. The pastor continued his prayer, but opened his eyes to glare at Sam. She mouthed "Sorry" and pointed at her aunt, who shrugged. Pastor Ed shook his head slightly, never missing a beat while beseeching the Creator for all manner of things.

Sam elbowed Teresa in the ribs. "You're gonna get me in trouble."

"With him? Nah. If we get out of this without any real

shenanigans, he'll be surprised. How did the job go the other day?"

"Fine."

Pastor Ed concluded the prayer, and another chorus of amens filled the sweltering air. He stepped forward to hug Jeb, then Buddy, who were both sobbing, mourning the loss of their father. A pang of guilt stabbed through Sam's belly. Daddy had it coming, and she'd have done it regardless, but she did feel bad about the pain she was causing her brothers.

"Actually," Sam followed up with her aunt, "it wasn't totally fine. There were a couple of hiccups, and I came home with a dog."

Teresa's demeanor changed. Her eyes narrowed, and she clenched her jaw. She dragged Sam out of the receiving line and away from the tent. Sam heard Buddy ask where she was going, but she couldn't turn to respond for fear she would trip. Teresa didn't let go of her arm until they were under the shade of a large oak, well removed from the procession.

"What's your problem?" Sam fussed.

"My problem? My problem is that you did something stupid. What's one of our rules?"

There's a lot of rules. Sam wasn't loving being dressed down like this. "You'll have to be more specific."

"We don't bring anything back from a job. Why? Why don't we do that?"

"I couldn't leave her th—"

"Answer the question," Teresa demanded.

Sam sighed and folded her arms across her chest. "Because we don't want anything that can connect us to the scene."

"Yeah, that's right. So you didn't bring home some trophy. You took their dog."

"And?"

"And people microchip their dogs so they can find them when they go missing."

Sam deflated like a kid's punching bag that had been hit too hard. "Oh." All the blood left her face like it didn't want to be associated with such a fool.

"Yeah."

Sam peeked over her shoulder toward the graveside tent. Lots of folks were still milling around, but the line had almost run its course. *I may have the police waiting for me when I get home, but at least I avoided that line. Silver linings and all that.*

"What do I do?" Sam asked meekly.

"Take it to the vet to have them check it for a tag, and hope for the best."

"That's it? I shouldn't … you know … I can't say it."

"That's it," Teresa said. "It's GPS, so they can figure out where she is and where she's been. So killing her—"

"Hush. Don't say that. I'm not doing that. Couldn't if I wanted to."

"Oh, so offing her human is fine, but dogs are out of the question."

Sam shrugged. "Yeah, pretty much. You want to come meet her? She's made things tense around the house. Desiree would never let us have an indoor pet, so the boys think that's some kind of hard-and-fast rule. Also, she likes Buddy but is pretty stand-off-ish toward Jeb."

"Sounds like she's a good judge of character," Teresa said. "Except for the part where she took to you."

Sam grinned. "Not nice."

Teresa's expression went dark, and she grew rigid.

"What?" Sam refrained from conspicuously looking over her shoulder at whatever Teresa had locked her eyes onto.

"Looks like Bennett Clayton isn't content to wait for us to finish our conversation. He's walking over here. And I guarantee you, it ain't to talk to me." Teresa started to step away from Sam. "I'll leave you to it."

Sam grabbed her arm. "By myself?"

Teresa leaned back in toward Sam and said in a low voice that was very nearly a growl, "Let go of my arm, and get yourself together. Show nothing but strength to this man. You want to be the HBIC? This is your first moment."

Sam dropped her hand. She waited several seconds after Teresa had cleared the area before turning to face Clayton. This was a man who knew how to wear a suit. He may have been the only man at the funeral who didn't shop at Men's Wearhouse or some department store. The trouble was, it lent even more credence to the idea that had formed in her head that he was the devil in black come to collect his toll. Her palms grew sweaty, and she hoped he didn't offer to shake hands.

"I'd say I'm sorry for your loss, but on account of I hear you're the one brought about his end, that doesn't seem like the appropriate sentiment."

Sam hoped the surprise didn't show on her face that he knew. She ought not to have been surprised, though. Four people other than her knew. Word was bound to leak, even if it was only a rumor. A rumor that might serve her ends.

"Well, I'll be honest, Mr. Clayton—"

"Bennett. Please."

"I would've been disappointed if you fed me the same spoonful of hot garbage as everyone else. Your relationship with your Daddy was ... complicated, but I understood y'all were always straight with each other. For better or worse. I expect the same."

He was appraising her. The deep shadows cast by the early afternoon sun worked to hide the depths of his black eyes. He nodded. "I want you to come work for me."

"And you think this is the time and place for that? When I'm supposed to be over there with my grieving brothers?"

"If you would rather rejoin them," he turned his body sideways to her as though opening a door for her to go back to the funeral.

She stood firm.

"That's what I thought. I know how valuable you were to your father. There is no need for you to squander your talents working for your brothers. They are …"

"… incompetent jackasses." Sam finished his sentence for him.

He nodded.

"I won't be working for them. I'll be taking over."

Clayton's lips turned up at the corners. "Is that so?"

She glanced toward her brothers and back to Clayton, forcing herself to improve her posture. "They're sheep. Jeb don't have the wherewithal to carry out whatever ambition he's got, and Buddy wasn't born with an ounce of ambition in his body. They'll fall in line."

"Perhaps. What of the others? Are you willing to do what is necessary to persuade them to accept you as the head of the family? This is a far cry from your grandmother being the puppet master behind your grandfather for all those years."

Sam said simply, "I'll manage."

He gave a mock salute and turned to walk away.

On an impulse, Sam said, "Someone put a hit out on Daddy right before he died. You know anything about that?"

Without turning back to her, he said, "I'd heard something about that. Occupational hazard, Sam."

CHAPTER 16
FISH CAN'T HEAR YOU

SAM

"Jiminy Christmas!" Buddy yelled after his rod nearly smacked him in the face. "Did you see the size of that thing?"

"That's what she said," Jeb mumbled.

Sam roared with laughter. Three beers deep, everything was funnier than it would be otherwise.

Buddy sighed. "That catfish. It was like trying to reel in a cinder block. But made of muscle."

"Fish don't have muscles," Jeb said.

Sam stopped cackling and slowly turned her head toward her oldest brother. "Say what now?"

Jeb clenched his jaw and focused all his attention on his bobber. Having realized that he must've said something dumb, he refused to acknowledge her.

Pride goes before destruction, and a haughty spirit before a fall, Sam thought in his direction. Desiree used to quote that at her all the time when she was a teenager and made a show of being smarter than her step-mother. Of course, nobody had ever bothered to explain what *haughty* meant, so she still didn't know what was going to cause the fall.

"He said fishes don't have muscles," Buddy offered helpfully.

"Thank you, Buddy. I thought that's what he said." Using her bare foot, Sam nudged the cooler sitting between her and Jeb. "When we clean these fellas later, what part of them do you think we'll be eating?"

"The meat," Jeb said sullenly.

"Uh-huh," she said in her most patronizing tone, "which is made of?"

Jeb stood up and walked toward the edge of the lake. "Y'all are gonna scare off the fish with all this talking."

"That's a myth," Buddy called. "Fish can't hardly hear you talking. Daddy just told us that so we'd shut up."

Ignoring Buddy, Jeb tucked his fishing rod under his left arm and pulled a cigarette out of his shirt pocket. He lit it and took a drag without ever looking their way. He couldn't have been more done with their conversation.

Sam considered poking him a little more but wanted to avoid making him mad. Everyone was doing such a good job of compartmentalizing their father's funeral that they were only a few hours removed from. Aunt Teresa would have words for them later for giving the post-funeral luncheon an Irish good-bye, but they'd all needed to get out of there. Old family and old friends and people who were neither family nor friends all wanted to relive Daddy's past and tell stories they'd heard a dozen times or more. There comes a time when you can't hear anymore of it without screaming.

The burnt tobacco smell activated something in Sam and provoked her to pull out her own cigarette.

"Those things are gonna kill y'all," Buddy said.

Jeb replied with a sense of bravado. "Got to die of something."

Sam tilted her head way back and blew a plume of smoke into the air. "Family history says I won't live long enough for the cancer to get me. So I've got that going for me."

Jeb laughed and pointed his cigarette at her emphatically.

Buddy's dour expression suggested he found the comments distasteful. He had always been too gentle a creature to enjoy gallows humor. She loved him for it, but his docile nature had not made for an easy upbringing. Daddy and Jeb had ribbed him mercilessly about being sensitive.

"I've got to tell y'all about something that happened at the funeral," Sam said. Both men stopped fiddling with their fishing gear and waited on her. "Bennett Clayton pulled me aside and had a word."

"Saw that," Jeb said.

His tone had unspoken implications. Sam wondered if he would have ever brought it up or instead, nurtured resentment and suspicion over it. She had a pretty good idea about which answer was closer to the truth.

"He offered me a job to go work for him."

Buddy leaned forward in his camping chair. "And?"

"And what do you think? I told him to go kick rocks. I'm taking over for Daddy."

"You—"

She waved an arm in Jeb's direction. "Oh, can it. Your objection is noted."

His face reddened, and he started chewing on his upper lip.

"What did he say about that?" Buddy asked.

"Suggested I'd probably get killed."

"He threatened you?"

"Nah," Sam said. "Felt more like he was telling me as a professional courtesy. But that's not all. Now, he wants to meet." She pointed at her phone.

"Oh, he's definitely going to kill you," Jeb said. "Not himself, obviously. He'll have Marcus or one of the other guys do it."

"Obviously," Sam said. But it hadn't been obvious to her, not right away.

Buddy asked, "So what are you gonna do?" He immediately returned to chewing the side of his finger, a nervous tic that

Daddy had tried all manner of methods to discourage without success.

"Figure something out."

"So you're going to meet him, then?"

Sam shrugged and nodded, having not decided until that moment. She couldn't be seen ducking the other big player in town. She smirked at herself. *Other* insinuated she was counting herself as a big player already. Kind of ridiculous. But also, it wasn't. Whatever power or status she had or could assert wasn't about her. It wasn't about the person Samantha Ray. It was about the position she occupied.

A new king wasn't respected because of his own merits, but because he sat on the throne. Here she was, the newly (self) appointed heiress, and if she wanted to keep her head on her shoulders, she had darn sure better walk around like it. Oh, and not get murdered in her first meeting with an opponent.

Jeb shook his head. "So what happens to all the stuff Daddy gave you when ole' Bennett gives you the ax?"

"I reckon whatever I want. So you two clowns better be nice to me."

Jeb grunted. "I ain't groveling at my little sister's feet. I can tell you that right now."

Sam grinned. "I'd say things are looking shiny for Buddy, then. How's that sound, brother?"

He stared into the dirt at his feet and shrugged. "If it's all the same, I'd rather have you around."

His sincerity was almost too much for the moment. A little place in her chest ached a bit. Sam reached out and patted his arm. "I ain't going anywhere, Buddy. Jeb would get too much satisfaction out of it, and I can't have that."

He didn't respond right away. "Hey," she said, keeping her gaze on him until he looked her way. "Ain't nothing going to happen to me."

Buddy finally nodded, almost imperceptibly.

Sam dropped her cigarette butt into the empty beer bottle beside her chair and stood up. "Now, if y'all will excuse me, I've got some business to attend to." She walked straight ahead and into the lake.

"What the heck are you doing?" Jeb said. "You're gonna scare all the fish away."

"Gotta pee."

Jeb sighed. "You're the worst."

CHAPTER 17

AN OPEN INVESTIGATION

CHASE

CHASE SLID INTO THE CHAIR THAT THE SHERIFF HAD directed him to in Interrogation Room 1, an amusing attempt at intimidation. Or at the very least, informing Chase where he stood in the pecking order and where the real authority lay, even if Chase was asking the questions.

Without any preliminaries, Chase plopped his digital recorder on the table and clicked record. "I'm Chase Williams, here with Sheriff Jerry Tompkins at the Sheriff's Department in Jasper, Alabama. Sheriff, can you state your name and acknowledge that you consent to being recorded?"

The sheriff grunted his assent. "I'm Jerry Tompkins, and I know you're recording this conversation."

"Thank you. I'm here today to ask you questions about the disappearance of Valerie Wilson."

Tompkins wrinkled his nose and snorted.

The producer's going to love that.

"I told you before you started recording, and I'll say it again now — I ain't commenting on an open investigation. I shouldn't have even agreed to do this much, but I figured this is the quickest way to get you out of my hair."

"Understood," Chase said. "I appreciate your time."

"If you appreciated my time, you'd let me get on with the work the people of this county pay me to do, rather than this here podcasting business. Can I ask you a question?"

"Sure?"

Tompkins leaned forward, elbows on the table. "You said sure, but you made it sound like a question. Like maybe you weren't sure if I could ask you a question."

No one had ever accused Chase of being the most respectful person, but he was trying his best here. Being surly rarely got you more information. Even so, the sheriff was testing the outer limits of his patience. "Sure, yes. You can ask a question."

"When you — a stranger — come into town with the notion that you're going to solve a murder that law enforcement, with all our training and infrastructure, haven't closed out yet, what kind of message do you think that sends?" Having made his point, Tompkins settled smugly back into the chair.

Chase stammered into an eventual answer. "I, I hadn't considered it from that perspective before, sir. I gue—"

"Sheriff."

"Sir?"

"Not sir. When I was in the Army, 'sir' was only for officers. 'Sheriff' is fine."

"Thank you for your service."

"Don't do that. I didn't do it for thanks, and it wasn't some selfless act. I was an eighteen-year-old knucklehead looking for adventure and trying to get away from my daddy because he wouldn't get off my back. And yes, I can appreciate the irony of that now. Uncle Sam had more rules than my daddy ever did, and he wasn't much for explaining why, either. But you didn't come here for my life story, so let's get on with it."

He knew this was going to be a tough interview. Cops usually were. He'd prepared and rehearsed it in his head any number of times, but none of the rehearsals had gone this poorly. Not even close. Chase tried to clear his head and jumped into the next question. "What happened the night that Valerie Wilson went missing?"

"You could go read about it in the *Daily Mountain Eagle*. It may not be the *New Yorker*, but it's a good paper."

Chase said, "I've read it, Sheriff. I wanted to hear it from you."

"Fine. I'll tell you what's already public information. The night she went missing, the doctor got a call—"

"Dr. Dennis Wilson?"

"Yes, Dr. Dennis Wilson." Tompkin's clipped tone suggested that he wasn't accustomed to — nor did he appreciate — being interrupted. "He got a call on his cell phone that evening saying one of his patients had been admitted at Walker Baptist and he was needed."

"Who was the call from?"

"That's not public knowledge, and I can't comment on an open investigation."

"Is it not public knowledge, or do you not know either?"

The sheriff repeated, "That's not public knowledge, and I can't comment on an open investigation."

Your lack of knowledge isn't public knowledge? Chase filtered his internal monologue so that it didn't become external. "Have you checked his phone records?"

"That's not public knowledge, and I can't comment on an open investigation." Tompkin's smirk as he delivered the line for a third time was clearly intended to convey, *I told you this would be a waste of both of our time.*

Chase was unfazed. This wasn't his first rodeo. *Actually, it would be my first rodeo in a literal sense.* He reprimanded himself. *Focus.* "Is the doctor a suspect?"

The sheriff sighed heavily. "We have not publicly identified any persons of interest."

"What happened after he got the call?"

"What call?" He'd been so devoted to his non-answers that he appeared to have lost the line of questioning. "Oh. Uhh. He got up from the dinner table and told Valerie he was headed to the hospital to check on a patient."

"According to Dr. Wilson, that's what he told her."

"Yes, according to the doctor," Tompkins said with obvious hostility. "And it's going to be might hard to corroborate unless you're aware of somebody else being at their dinner table that night or how I might get in touch with Val."

"Is that normal for a pediatrician to go to the hospital after hours like that?"

"Beats me, kid. I'm a sheriff, not a doctor."

"What happened next?" Chase pushed on now that he found a topic that Tompkins was willing to talk about.

"When he got to the hospital, he found out that the patient hadn't been admitted. In fact, he didn't have any newly admitted patients. So he went back home thinking there was a mistake. When he got there, the place was ransacked, and Valerie was missing. No one has seen her since."

"What date was that?"

The sheriff looked at his watch. "About three weeks ago. A little more. August 10."

"What about the family of the kid that was reported to be at the hospital?"

"What about them?"

Chase clarified his question. "Did you check them out?"

"I can't comment on an open investigation."

"What was the child's name who was supposedly at the hospital?"

"That's a HIPAA violation. I can't tell you that."

Now for the *well, actually* part of the program. "It's not individually identifiable health information if the kid wasn't actually receiving medical treatment."

Tompkins leaned forward again. "Don't get cute. But since you're technically right, I go with my old standby — I can't comment on an open investigation."

Chase thought back fondly to his days of watching Futurama, where one of the characters said, "Technically correct is the best kind of correct." The sheriff didn't seem like he'd appreciate the reference, so Chase kept it to himself.

The sheriff's watch buzzed on his wrist. He looked at the screen, and then back at Chase. "Are we about done?"

"One more line of questions?"

"Shoot."

"Was Dr. Wilson ever investigated for any kind of child sexual abuse?"

A bark of unexpected laughter came out of the sheriff. "That's a helluva accusation to throw at someone."

"Not accusing. Just asking."

"Before I dignify that with any kind of response, how about you tell me why you're asking?"

Chase said, "It's my understanding that he married a former patient, who also babysat his youngest daughter, when she was right out of college, and he had kids her age. It's not farfetched to wonder if something started up when she was younger. And if that's possible, were there others? So, were there ever any investigations or even accusations against him concerning anything of that nature?"

"Here's what I know. His practice is in Jasper city limits, so you'd need to ask Chief Richards about that. So if that's all, I've got some things to get back to. You may have noticed we're kind of busy around here."

"If you ever want to talk about the congressman, you know how to reach me."

Rather than respond to the prompt, the sheriff stood up and walked to the door of Interrogation Room 1. Standing in the door frame, he said, "If you've got any sense about yourself, you'll hit the dusty trail back north of the Mason-Dixon."

Chase couldn't tell if that was only a recommendation, or if there were some teeth behind it. He clicked off the recorder and shoved it into his bag.

CHAPTER 18

THIS IS HOW YOU DIE

SAM

THIS IS HOW YOU DIE. STUPID, STUPID, STUPID. TERESA'S GONNA BE pissed if she has to arrange another funeral. Jeb had wanted to come with her, but she'd insisted on handling her business alone. In preparation, she had rewatched *The Godfather*, confirming her suspicions that Clayton planned to have her killed at this meeting if she didn't give in to whatever demands he had in store. She didn't intend to concede anything. This is where she would die. At the gaudiest, most out-of-place, Spanish-style mansion on Smith Lake.

She didn't love the idea of her corpse being eaten by catfish and whatever other scavengers lived at the bottom of the lake, but that seemed like a highly probable outcome. Still, here she was, because if she did survive the meeting, it would go a long way toward securing her legitimacy. That alone would minimize where future threats came from. Right now, her hold on things seemed tenuous. The smallest wave could displace her. She needed something — even if it was a long shot — to shore things up.

Sam opened the door of the truck and slid out. She pulled her phone out of the belt pack that was lying on the bench seat, leaving the .380 zipped inside and feeling naked without it. In fact, she'd rather be entirely naked and have only the gun than the other way around. But there was no point in carrying it in. They would take it away. Not bothering to carry the gun in the first place and stripping them of the opportunity to disarm her was the stronger move. It projected the confidence she needed to portray.

Probably. Maybe? Whatever. The end result would be the same — in a house full of Clayton's people, she and Clayton would be the only ones not carrying. That was a guess. He would want to be seen as a business man with clean hands, not the grimy, cut-throat she knew him to be.

Sam shut the door of the truck and tossed the keys to the giant of a security man approaching her, as though he were the valet. Surprise flashed across his face. "Take good care of her. I'd hate to have to whoop you when it's time to leave."

She strutted toward the front door, where another security fella waited with a wand. "Let's have at it, Harry Potter. And don't get too handsy."

He nearly smiled, but caught himself in time to reapply his expressionless demeanor. After she passed inspection, he opened the ridiculously large front door, letting her into a foyer with the most pretentious decor she'd ever seen. *This is what running sex workers and drugs buys you. Might be Papaw chose poorly.* In the generations before the Claytons had dealt in the vice trades, they had built their country empire on the backs of others through sharecropping and slavery. Exploitation was in their blood.

When Bennett entered the foyer with a small entourage trailing him, he greeted Sam with a warm smile and a hug, like they were old friends. She was half tempted to check one of the full-length mirrors to make sure he hadn't planted a knife in her back. And she was definitely curious who he was putting on a show for. It was only his people and her. Everyone in the room knew he was a monster.

"Didn't a pretty plantation manor used to sit here?" she asked.

Bennett nodded. "It did. But the upkeep was a bear. Maintenance on a house that's older than half the states in the country is absurdly expensive and inconvenient. So once my parents and everyone else who was attached to it died, I replaced it with something … more modern."

And fugly. Sam smiled politely, realizing as she did it that she was evolving. Old Sam — as in two weeks ago — would have sniped about getting on with whatever this was also about. New Sam was willing to feel things out a bit. *No reason to be the cow leading the herd through the shoots to the slaughterhouse.*

"Would you like a tour?" Bennett offered.

"I'm good, thanks." *Old Sam isn't totally dead.*

"Straight to business then? Let's go out to the back veranda. It'll still be cool, and I like seeing the alpacas."

Also, it's easier to hose someone's blood off out there than have them clean it off the fancy tile inside. New Sam remained very cynical about Bennett's intentions, regardless of his manners. Nevertheless, she followed him and his gaggle of men followed her. *I'd give my left ovary to have a pistol handy.* The outcome might be the same, but at least she'd take a couple of hombres with her.

Two men opened a set of French doors at the back of the palatial home. Bennett strode directly to a table holding a spread of fruit and pastries, and gestured for her to take a seat opposite him.

Sam sat, resisting the impulse to slouch down into her natural posture. *Desiree would be so proud. No, not proud. Her stepmonster would never be proud of her. Less disappointed.*

Bennett sat across from her as his half-dozen men became part of the landscape along the wall. Sam gestured at them with a thumb. "They tag along with you everywhere?"

He smiled. "Your reputation precedes you …." He didn't

quite finish his sentence with the right intonation. "What do you prefer I call you?"

I prefer you don't call me. "Sam is fine."

"Your reputation precedes you, Sam."

"I've heard that before, but it's not usually intended as a compliment."

"Certainly it is this time. I want you to make them irrelevant."

Sam leaned forward and moved some pineapple and cantaloupe onto her plate, giving herself a few seconds to figure out what he was asking. "You want me to be your bodyguard? That's not really my thing. Wouldn't know the first thing about it."

"No, no," he corrected her. "I want you to come work for me and eliminate my need for security altogether."

"I appreciate the offer. Really, I do. But I think you'd find that I'm what they call unemployable. Too much independence for my own good." Sam thought that if she declined him in a self-deprecating way, he'd take more kindly to it.

"I will pay you handsomely."

"I have no doubt about that, but I don't much care for doing others' bidding. It's a me problem."

Bennett leaned forward. "I disagree. Are you not a contract killer, doing other people's bidding all the time?"

"Sure," Sam said, sitting back in her chair, trying to appear casual, even though all her senses were on full alert. "But I'm an independent contractor. I can take or decline jobs as I want. You don't strike me as the kind of man who lets his employees dictate their terms to him."

"I am unaccustomed to being told no," he agreed.

Sam nodded. "Yeah, I don't much cotton to that."

His upper lip twitched. The first outward sign of his displeasure with the way the conversation was going. It wasn't quite a sneer, but it was definitely in that family. "I have twice offered for you to come work for me, and you've turned me down twice."

"I am flattered. It's just that I don't think it's a good fit. I've got my brothers to think about. There's the other businesses. A lot going on right now."

Bennett held his hands out and plastered on a thin smile. "As it turns out, I am in an acquisitions phase. I can buy your other businesses and take on your brothers as well."

So generous of you. "Like I said. Not a good fit." Sam pushed back her chair, which made an awful noise on the presumably expensive tile, and stood up. "So if that's all there is, I think I'll be off now." Neither of the men in front of the French doors moved aside as she approached. She turned to face Bennett. "Could you have your monkeys stand down?"

Bennett took his time responding. He stood slowly, placing his fingertips on the tables. His knuckles whitened as he leaned forward. "I do not intend for you to leave here without us having reached an agreement."

Sam pursed her lips and nodded. "I kinda figured you'd say something like that." She reached into her back pocket, and there was a clatter of assault rifles shifting in the men's hands. "Calm down," she said over her shoulder. "The gorilla at the front already checked me out. I'm harmless." Turning back to Bennett, she said, "Before either of us says anything we can't walk back, I'd like to make a phone call. You good with that?"

He nodded.

Sam walked back to the table and tossed her phone down. She punched the screen a few times until a phone on the other end began ringing. "I'm gonna put it on speaker. I think you'll want to hear this." Bennett stood upright and folded his arms across his chest.

"¿Que?" a voice answered.

"Rodrigo, can you tell me where you are right now?"

"XL Gymnastics."

She was super tempted to look up at Bennett's expression, but restrained herself a little longer. "Uh-huh. And are Mr. Clayton's daughter and sweet little grandbaby in there?"

"Si."

"Alright. Thanks, Rodrigo. You hang tight. I'll call you when I get home."

She had no sooner hung up than a red-faced Bennett said, "How dare you threa—"

"Oh, shove it." She turned her back to him. "I didn't threaten anybody. I don't make threats. But you needed to know you're not the only one with a plan. Now, tell your boys to move aside."

CHAPTER 19

WE'RE NOT PREPARED FOR THAT

SAM

THEY'D ACTUALLY HAD A NICE DINNER, FOR ONCE. SAM had been skeptical about having sushi in Jasper. Before tonight, she couldn't recall having ever seen a Japanese person in town, but sure enough, there they were. Now, it was time to talk shop. She had limited Jeb and Buddy to two beers, and Rodrigo was a teetotaler, so everybody would be sober enough for a business discussion by the time they got back to Daddy's house. *Nope. Your house.*

In the den now, with the Braves game on the TV for some background noise, Sam flashed back to the subject of her most recent contract as she scratched Waffles under the ear. She shook off the memory and said, "We've got a problem. Bennett Clayton is looking to rid himself of us and take over our side of things."

Buddy scrunched his brow. "I thought everybody agreed to divvy things up and stay in our lanes."

Sam shrugged. "Clayton's got ambitions. He'd planned to get shed of me today, but Rodrigo and I dissuaded him of that notion."

"How'd you manage that?" Jeb asked.

"I had Rodrigo sitting outside his granddaughter's gymnastics place when I went to meet with him. And when he got ready to have his fellas blast me to bits, I clued him in on what was going on."

Buddy's eyes bugged, and he turned to Rodrigo. "You were going to kill a kid?"

"Ask el jefe." He jerked a thumb in Sam's direction.

"Well?" Buddy insisted.

"I didn't think it would come to that."

"And if it had?"

Jeb shoved his little brother's shoulder. "Don't be naïve. If it came to that, she'd be dead. And we'd be dead. And it wouldn't matter anymore. So what's the plan, Little Sis?"

"Not to get killed. I'm working out the kinks. But in the meantime, we need some ideas for additional revenue. I've been looking at the books, and Daddy had been letting the business slip for years. We're falling behind the other families."

Jeb sat forward in his chair and pointed his finger at her. "I won't sit here listening to you bad-mouth Daddy."

Sam leaned toward him, matching his increased intensity. *Can't let him think he can get all aggro on me.* "Brother, I'm not talking ill of him. I'm telling you the state of the business. It's not good. So unless we all want to go get nine-to-fives, we gotta figure out how to diversify our income. Relying so heavily on hitman work isn't sustainable."

"Sustainable?" Buddy chuckled. "Diversifying income? You going to business school all of a sudden?"

Her cheeks grew hot. She *had* been reading business books and even considering going to night school. Her first instinct was to hurt Buddy for embarrassing her, but she restrained herself. She was proud of herself for showing restraint. It wasn't all that long ago she would've lashed out first and dealt with the fallout second.

"I'm evolving," she said.

"I got another question. Should Rodrigo even be here seeing

as he ain't family?" Buddy said, then gestured to Rodrigo. "No offense."

"No problemo," the man said.

"Rodrigo stays," Sam said, not offering to explain herself further. The man had been more loyal to her than either of her brothers, and he was more competent by a country mile. "Now, anybody got ideas for how to make some money?"

"How about crystal? I know some people," Buddy said.

You know some people. That was an understatement. Trouble was, they all knew him as a consumer, not a distributor. She shook her head. "Between Clayton and the Davises, they have that pretty well locked down. I don't want to step on anyone else's business and kick off a war. We're not prepared for that. Besides, drugs draw too much unwanted attention."

"I got an idea," Jeb said. "How about getting into the skin game, if you catch my drift?"

"I don't."

"A strip club."

"Yeah," Buddy chimed in excitedly. "We could re-open Wesley's Booby Trap."

Jeb giggled. "I can manage the talent. You can work there too," he said to Sam.

"I don't think so."

"Not as a stripper," Buddy said. "You don't have the ... uhh ... assets for that. And by assets, I mean jubblies."

The boys cackled.

She was getting real uncomfortable with the direction of this conversation. Them assessing her body like that tread awfully close to why she'd put Daddy in the ground, and she'd like to avoid doing that to the boys.

"We're not doing that." Sam stood up. "I tell you what. I'll figure it out and let you know."

Neither brother took their cue.

"This ain't a dictatorship. This is a family decision," Jeb complained.

"You're right and you're wrong. It is a family decision, but seeing as I'm the head of the family, I'll make this decision."

"The hell you are," Jeb said. "I'm the oldest."

"You're dismissed," she said, staring him down.

At first, he didn't move.

Sam maintained her unflinching gaze.

He looked away. "Whatever. You can pretend to be in charge." He got up and slapped Buddy on the leg. "Come on, bro."

Buddy looked up at Sam. She flicked her head toward the door.

After the boys left, Rodrigo said, "Business is bad, eh?"

"Nah. It's not so bad. But I don't want them getting too comfortable either, thinking I'm going to be their mama."

"You have a plan?"

"Not yet. But I met with the lawyer again. He said we own most of the laundromats and dry cleaners in the county. Daddy bought them to clean his money, but they turned into cash cows. Lawyer said they made enough money that we could probably go totally straight if we wanted to."

"Why no do that?" Rodrigo asked.

"Well ...." That was as far as she got. She hadn't actually considered it before. A life in which she wasn't an outlaw wasn't something she'd ever entertained. Living outside the law was so ingrained into her identity, having been passed down through a half-dozen generations, that thinking of being legitimate kind of broke her brain a bit. It took her several minutes of mucking about in that quagmire of thought before she finally said something. "I don't know."

Rodrigo had lost the train of the conversation. "No se what?"

"About leaving this here life of crime."

Rodrigo nodded and stood up.

"You headed out?" she asked.

"Si."

Sam followed him out and sat in one of the rockers on the front porch.

As he hit the bottom stop, Rodrigo asked, "You not worried he come tonight?"

"Not really. He's not spontaneous like that. He'll want to make a plan."

"You want I should stay?"

"Hell no," Sam said. "I don't want Maria mad at me."

"Same." He waved and sauntered toward his Bronco.

After his headlights disappeared, only the glow from the windows and Sam's cigarette shone any light. The moon hadn't come out to play with the stars yet. She pulled her phone out of her pocket and tapped her text messages. She found it curious that the person she most wanted to talk to was the one she had the least certainty about her status with.

Sam typed out six or seven different messages that she immediately erased, her self-loathing growing with each occurrence. She finally sent, "Wanna hang out?"

The immediate appearance of gray-shrouded ellipses kept her from dissecting her decision. But when the dots disappeared just as quickly, she decided to set the phone down on the side table instead of chucking it into the tree line.

The glass tabletop rattled a moment later.

"Sure."

She dropped a GPS pin into the text message and typed, "30 min."

CHAPTER 20
FIGURATIVELY OR LITERALLY

CHASE

CHASE SHUT THE CAR DOOR, WONDERING WHAT HE'D agreed to. While a host of stars decorated the night sky, inky nothingness spread out before him. He knew he was in the right place because Sam's red truck was backed down the boat ramp. But if it hadn't been for that, he'd have gotten right back in the car and hoped to avoid hearing the music from *Deliverance* chasing after him.

Sam came around the far side of the boat and hopped over the trailer's tongue. "I didn't think you had a car," she said, skipping any semblance of a customary greeting.

"Turned out to be too much of a hassle to get anywhere without one."

"Yup." She nodded her head toward the boat. "Can you back a boat off a trailer?"

Instead of a flat *no*, Chase said, "Put it in reverse and hit the gas?"

Even though the sole streetlight in the parking lot cast a shadow over Sam's face, it didn't hide her bemused expression. "I think I know the answer to this next one — how about backing a truck down a boat ramp?"

"Is it any harder than driving in ice or snow?"

"Nope."

"Then I think I can manage to back up in a straight line for a short distance."

Sam considered things for a minute. "You understand that if you drown my truck, I'll have to kill you?"

With most other people, he'd assume it was entirely a joke. "Figuratively or literally?"

"I don't rightly know yet."

Chase decided to take his chances and held out a hand palm up as he walked toward the truck. The keys jangled as they slapped his skin. He hopped in the truck and rumbled it to life. Cautiously — very, very cautiously — he put the truck into reverse and eased his foot off the brake, keeping his eyes on the rear-view mirror the whole time. Sam was cast in a harsh red light, but he could see her well enough.

When the trailer was mostly submerged, she held up a hand for Chase to stop, started the bass boat's engine, and backed it off the trailer. She didn't give Chase any more signals, but he figured it was safe now to go park the truck. He'd already decided to pull headlong into a spot. There was no way he was going to have her watching him try to back a trailer up. He'd seen several of the dozen ways that could go wrong and had no interest in providing the evening's entertainment.

By the time Chase had finished parking, Sam had sidled the boat up to the dock. He jogged across the parking lot toward her. "You're like a poor man's David Hasselhoff," Sam called. "But not shirtless."

"Thanks?"

He took a tentative first step from the dock onto the boat.

"You're not gonna tump it over. Come on."

With more confidence than he felt, Chase planted a second foot on the boat. Sam hardly waited for him to get his balance before engaging the throttle, causing him nearly to tumble into the seat beside her.

She slapped him in the chest with a life jacket. "Put this on."

"I didn't see you as a safety-first kind of girl."

She raised her voice to be heard over the wind as the boat picked up speed. "If you fall into that and bump your head, nobody'll ever see you again. There's enough dead bodies in this lake without adding you to the mix."

He wondered how many bodies she'd contributed to that number, but thought he didn't want to know. So he redirected. "Tump? What the heck does that even mean?"

"It's not my fault you're an uncultured swine. Look it up on your phone."

Chase fiddled around with his phone for a minute before saying, "My dictionary app says it's not a real word. Or at least not the way you're using it. It's not a verb."

In the dim glow from the boat's console, Chase saw her shake her head. "Of course you have a dictionary app."

"It's really for the thesaurus, not the dictionary."

"If you think that makes it less nerdy, it doesn't."

He'd accepted the mantle of nerdery long ago. He'd had plenty of folks tell him it was incongruent for him to be both an athlete and a nerd, but what they didn't understand was that the base tendencies that underlined both groups had a lot of crossover.

Sam slowed the bass boat and brought it to a stop about forty yards from a dock. A green light illuminated the water at its end.

"What do you know about night fishing?" Sam asked.

"About as much as I know about day fishing."

Sam reached behind her, grabbing a fishing rod and handing it to him. She pointed at the reel. "This is a spincast reel. It's pretty much fool-proof. Click that button down on your back-cast. Release it on the forward cast. You're gonna want to land your crankbait in the middle of that circle of light. When it hits the water, give it a few seconds and start reeling. We'll know pretty quick if the fish are here tonight. If not, we'll move on to another one. Got it?"

"So you didn't come out here to talk?"

"The exact opposite. I came out here *not* to talk."

After Sam baited her hook with a big worm and as she moseyed up to the front of the boat, Chase made his first cast while her back was still to him. Growing up in the city hadn't provided him with a lot of opportunities for fishing. Relief washed over him when his lure plunked down in the circle of green light.

He began reeling, first fast, then slower. His thinking was that a little fish wouldn't always swim at the same speed. Being mostly ignorant about fish behavior, this wasn't based on anything solid. Once he retrieved his crankbait, he reared back and cast. Again, the bait landed within the target range.

Trying to be discreet, Chase peeked out of the corner of his eye to see if Sam was watching him. He didn't want to care what she thought of him — his feelings about her were as compli-cated as anyone he'd ever known for only a week. *We're from entirely different worlds. She's a killer. A contract killer, no less. Not even like a justified thing where you could be like, well, sometimes people find themselves in terrible situations and bad things happen. Nope, she does it for money. As if she's another millennial in the gig economy. Yet, we still have a kinship.* He shook his head at himself. *Kinship. Who uses that word anymore? Nerd alert!*

Something prodded at Chase's bait. He jerked the rod in surprise.

"Easy does it," Sam said, surmising what was happening. "Somebody's testing it out down there, seeing if they want to eat what you're offering. Don't scare them off."

For another ten minutes or so, Chase cast and retrieved. Cast and retrieved. But to no effect. He never got another nibble. Sam was playing at the edges of the light with her bait, but she couldn't entice anything, either.

"So," Chase broke the extended silence, "what is it you came out here not to talk about?"

CHAPTER 21
NEARLY BEING MURDERED

CHASE

"Nearly being murdered today." Sam said it mid-cast. She didn't turn to look at him. She said it as if she'd been telling him she ate a cheeseburger for dinner.

Chase waited for … what? A punch line? The other shoe to drop? Something. It wasn't every day somebody tried to kill you. Of course, that had been *his* life experience. *Your mileage may vary.* "Care to elaborate?"

She reeled the line in wordlessly, then abruptly set her rod down and pulled out a cigarette and set it between her lips. Reaching for her lighter, she said, "You mind?" The cigarette bobbed like a see-saw when she spoke.

"Does it matter?"

She thumbed the flint wheel on her black Zippo. A flame danced in the light breeze before she clicked it shut and pocketed the lighter. Sam slouched into the pilot's seat and exhaled smoke into the night. "Not really. A girl's got needs."

Feeling awkward still standing at the back of the boat, Chase slid into the chair beside her and relied on his time-tested technique of letting someone else work themselves up to speak without his prompting. When there was an open question hanging out there, if you were patient enough, they would usually fill the void.

"It wasn't personal. Just someone doing what they thought needed done."

"That's about the least specific thing anyone has ever told me."

A smirk slipped over one side of Sam's mouth. "You want all of it?"

"As much as you're willing to tell."

"So, here's the problem. I can tell my lawyer anything because he can never tell anyone else. It's all going to the grave with him. My pastor. I can even talk to him about anything. Same reason. If I saw a shrink, I could confess most anything to her. You, though — I like you. Don't get me wrong. I even trust you to a degree. But, like I said before, if some judge says they're gonna toss you into the clink on contempt charges until you talk, I got no cause to think you're going to take that kind of rap for me. Even my brothers wouldn't do that. Buddy might want to, but I don't think he has the … fortitude for it. Heck, I think the only other person that has that kind of privilege is a spouse."

"Whoa," Chase held both hands out in front of him. "If this is some kind of marriage proposal, I may have been sending mixed signals."

Sam rolled her eyes and laughed. "Shut up."

Chase reclined in his chair and hung his legs over the side of the boat. He scanned the night sky to see if any planets were visible. "I would though."

He didn't look her way, but heard her exhale.

"Would what?"

She knew what, but she wanted to make him say it.

"All I'm saying is, you can trust me if you need to talk through something."

"Why?"

"The family I was born to was ... not great, so once I got old enough, I figured out that the people you're related to by blood aren't necessarily the ones you're willing to go to the wall for if things get tight." Chase grew suddenly uncomfortable with the amount of sentiment he'd been expressing. "Not that — you know what I'm saying — right?"

Sam licked her thumb and forefinger, and used them to put out her cigarette, which had burned down to the filter. "I hear you, cuz." She turned the boat's engine over and drove what felt like a couple of miles to another dock that looked more or less identical to the one they'd left.

The otherwise quiet travel time meant Chase had several minutes to parse through what he'd said and regret learning to talk in the first place, because if he'd never learned to speak, he wouldn't have had the opportunity to embarrass himself like that.

Sam killed the engine, grabbed her fishing rod, and walked to the front of the boat. She immediately cast, unlike the last stop where she'd scouted for a bit before doing anything. "One of my father's rivals — Bennett Clayton — approached me at the funeral and offered for me to come work with him. I basically told him to pound sand, so he figured trying to kill me was his best bet. But I was a step ahead of him and had my man following Clayton's family around. So when I went to meet him where he thought he was going to execute me like some hostage, I called my guy and put him on speaker phone so he could tell everybody who he was watching. Seeing the surprise and fear on his face was delicious. He's used to dealing with chumps, but he learned real quick that I'm cut from a different cloth. 'Course, that creates its own problem."

"What's that?"

"Well, now he's already tried to kill me and failed. In front of his people, no less. A whole crew of 'em heard that call. He figures I ain't the kind of person to let a thing like that lie, and not that long ago, he would've been right."

Chase didn't want to break the spell of whatever was happening here, so he interjected himself only enough to encourage her. "But now?"

"But now, I've been having a crisis of conscience. Or something. I'm not real sure what's going on up here." She nodded her head quickly, since her hands were occupied. "The accountant says our legit businesses make enough money to stand on their own, besides what Daddy squirreled away over the last couple of decades. I don't really know how to go straight, but I thought I might give it a shot. See how it goes."

Chase's heart leaped at the idea that the moral dilemma he'd been experiencing might be lifted. "What about Bennett? Would he believe you if you told him?"

"That's still a problem." Her slouchy posture suddenly changed, and her eyes widened a bit. "Hang on. I need to have a think." She set her rod into a holder, fished another cigarette out of her fanny pack, and lay on her back with her legs dangling over the side of the boat.

Standing there watching her, Chase felt like a creeper, so he occupied himself with tossing a lure toward the dock light. Several casts later, Sam sat upright. "I think I have an idea."

"Alright."

"Let's say, hypothetically, that we use our dry cleaners and laundromats to clean the money from our other ventures. It's a little on-the-nose, I know. If we're not in those other lines of business any more, we could offer those laundry services to others. Help them clean their money and take a small percentage for our troubles."

"Others like Bennett?"

"If we're business partners instead of being competitors, he doesn't have a whole lot of motivation to turn me into chum.

I've got to figure out all the details and make a proposal in a relatively neutral space."

"So much for going totally clean, huh?"

"Eh," Sam said with a smirk. "Tigers and stripes and all that."

He laughed at the very Sam-like perspective on the matter.

"What about you?" she asked. "Any problems you need solving?"

"I'm interviewing the chief of police tomorrow."

Sam scoffed. "He's a real peach. I think you'll really enjoy his company." Her tone was thoroughly drenched in sarcasm.

"That's all you've got for me?"

"No. One more thing — don't mention my name. He's never been a member of my fan club."

"That's hard to believe. You're such a gentle and inviting creature."

She flicked a cigarette butt at him and returned her attention to fishing.

CHAPTER 22
A STORY ABOUT STINGING INSECTS

CHASE

Chief Richards leaned back in his chair and propped his feet up on his desk. After he'd folded his arms across his chest and gotten himself situated, he said, "So I guess you're here to talk about Val? I hear you've been pestering plenty of folks about her."

Chase adjusted the recorder on the desk, concerned that the chief's nonchalant posture would put him too far from the mic for the sound levels to be right. Nobody had any appreciation for the difficulty it created in editing when they prioritized their comfort or how they wanted to be perceived over their proximity to the microphone. But hassling them about it wouldn't do any good either. That was a quick way to get the interview started with someone who was already annoyed. "Actually, no," Chase said.

"Oh?"

He appeared to be genuinely surprised, perhaps even relieved, though that wasn't likely to last. "No. I wanted to ask you about Dr. Wilson's first wife."

"Beth?" He swiped a hand across a forehead like he was sweating.

But if anything, the air conditioner was working overtime to keep it too cool inside. That's something he'd noticed since being in Alabama. Everywhere was cold inside, like they were still trying to make up for the first two hundred years of settlement before they had air conditioning.

"I haven't thought about her in a stone's age," the grizzled old policeman said. "What is it you want to know?"

"Let's start with this — don't you think it's strange that he's had two wives disappear?"

Richards shook his head. The rubber-soled boots came off the desk, and he sat rigidly in his chair now. "Hold it right there. You don't know what you're talking about."

"Care to enlighten me?"

"I don't suppose that if I say no, you'll leave well enough alone, will you?"

Chase didn't have to think before answering. "Probably not."

Richards considered his options before sighing. "Beth was too big for this place. Always was. I knew her my whole life up until she left. She was like one of them wild mustangs out West. Just born wild and can't be tamed. She tried. She got married and had babies. Did all the things a Southern woman is supposed to do, but if you looked in her eyes, you could see them getting dimmer."

"With all due respect," Chase said, "you don't think you're romanticizing it a bit?"

"Wasn't anything romantic about it. You ever see one of those mustangs up close when they're in captivity? They're made for something bigger than that cage. You know it, and they do too. Even if they've never seen a prairie, they know there's a part of them missing. Beth was like that."

"So you think she skipped town one day and left her family behind?"

"That's exactly what I think happened. Some women aren't fit to raise a family."

"I wonder if you'd say the same about a man who left." *Whoops. Didn't mean to say that out loud.*

Richards asked indignantly, "What's that supposed to mean?"

"Sorry. Forget it. I didn't mean anything by it. Did you do any kind of investigation that led you to the conclusion that she left of her own accord?"

"Of course we did. This ain't some fly-by-night operation here. We're real police who do real work to take care of our people."

He clearly still had his guard up. Chase patted his own chest. "My fault. I asked that poorly. I only ask because I'm sure you don't get called out over every domestic situation where somebody splits."

"Uh-huh," the police chief grunted and relaxed his posture. "Most times we don't. But Doc was worried something had happened to her, so we checked it out. This was …" He looked at his watch as if it would help, "… about fifteen years ago. Twenty at the most. Their youngest wasn't much more than a tyke."

"What did you find?" Chase prompted.

Richards took a minute to consult his long-term memory. "She'd taken a couple of suitcases and most of her summer clothes. Swimsuits too. Withdrew a shade under ten grand from their bank account. Not at a local branch. Everybody here would have known her. She went a couple towns over. Her car popped up in Texas a few months later, but not her." He shrugged. "She's never been seen since. Probably living the good life down in Costa Rica or Belize or somewhere."

On ten grand? Not likely. "None of that felt staged or set up to you?"

The police chief's face grew more stern. He'd expected his account to be the end of things. He wasn't accustomed to being questioned and didn't care for it. Richards was a man who'd had the last word on things for a long time.

"Doc was a broken man for a long time after Beth left. As anybody would be. It was years before his old self resurfaced."

Before or after he started making moves on the babysitter? Chase realized he was assuming the worst about Doctor Wilson but had nothing more to support it than his own intuition, which is basically the same as what Chief Richards was relying on in his belief that Beth had left everything behind. Richards actually knew these people, while Chase was hanging his hat entirely on the highly improbable coincidence of the same man having two wives vanish and him being uninvolved. He needed to adjust his own thought processes. Be more open to possibilities, rather than looking for things to support his conclusions. He had to be in the business of asking open-ended questions, not approaching things with an agenda.

"Did you turn up any evidence that suggested foul play?"

"No."

A long silence settled in between them and made itself comfortable.

"Can I give you some advice, son?" the chief asked.

Was there anything more patronizing than someone calling you *son*? There's no doubt when that happens exactly where you stand in that person's estimation. And even more telling, they want you to know it. Chase waited, neither consenting to nor denying the request.

Chief Richards leaned forward, elbows on his desk, hands clasped in front of him. Then he broke them apart and turned off the recorder. "There's a whole lot of history in these hills and hollers. Some of it buried deeper than others. You take a shovel out there and start digging, and there's no telling what you're like to turn up."

That's kind of the point. Chase knew better than to speak it. He nodded curtly.

The police chief continued, "People don't like dwelling on the past."

Chase thought that the dozens of Confederate flags he'd seen flying in front yards since landing in Alabama kind of contradicted that statement.

Richards hadn't finished his admonishment. "What I'm trying to say is … look, are you familiar with yellow jackets?"

"As in the Georgia Tech mascot?"

"Yeah, like that. What you need to know about yellow jackets is that they're assholes. They're not like bees. Even paper wasps won't usually bother you unless you give them cause to. Nah. Yellow jackets will go out of their way to sting a fellow. Another thing is they burrow in the ground — that's where they build their nests."

Chase shook his head, at a loss for where this was heading. "Okay."

"If you ain't careful when you're walking through the woods, you might stumble onto a yellow jacket hive. If you do that, they're going to come after you. And I mean, they'll chase you down. You'll be lucky if you only get dozens of stings. If you ain't lucky though, you could get stung hundreds of times. Might even die from it."

Chase tilted his head and considered his next words. "I suspect you're trying to tell me something, other than a story about stinging insects."

Chief Richards stood up and stuck his right hand out toward Chase.

Thus ends the interview. Chase stood as well and took the offered hand.

"Tread lightly and watch your step."

CHAPTER 23
MINE IS PRETTY

SAM

THE LAWYER SUPPORTED THE IDEA THAT SHE GO legit, and frankly, she thought she saw some relief in his eyes. Of course, she only told him half of it. The straight half, not the laundering bit. As she understood it, she couldn't tell Nick that she was *going to* break the law. She could only involve him *after* she'd done it. But what if it was an ongoing operation like money laundering for other criminal enterprises? When could she tell him about that? She could pose a hypothetical question.

As for Stan the accountant, he would undoubtedly notice a significant uptick in business with the laundromats and dry cleaners. But he wouldn't ask more than the necessary number of questions. He would carry on fiddling with his spreadsheets or whatever he did all day and make sure everything looked right and Uncle Sam got his share.

For all his (many) faults, Daddy had been shrewd about business, and he hadn't been selfish with his accumulated wisdom. "Pay your taxes. All of them. We make enough money that a few thousand going to the feds that you might could quibble over ain't worth getting audited by the IRS. That'll bring hellfire down on your head real quick. And that's the last thing you want. Scalawagging bastards." So they paid the feds and the lawyer and the accountant and local law enforcement. And nobody came calling. Staying on the right side of justice was an expensive business.

Speaking of business, it's time to quit procrastinating and call Bennett. "What do you think, Waffy? Will he go for it?"

At the sound of her name, the dog flopped onto Sam's bare feet and wriggled around, urging Sam to wiggle her toes. Sam complied. What good was a dog if you couldn't spoil it rotten and give it everything it wanted?

Sam sighed and punched at the screen of her phone until it started ringing on the other end. Anxiety tried to gnaw its way through her body for the twenty seconds or so it took for the call to ring all the way through to voicemail. After Clayton's terse suggestion to leave a message, Sam said, "This is Sam. There's something I want to talk to you about. Call me."

Sam stood up, and Waffles rolled on her side with a grunt. "You wanna go see the cows?"

The dog hurried to her feet and bolted down the steps into the yard, before whirling and panting impatiently at Sam.

"You're gonna have to wait until I get my boots on at least. Hang tight." Most dogs that didn't grow up around cattle were shy about thousand-pound cows. But not Waffles. There was definitely herding blood somewhere in that animal. She had taken right to the cows and started trying to boss them into going whatever direction she had in mind, whether they liked it or not.

After pulling her socks and boots on, Sam stepped inside the door and grabbed a set of keys. She yelled to Buddy, "I'm going to the back pasture to check on the cows."

He murmured a response, too immersed in a video game to use actual words.

"I'm taking your truck."

That got his attention. "What? Why?"

"'Cause it's a piece of junk, and mine is pretty."

He protested, but she didn't stick around to hear it, letting the screen door slam behind her. Desiree had always gotten pissed about the door slamming, so she'd made a habit of it.

As Sam crossed the porch and strode down the steps, Waffles chased her tail in excitement. Sam opened the door of her truck to retrieve her belt pack and holstered the .22 that was lying in the middle of the bench seat. Waffles waited expectantly at her feet. "Not this one. We're taking Buddy's." The dog tilted its head in confusion.

The dog pranced alongside Sam as she went to Buddy's truck and opened the passenger door. A wave of superheated air poured over her. "Come on." Waffles sprang up into the truck and took her place by the window. Sam joined her seconds later, firing it up and powering all the windows down. A chaotically wagging tail was all the thanks she needed.

She drove around the back of the house toward the first gate, put the truck in park again, and got out to open it. Waffles gave her two impatient barks.

"Oh, shut it." The gates were always a hassle with only one person. Park to open. Drive through. Park to close. Get back in the truck. And when the cows were all the way in the back pasture, there were three sets of gates to deal with. It's not that it took an extraordinary amount of time, but she always found the stop-and-go irritating.

As they drove the well-worn path past the hay barn, Sam fondly thought of countless summer days of hide-and-seek and rope swinging from the rafters onto stacks of hay bales. She'd even had her first kiss in that barn. The boy hadn't been expecting it, but it didn't take him long to get with the program either.

At gate two, Waffles barked again. Sam fussed, "Don't get impatient at me. You could get out and do it yourself."

Waffles repeated her ritual at the third gate, leaning so far out of the truck in her excitement that she came perilously close to tipping out. Sam parked when they came within sight of the cows, most of whom were either shading themselves under trees or cooling themselves in the pond. A few of the cows lay in the tall grass. Sam said, "Might rain later."

The dog stared at her with desperate hope.

"Alright, I've made you wait long enough." She pushed the truck door open, and Waffles bounded out, charging toward the cattle. The first few times they'd done this, Sam worried the pup would catch an annoyed hoof in the head or ribs. But the cows seemed to tolerate her well enough, and she had a knack for staying just out of range.

Sam slipped out of her brother's truck and lowered the tailgate, finding what she hoped for — a camping chair. She grabbed the chair, popped it open, and sat down. She unzipped the pouch in the arm of the chair, curious what she would find. True to form, Buddy had a small stash of weed and papers tucked away.

It was mildly tempting to light one up and blaze away. But then her phone buzzed in her belt pack. Her heart rate doubled. Sam fumbled with the zipper and yanked the phone out to check her text message. She didn't know why Clayton would text instead of call. She wouldn't expect him to commit anything to writing.

A green message said, "Want to improve your residence's value? Let's discuss enhancements that get the job done near Jasper. Reply YES for tailored guidance. Reply STOP to unsubscribe." It was signed off with the name of an LLC. In a flash of anger, Sam pulled up her internet browser to find the company's address on the Alabama Secretary of State's website, so she could have Rodrigo pay them a visit or maybe mail them a glitter bomb instead. She slammed the phone into the cupholder in frustration that good cell coverage didn't extend to the far reaches of the farm.

Waffles started machine gun barking. Sam looked up to see

the hair on her neck standing up as she crouched between a cow and the waterline. It could only be one of two things.

"Waffles, no!"

The dog didn't back down. A black rope flashed toward her. Waffles yelped. Sam ran forward, drawing her .22. A dozen yards away, she paused. A large water moccasin lay coiled on the bank.

Sam raised the pistol and slowed her breathing. With two successive rounds, the snake fell limp, its head barely still attached. She hurried to Waffles, who was holding a foreleg in the air and panting. Sam scooped her up. "You poor, sweet, dumb thing. The cows would have been fine. You won't be, though."

She reached through the open window and laid a whimpering Waffles on the seat. As she ran around the back of the truck, Sam snagged her phone out of the camping chair and scrolled for the vet. It rang twice.

"Dr. Hanks."

"It's Sam." The truck roared to life. "Waffles got snakebit. Cottonmouth. Front leg. We're coming in hot." She hung up and bounced the truck over the bumpy trail, arriving at the first of three closed gates.

CHAPTER 24
JUST BELOW RECKLESS

SAM

Waffles had snuggled up as close to Sam as was physically possible, then fallen asleep and not moved the entire drive home. Sam kept one hand on the steering wheel and rested the other on the dog so she could feel its breathing.

The vet had warned her that the antivenom was expensive, as if that might cause her to change her mind and leave the poor little creature to its fate. She expressed in forceful and explicit terms what might happen to him if he didn't give Waffles the shot. Despite her vulgar description of sudden violence, he seemed unfazed. Apparently, people are prone to acting out when under stressful situations involving animals.

Between the ordeal, the antivenom, the antihistamines, and the steroids, Waffles was tuckered out. Her limp body was so pitiful. "How about let's stay clear of dirty, rotten snakes from now on? Okay, Dubs?" She stroked Waffles' fur, as much to soothe herself as the dog. She'd never have thought that in a matter of less than a week, she'd have become so attached to an animal, yet here they were.

Sam didn't even want to think about the decision she would have had to make if their first trip to the vet, the day after

Daddy's funeral, had turned up a microchip. Fortunately, Waffles' previous owner wasn't that committed to the animal. Still, it was foolish of her to bring the pup home.

When Sam topped the last significant rise between herself and home, she saw smoke billowing above the treetops several miles away. Some farmer was probably losing his crop of soybeans or corn. Once she got closer, she'd be able to tell whose land it was. As hot and dry as August had been, it was no surprise that something was burning. It didn't take much to turn things into an inferno.

As she churned up the asphalt, a knot formed in Sam's belly. It tightened and twisted with every passing second that the gray cloud ascended from approximately the area where she figured her house to sit. She hit her turnoff going a lot faster than she should have, and pulled Buddy's truck up on two wheels for a brief second. With a flick of the steering wheel, it settled back on all fours, spitting gravel in all directions. Waffles whimpered and slid down to the floorboard.

"Sorry, girl."

On the remaining county roads that led to her driveway, Sam kept a speed that hovered just below reckless. The trees that grew up on either side of the roadway mostly obscured her view of the sky. But one thing was sure. The closer she got to home, the bigger the swatch of sky that it blanketed.

Slowing to an appropriate speed, Sam turned off the country lane onto the winding driveway that led to her house. As a teenager, she'd told Daddy she wanted a Camaro and that he'd need to pave the driveway. She got a truck like her brothers. Daddy gave her step-mother the roadster she'd wanted, but not the driveway.

Sam burst through the tree line and hit the brakes. A nightmare unfolded in front of her. Flame and smoke poured out of the house, through every burst window and vent in the eaves.

Sam's hands covered her mouth as she watched her family's history burn. The quilts her great-grandmother had made. Her mother's pearls. Daddy's collection of rifles and shotguns. The weight of it was too much. It pressed her into the seat of Buddy's truck.

Buddy.

Her truck was still there.

He hadn't gone anywhere.

She sat upright. Scouring the scene for him.

For the first time, she noticed a lump of clothing lying across the threshold of the front door, with the screen door propped open against it. Sam kicked the truck's door open and sprinted toward the blaze. Waffles barked and nipped at her heels as she ran.

The dog stopped in the yard as Sam charged onto the flame-licked porch. She dropped to her knees beside the body that was face-down. She gently rolled it over.

Buddy's eyes fluttered open. "Hey, Sis," he said hoarsely.

"Hush. Let me look at you." She couldn't tell anything through his blackened shirt. She unbuttoned it and pushed it to the side, recoiling at the sight of a half-dozen bullet holes.

A crash came from within the house, and a blast of super-heated air pushed over them. Waffles whined from the bottom of the steps.

"I gotta move you."

Buddy clenched her arm. "Please, no, Sam. It hurts." A tear rolled out of one eye, leaving a trail on his soot-covered face.

Sam looked away. "I have to. We're roasting."

He released her arm and closed his eyes. That was worse than him arguing. Sam stood at Buddy's head, grabbed him under the armpits, and pulled. Buddy moaned in pain. Maybe it was a whimper. It was a pitiful and terrible sound that was nearly drowned out by the fire.

Sam tripped as she struggled to pull him backwards, falling against the porch rails with Buddy pulled partially across her lap.

"No more," he whispered.

"Stay with me," Sam said. She felt in each of her pockets for her phone, but it was still in the truck. "Help is coming." It was a lie, but it didn't matter.

"There were too many of them," Buddy said. "I got a couple, I think." Every phrase was an effort that was punctuated by gasps. "Made me feel bad. They waited 'til the fire made me come out."

"Who?"

Buddy squeezed his eyes and grimaced. A weak cry escaped his lips. Waffles crawled up the steps in a crouch and pushed up against Buddy.

Sam realized with a start that both of the dog's owners had now had their houses burned.

"Sam, I'm scared."

Her heart broke in a way that she thought she'd never recover from. May not want to. She took a deep breath, searching for words. "You got no cause to be scared, Buddy. You remember when you were eight and when we got home from Vacation Bible School, you told Daddy that you gave your heart to Jesus? Jeb made fun of you, and Daddy slapped him? I didn't think I believed in Jesus, but it was worth you believing so we could see Jeb get smacked. Can't nobody take that away from you."

Buddy didn't respond. Lying across her as he was, she felt his breathing get ragged and erratic. Sirens screamed in the distance. She hadn't lied to him after all. Actually, that wasn't true. She had lied. It just happened that she was wrong.

Buddy laid his hand over hers and squeezed.

Sam's throat hurt from the smoke and the heartbreak.

"It'll be over soon, big brother. You can go see Momma and Jesus."

Sam leaned her head back against the post behind her and waited for either the fire to consume them or the first responders to get there. In that moment, she didn't much care which got to them first.

CHAPTER 25
THE GATHERING DARKNESS

SAM

THE AMBULANCE'S TAILLIGHTS DISAPPEARED DOWN the lane. Sam wiped her eyes with the backs of her hands. It was only then that she realized dusk had descended on them, and the gathering darkness would soon envelop them entirely. It had already consumed her. The sky might as well be next.

She peeked inside her truck and gave Waffles a pat through the open window. "You're a good girl." The dog rolled onto her side and extended all four legs in a cozy stretch before settling back into her nap, one paw still visibly swollen under the bandage wrap.

Sam strode toward the place where Jeb stood with Sheriff Tompkins, the fire marshal, and a cluster of other deputies and firefighters. Her phone buzzed in her back pocket. She pulled it out. The text from Rodrigo read, "You want I should come?"

How did he hear? She made a point not to call him. She couldn't even make herself call Jeb when the time had come. Tompkins had to do it. Jeb had given her a hug when he'd arrived, for maybe only the second or third time in their post-childhood lives. She'd nearly come apart then.

Sam whistled at the congregation of people. "All y'all can

go." She pointed at the three she wanted to speak with. "You three stay."

The firefighters and cops looked at their respective bosses, who nodded, and the huddled mass drifted away from the remains of the house.

Sam already had a pretty good guess about what had happened and who had ordered it, but she needed some affirmation. Looking at the fire marshal, she said, "Well?"

He nodded solemnly and pointed at the side of the house closest to them. "Most of the downstairs windows are broken to the inside. If the window breaks had been caused by the fire, they'd have broken outward, and you'd have more glass on the ground out here. There's also indications of accelerants being used at those locations. We can come back tomorrow and take samples to do a more thorough analysis. If I had to guess, the fires were started nearly simultaneously on each side of the house."

He'd worded it precisely, not accusing anyone of anything. He was a man matter-of-factly stating the results of the preliminary investigation. He had worked in the county for a long time. His findings wouldn't be made final until he received further instructions.

"So what are you saying?" Jeb asked.

Sam held up a finger. "Hang on. Let's see what the sheriff has to say."

Tompkins chewed on his lip for a minute before he started. "The deceased had—"

Sam's fury flashed white hot. "Don't you dare call him that, like he's some random person you haven't known since he was in a cradle."

The man held up a hand in apology. "Sorry, Sam. Buddy. Buddy had a half-dozen gunshot wounds in his torso. Could be more in his extremities. We'll know later. Second and third-degree burns were also present. We didn't find any casings yet. We can come back out in the morning to search."

Jeb's eyes welled up with tears. Sam had to look away from him. She was working hard to keep herself in check. Otherwise, she'd be an emotional ping-pong ball.

"How do you want us to write this up?" the marshal asked.

"I would expect you to write it up exactly like it happened. Bennett Clayton's men came here, set my family home on fire to smoke out my brother, and murdered him in his doorway."

Tompkins looked down and scuffed at a patch of grass with his boot. "Sam I can't put Bennett's name on this report. Ain't any evidence saying he done it."

Jeb said, "Isn't a person's testimony evidence too?"

Look at big brother's criminal history paying off. She nudged him with her elbow and nodded. He smiled down at her and looked proud.

"Well, yes … in a manner of speaking," Tompkins said.

The fire marshal chimed in. "What he needs is forensic evidence."

"No." Sam stepped toward the men so that she was uncomfortably close. Buddy would've said that she was in his personal bubble, but she had to push Buddy out of the frame for now. "What he needs is to remember who his friends are."

"*Friends* is a funny word when you use it that way." The sheriff crossed his arms over his chest, and his elbow nearly hit Sam's chin. She didn't flinch and didn't remove her gaze from his. He took a half-step back. "You mean you pay me money and I do what you say? Well, let's say I have other friends, maybe even better friends. And what they want and what you want is different things. What then?"

Sam looked at him a hard minute before answering. If she lost the sheriff, life could get more difficult. So she had to figure out real quick whether strength or ass-kissing was the better strategy. If there was ever a time that she didn't need the law scrutinizing her, it was coming soon.

"I understand how things look to you right now," Sam said. "Daddy's dead. Buddy's been killed. It's me and Jeb now. You don't know if maybe we're gonna go the same way. And you don't want to have been caught backing the wrong horse. How am I doing so far?"

Tompkins said nothing.

The fire marshal looked like he'd rather be anywhere else.

All four of them stood in the stark glare of floodlights and were otherwise islands in the darkness.

"Answer her," Jeb said.

"It's okay." Sam put a hand on his wrist. "The thing is, this ain't a horse race. This is an inflection point. You can decide what this county's going to be. The Colemans have been here a long time and we haven't once traded in skin or in drugs."

Jeb cleared his throat.

"For the most part," she added. "The family hasn't sanctioned it anyway. And as much as possible, we do our business out of town."

"Martin Welker? That wasn't somewhere else. And it's causing me no small amount of problems." Sheriff Tomkins said. A question that was more of an accusation.

"I thought Marty had a fishing accident?"

"Uh-huh." He was not convinced.

"We've stayed clear of peddling in vices, and we'll continue to do so. Your boy Clayton has built that big hacienda of his trading in things that people used to have to go to Cullman or Birmingham to get. And that's happened on your watch."

"Now, you list—"

Sam stepped into his space again. "I'm not done talking. You write this thing up exactly as it happened, but you don't have to use names if it makes your tummy a little upset."

She couldn't see the color in his face. Things were mostly

various shades of black and gray in this light, except for the embers that used to be her home. They glowed a bright orange. But she suspected there was a whole lot of red in the sheriff's cheeks right now.

"If my report says what you're asking, it's going to set things off."

"Jerry, things are already popping off. Your paperwork ain't got anything to do with that."

He shook his head. "We can't have a war. *You* can't have a war. You don't have the people for that."

"There won't be war. I already promised you that."

Relief replaced some of the tension in the man's face.

It didn't last.

"But you can be sure as hell there's going to be a reckoning."

CHAPTER 26
DARK, COLD, AND ETERNAL

CHASE

PAINFULLY BRIGHT LIGHT PRIED AT CHASE'S EYELIDS, and the most grating of noises clawed at his ears. He removed the pillow from under his head and buried himself under it. This solved the light issue, but a muffled version of the shrill racket permeated through the cotton. A hand slapped at his back, raising his level of alertness.

Chase sat up and opened his eyes. Sunlight seared his brain. There was someone on the bed with him. She smacked at the bed where he'd been. *What was her name? Amber? Tiffany? No. "Britanni, but with two I's."* He sighed. The sound of regret.

"Phone," she croaked. "Answer."

Still in a funk, he picked up his cell phone off the nightstand. It was dormant, but the ringing continued. Realization broke over him. He grabbed the receiver from the motel phone and cradled it to his ear. "Yes?"

"Mr. Williams?" The man's voice was far perkier than was appropriate.

"Yes."

"There's an envelope with your name on it at the front desk."

"Who from?"

"Doesn't say."

"Can you bring it to my room?"

There was silence on the other end of the line for several seconds. "Uhh. No. It will be at the front desk when you get here."

A click told him the conversation had ended. *I guess Southern manners doesn't cover extended-stay motel clerks.*

Chase stood and shuffled to the bathroom, where he took what must've been the longest pee of his life. The kind where something inside you, probably your bladder, still ached afterward for having been distended for so long. During the midst of it, Brittani grumbled, "Too loud." With his free hand, he reached for the bathroom door and swiped it shut.

With any luck, the tumult of the morning would encourage a quiet exit while he went downstairs. He didn't think either of them likely remembered enough about each other or the night before (courtesy of Herr Jägermeister and all the poor decisions that accompany him) to want to make a whole thing of it.

He slid into the closest clothes and footwear he could find and let the door clang shut behind him. The worst part of Alabama greeted him outside — the humidity so sticky that it nearly necessitated a couple of showers a day and air so warm it felt like stepping into someone's mouth. By the time Chase trekked all the way along the corridor, down the flight of stairs, and into the motel lobby, he mostly had his wits about him.

According to his name badge, Donald greeted him. "How can I help you?"

"I'm Chase from Room 231. You called me a few minutes ago."

"Right." Donald pointed to an envelope that was sitting on the counter a few feet away.

It was a plain letter envelope that had only "Attn: Chase Williams" printed on the front.

"Who left this for me?" Chase asked.

"Dunno. It was sitting there when I came on duty this morning. I waited 'til a decent hour to call you."

Chase looked at his watch. "7:15 on a Saturday is a decent hour?"

"It is if you weren't doing shots at the bar like you're a coed again."

The surprise on Chase's face must have been transparent.

"I saw you last night. Of course, since I'm a grown-up with an actual job, I left before you did."

"You're awfully judgy for …" Chase let the sentence die on his lips.

But Donald finished it for him. "… for a motel clerk? Son, judging people's life choices that bring them to a place like this is one of the few perks this job has."

Chase trudged back to his room, dreading two things now. That it would still be occupied by someone other than himself. And the contents of this envelope. He looked at it again as he walked. Whatever it was, would not be good. People called or texted if they had something good to say.

He reached into his pocket for the keycard and came up empty, having not grabbed it on the way out. *Great.* Now, he had to hope Brittani-with-two-I's was still here or face the judgment of Donald again. *This day already sucks.*

Chase knocked on his own motel room door. A moment later, Brittani answered, wearing one of his t-shirts. And not one that had been laying out from the night before or in the dirty clothes pile. She'd gone through his stuff to get it. She'd probably seen it in a movie and thought it was cute. It wasn't. Well, she was, but the bit wasn't.

"What was that all about?" she asked when he entered without a word.

Chased crossed the room and sat in the desk chair, elbows on his knees. His stomach was in fourteen different knots, and he felt like he was on the edge of throwing up whatever was in there. The nausea was only partially due to the recent onset of anxiety. "I don't mean to be rude, but I got some bad news, and I need you to go." It wasn't really a lie, more like a delayed truth. He hadn't gotten bad news yet, but he assumed it was in his hand. There might have been a nicer way to say that, but he hadn't been able to figure it out in the moment.

Brittani was unfazed. She sat down in front of him on the floor. "Oh no. Are you okay?"

"Yeah. I … uhh … I'm gonna take a shower." He stood and stepped around her, envelope still in hand, headed toward the bathroom.

"Do you want some help?" she said coyly. "You can make up for last night."

Aside from the shower being hardly large enough for one person, he absolutely didn't want company. He wanted to be alone. Then the second part of what she said landed on him, adding a couple more knots. "What happened last night?"

"Nothing. Literally, nothing." She pointed at his midsection.

"I don't—oh. Uhh. Sorry?" Heat rose to his cheeks.

She shrugged. "Happens."

Chase nodded. "I'd like to be alone when I get out, you know?"

Brittani smiled. "I get it."

"But it was nice to meet you." He knew immediately that he'd think about how stupid a thing that was to say for the rest of the day, probably tomorrow too, and regret the line for the rest of his life.

He closed and locked the bathroom door, setting the envelope on the counter and turning the water temperature to slightly less than scalding. He could burn off several layers of skin and get a new start to a loathsome morning.

Ten minutes later, with skin as pink as a newborn's, Chase emerged feeling no better. But when he opened the bathroom door and saw that Brittani had cleared out, he felt slightly better. Until he realized that she'd taken his t-shirt with her. Then he felt less improved, but still better than if she hadn't left. All of these variations were of little consequence to him compared to the dread that accompanied the letter.

He paced around the room, remembering stories of anthrax and letter bombs, and chastising himself for thinking he was significant enough that someone would go to those lengths to kill him. There were much easier ways to go about it. Having gotten fed up with himself, Chase sat on the end of the bed, ripped off one side of the envelope, reached in and tweezered out a letter.

He opened the tri-folded page, unveiling a short, typewritten message.

Stop your investigation and leave town, or you'll find out how dark, cold, and eternal the bottom of a mineshaft is.

Chase flipped the paper over to make sure there was nothing on the back. There wasn't. That was it. Twenty-ish words containing what seemed pretty clearly to be a threat. The journalist in him appreciated the conciseness of the message, while the double-major-in-English side noted the colorful description that avoided any trite expressions. While those two sides were admiring the death threat's technical aspects, the humanity in him worked to shove down a panic attack.

He threw on some clothes and hurried back to the motel lobby. Donald greeted him with a plastic and well-practiced smile. "You're looking somewhat improved, though your coloring is still ... poor."

Ignoring the flippant insult, Chase asked, "You didn't see who left the letter for me?"

"I already told you I didn't. It was here when I got here this morning."

"What time was that?"

"About 5:00am. Is something wrong?"

YES, SOMETHING IS WRONG. "What about the night clerk? Would they have seen anything?"

Donald shook his head. "I wouldn't count on it. Richie was probably either asleep or trading meth for sexual favors from one of the lot lizards."

"Lot lizards? You know what, never mind." He could figure that one out later. Chase looked around the lobby and spotted his first dash of hope. Turning back to Donald, he pointed at a darkened dome affixed to the ceiling. "What about the security camera? It would show who dropped the letter off."

Again, Donald shook his head. "Don't work. It's more there as …" He paused as he searched for the right word. "… a deterrent."

Chase restrained himself from reaching across the counter, pulling the smarmy Donald across it, and pummeling him. But the temptation was real. Instead, he stormed out of the lobby and under the drive-through awning, snatching the phone out of his pocket. He looked around to see if anyone was watching him. There were no signs of human activity in the parking lot.

Chase scrolled through his recent calls, uncertain who to dial. He had several outgoing calls to Sam over the last few days, none of which had been answered or returned. He tried her again. Four rings later, he got the same snarky voicemail instructions he'd heard before: "You know who this is, and you don't need me to tell you what to do."

This time, he left a message.

CHAPTER 27

A LONG LINE OF BLOOD FEUDS

SAM

THE SHEET OF RAIN THAT LOOMED TO THE WEST WAS close enough to smell. It had always been one of her favorite scents, as far back as she could remember — the smell right before it rained in the summer. And oranges — there was nothing better than a freshly peeled orange. Sam worried briefly that the scent of rain would now be spoiled for her, that she would always associate it with Buddy's funeral.

It was an altogether different crowd than the group that had assembled eight days ago, however impossible that seemed. In the past two weeks, time had slipped into a funk. Actually, time had probably stayed mostly constant. Her perception of it was a disaster, though.

Buddy's crowd was made up of stoners, burnouts, and people who would likely never amount to much when it came to counting stats. But they seemed to really care about each other. They'd all stayed together since middle school, making the same poor choices, losing the same dead-end jobs, and bailing each other out of jail for petty crimes. Together. Always together. Which was more than she could say for any group of people in her life.

Where Buddy had been a magnet that pulled everyone

toward him, she'd always been the opposite pole of that same magnet whose forces repelled everybody.

Sam's phone buzzed in her purse. She looked up at the casket and grumbled, "It's your fault I'm having to carry a purse." Of course, it wasn't his fault. Another theme that ran through the story of Buddy's life. It was rarely his fault. Any of it. A victim of circumstance.

Here, though, these circumstances didn't make sense. Killing Buddy didn't serve anyone's interests. Unless they wanted to inflame her rage and bloodlust, because they'd darn sure done that. No one had stepped up to take credit for killing him. Not that she necessarily expected them to. This wasn't a terrorist act that served some political end. It was another murder in coal country in a long line of blood feuds.

After the phone quit pining for her attention, she looked to see who'd called. Chase. He'd called several times over the last few days. Not more than once a day, though. He was persistent but polite about it. She didn't have the capacity to deal with whatever he needed, whether it was minimal or major. It had taken all she had to get her through to today. Now she was poured out.

With everyone gone to wherever it is they went after a funeral — Wal-Mart, back to work, to smoke a joint in their fallen friend's memory, or to the dinner for the family — she could sit here in her emptiness with the funeral tent sheltering her from the downpour.

"Samantha Ray," a man's voice called behind her.

Sam's hand shot toward her purse, before she remembered that Aunt Teresa had forbid her from carrying a pistol to the funeral. She stood and turned to face the speaker.

Bennett Clayton.

Her blood ran cold.

He walked around the edge of the tent, past the rows of

chairs. Rain spattered his exposed left side. He stopped after turning in at the front row. "I'm sorry about Buddy."

Sam spit at his feet.

Then she thought about his words. *I'm sorry about Buddy,* which is very different from *I'm sorry about what happened to Buddy.* The first version is what you say when you contributed to the thing that happened. Her heart pounded, and a tinny sound rang in her ears. She suddenly needed to pee.

Sam took two steps toward him, a sneer on her face.

"Don't." He held his left hand out while his right went to his hip, pushing his suit coat back and landing on the handle of his pistol.

Sam stopped. She flexed her hands as a surge of adrenaline coursed through her. If she acted rashly, she may not survive the encounter. And if she didn't survive, she couldn't get retribution. She slowed her breathing and reasserted control over herself.

"Seems like you only want to talk to me in situations where you think I'm helpless."

"I do like to be in charge of a situation."

"Is that how you get it up at your age?"

He shrugged off the coarse insult.

"You're a dangerous woman, Sam. I think I'd be a fool to put us on equal footing."

"You didn't come to pay your respects, so what do you want?"

Clayton cleared his throat, and an expression akin to shame, or at the very least shame's distant cousin, skirted across his face. He averted his eyes from her. "It was an accident." Before she could respond, he held up a finger. "*Accident* is the wrong word. Mistake. It was a mistake."

Sam's belly clinched tighter still and lurched up toward her throat. "What was?"

"Buddy. Killing Buddy was a mistake. It was supposed to be you."

The strength went out of Sam's legs, and she stumbled forward. Clayton automatically reached out to catch her. Rote Southern gentility. Sam batted his arm away. "Don't touch me," she growled. "Not ever." Rage and guilt tussled within her.

Clayton held his hands up in apology.

Sam recomposed herself and took a half-step back from the man who'd had her brother killed, possibly ordered the hit on her father — an open question she'd not had the time to answer — and would certainly kill her, if he had his druthers. But not here. Not today. Murdering a rival at a family member's funeral would be bad form. And while Bennett Clayton was definitely a monster, he was the kind of monster who carried out his misdeeds with a certain decorum that made him all the more sinister.

"Your truck was in front of the house," he explained. "The boys thought it was you in there."

She hadn't thought Buddy's death could sting more. She was wrong. That his killing was accidental was an exceedingly bitter pill.

"I wanted you to know I wasn't coming after your family."

The way he said it — he was searching for something. There was a question he hadn't asked yet. But she was too broken inside to suss it out. "How very courteous of you."

"I was hoping …" A sneer of disgust twitched across the lips of the man who wasn't accustomed to *asking* anything of anyone. He started over. "I want assurances that you won't come after mine over this." He pointed a finger loosely toward the rain-drenched casket.

Clayton had stayed long enough to convert Sam's despair back into a seething rage with the flippancy of his gesture. He had no remorse over Buddy, just concern for the blowback it would have on him and his.

"I was ready to walk away," she said. "From all of it. I had plans to go straight. I thought maybe we could—it doesn't matter what I thought."

"You can still do that."

"No." It was definitive. Until now, she hadn't thought in the last few days about the other business she'd been hashing out. It was ashes now. Those ideas, those hopes, had died with Buddy and burned with the house.

She stared Clayton in the eyes with all the steel she could muster. "There's only one thing now."

He didn't break her gaze as he slowly, but conspicuously, slid his hand back to his right hip. He could finish this business now, and there was nothing she could do about it. She could run. But she wouldn't. There was a part of her that knew what a relief it would be for everything to be over.

"Daddy," a voice said from the other end of the tent.

Both Sam and Clayton jumped in surprise.

His daughter stood there, umbrella still held over her. "Thomas is hungry."

Clayton said, "I'll only be another minute."

She planted one hand on her hip. "I'm not going back to the car without you."

Irritation played across his face.

Sam said, "I was thinking the other day. I wonder if on the night Judas betrayed Jesus, if he'd already decided to do it that night. Like, was he sitting there during that whole dinner knowing what he was about to do and knowing that was the last time they'd all be gathered together? Like, he didn't know exactly how everything would go. But that would have to weigh on a person. Knowing that his actions are what led to everyone else's suffering. Don't you think?"

Clayton watched her, trying to find the threat in her words.

"Daddy." A demanding whine that didn't befit an adult.

"We're not done," he said to Sam.

"You got that right, chief."

After Clayton had left to get his grandson a Happy Meal, Sam slumped against her brother's casket in the mud and rain, and mourned. She had to get it out of her system now. There wouldn't be any place for it in the aftermath to come.

CHAPTER 28
A RESTLESS EVIL

SAM

"Why do you think they called this area Booger Tree?" Jeb asked as they drove past the small houses and trailer homes that made up most of rural Winston County.

"Probably for reasons that are super obvious and gross," Sam said.

"Or maybe …" She could always tell when Jeb thought he had a great idea because his voice register would change, and he'd start talking faster. "… it was such a nice place to live that the people who moved here called it that to keep people away. Like how the people of Iceland called it *that* and Greenland *green* so people would move there instead."

His ideas were rarely as good as he perceived them to be.

Sam chanced a questioning look away from the roadway and in her older brother's direction. "I'm not sure that's historically accurate."

He shrugged, indifferent to the possibility.

The music rolled over to an atrocious evolution of bro country. Sam groaned and punched a preset button for another station.

Jeb said, "Hey! I like that song."

"First of all, my truck — my rules. Second, of course you do."

"What's that supposed to mean?"

"It means that your taste in music, as in all things, is beyond questionable."

He folded his arms across his chest. "You can be really mean sometimes. You know that?"

She knew. But she also had restraint, because she didn't tell him that he was acting like a titty baby by getting his feelings hurt so easily.

For her whole life, having a sharp tongue had been a defense mechanism at home. The boys had always been bigger and stronger, but she was clever and smarter. And she had never had any qualms about making sure they knew it. She'd caught a few beatings over the years, both from her brothers and Daddy. So as defense mechanisms went, it wasn't terribly effective. When she inevitably went too far, her stepmother would quote the Bible at her. *Samantha Ray, the tongue is a restless evil, full of deadly poison.* She seemed to recall only the parts of the Good Book that she could weaponize.

Sam drove through the rolling hills until the road turned to dirt and became a private drive that wound around trees and eventually ran out at the foot of an unexpectedly nice house with a wraparound porch.

Sam turned off the truck's ignition, but when Jeb reached for the door handle, Sam stopped him. "Hang on."

"What?" he said impatiently.

"Before we go do this, I want to make sure you're all in."

"You ain't the only one who loved Buddy, Sam."

"Alright, then." She nodded. "Oh, one more thing. We gotta mind everything we say. Shooter's fine, but his daddy's kinda squirrely."

"You mean like how he thinks birds aren't real and they're actually government drones that spy on us?"

Sam raised both eyebrows in surprise. "Yes, that's exactly what I mean."

Jeb shrugged. "I been around him some. They got a still they've been running since Prohibition. We used to get our 'shine out here in high school."

"In that case," she pointed toward Jeb's floorboard, "be a dear and grab that bag under your seat."

Jeb reached down and dragged out a bag, unzipping it enough to see its contents. He let off a low whistle. "What were you gonna do if you got pulled over with this much cash in the truck?"

"There isn't a cop in all of Walker County that's gonna pull me over. A privilege that comes with a pricey tag."

"We're not in Walker County anymore, Dorothy."

Sam got out before responding. She didn't want to spook Gaither Mann by sitting in the truck too long. Jeb grunted as he hefted the bag over his shoulder. "Why's this so heavy?"

"He won't take hundreds or fifties. And he wants an even amount of fives, tens, and twenties."

"I guess that checks out." As the front door to the house opened up, Jeb whispered across the hood. "You really want to get the old coot going? Ask him about aliens."

Sam tried to turn her laugh into a cough and eventually got there.

A plump man who completely filled his overalls, which he wore with no shirt underneath, waddled down the steps. Shooter, following behind, stood several inches taller but would never be mistaken for anyone else's kid.

"Jebediah, Samantha Ray, it's good to see you two. I am surely sorry to hear about all your troubles recently."

"Thank you, sir," Sam said.

"Y'all know Oliver."

Shooter glowered at being called by his given name.

"Yes, sir."

Jeb waved to Shooter and looked ready to launch into some tale about their teenage tomfoolery, so Sam shifted her weight and elbowed her brother.

Mr. Mann said, "Let's say a prayer of blessing over our business here today before we get started."

Sam smirked in surprise. "You're gonna ask God to bless you arms dealing to me so I can—"

Mr. Mann raised a hand. "I don't need to know what you plan to do with the merchandise you buy from me. You don't tell the folks at the Wal-marts what you're doing with your groceries, do you?"

Even though she was pretty sure the question didn't call for an answer, he paused long enough that she said, "No, sir."

He nodded. "And as for your question, would you rather the Lord didn't place his hand of blessing on our business together?"

"I can't imagine that He wants anything to do with it whatsoever."

"Suppose we leave that up to Him then. Fellas, remove your hats." Once Jeb had swiped the ball cap off his head, Mr. Mann bowed his head and was silent.

After a full minute passed, Jeb said, "Are you not gonna pray out loud?"

Mr. Mann didn't look up to answer. "I ain't talking to you, son, and I ain't a pharisee. You got no cause to hear this conversation." He resumed his silence, and presumably his prayer.

Jeb looked at Sam and silently mouthed, "Pharisee?"

She shrugged and tried to catch Shooter's eye to get a feel for his thoughts on all this, but he played the part of the dutiful son and complied with his role. Sam followed suit, bowing her head and closing her eyes. Several minutes more silence passed uneventfully.

Finally, Mr. Mann said, "This ain't no time for y'all to get caught up on your prayers. We got business to tend to. Jebediah, you give that money to Oliver, and he'll carry it up to the house."

Jeb reached down for the bag that he'd set down at the earliest opportunity and lifted it like a kettle bell. Shooter took it with one hand, like he hardly noticed the weight.

"Come on," Mr. Mann beckoned. "We'll take the mule."

Sam noted to herself that it was a good thing he was talking about the four-wheeler, because there wasn't a mule ever bred that wouldn't balk at being saddled with either of the Manns.

"Where we going?" Jeb asked after they'd piled into the mule.

From his place in the passenger seat, Gaither answered without turning around. "We're gonna go see what all that cash bought you."

Shooter drove them into the forest surrounding their place, using a well-worn path they followed for a couple of miles until it ran up against a bluff that rose out of the forest floor. The cliff housed a cave whose face had been boarded up generations earlier. A door within the facade stood off-center enough to be noticeable. Sam couldn't believe that in the hundred-or-so years that it had been there, no Mann had been born with compulsive enough tendencies to tear it out and start over.

Shooter unlocked the deadbolt that was latched to the door. Sam had little doubt there were several other layers of security that weren't immediately noticeable. As Gaither lumbered past the others, he flicked a switch on the cavern wall, and overhead lights illuminated the natural cathedral.

A crate sat unopened in the middle of the floor. Mr. Mann gestured at it. "Make sure we got your order right."

"We trust you," Jeb said.

"Don't. Make sure it's right. Like the Russkies say, 'Trust but verify.'"

Jeb slid the top off the crate, letting it clatter to the floor with a reverberating echo. Sam scooted up next to him and peered inside. Three shotguns, three assault rifles, twelve extra magazines for the latter. A dozen frag grenades and concussion grenades, along with some dynamite that looked like it'd been hiding in the mines for the last half-century. Added to all this were six pistols, three Kevlar vests, and enough boxes of ammunition to equip a militia.

"You got the other?" Sam asked.

Shooter reached against the wall and palmed a suede rifle case. He held it out in front of him, laid across his hands. Sam unzipped it and withdrew the black rifle from its fluffy woolen confines.

Mr. Mann said, "Winchester XPR .308 with suppressor and thermal scope. All ready to go."

"She's real pretty," she admired.

Jeb said, "So how come y'all had us come all the way out here for this stuff instead of having it ready to go at the house where we could just load it up?"

"We could have done that," the older man answered. "But what would have happened if y'all showed up without the money or with a half a dozen men and decided to relieve us of our wares?"

Jeb's eyes widened. "That never even occurred to me."

Mr. Mann clapped him on the shoulder. "I like that about you, Jebediah. But I can guaran-damn-tee you it occurred to your sister."

Jeb looked to her doubtfully.

Sam shrugged. "Those are called intrusive thoughts. We don't act on all our intrusive thoughts."

Mr. Mann laughed. "Told you she'd thought about it. That and a handful of other scenarios, I bet. But she still showed up with the money, because she's in it for the long haul. None of this short-sighted wannabe gangster stuff. That about right?"

"More or less."

Once they were loaded and on their way back to Walker County, Jeb asked, "You think it's gonna be enough?"

Sam kept her eyes on the road. "Hard to say, brother. It might be the last thing we do." A lump formed in her throat. She'd known that since she conceded to what felt like an inevitable path of vengeance, but she hadn't said it out loud until now. "Can you live with that?"

To his credit, Jeb thought about his answer a good long while before he gave it. "I suppose I can. I owe Buddy that. And who knows, we might get the best of 'em. If you got a plan, that is."

"I will have."

CHAPTER 29

COBBLING THINGS TOGETHER

CHASE

Dr. Wilson sat across the formal living room from Chase and gave him the same look that he probably reserved for panhandlers and vagrants. "I have a pretty good idea of what you're trying to do here."

"Oh?" He had grown accustomed to starting off with a bit of animosity from the person being interviewed. So *Oh?* was both innocuous and served as an invitation for them to express their disgruntlement. *Never mind that he volunteered to be here and do this.*

"You're trying to paint me as some villain so you can entertain people with your radio show and make a bunch of money selling the rights to my personal tragedy to Netflix."

He wasn't entirely wrong. Chase had big ambitions, and this had all the makings of a story that people would pay attention to. Not only podcast listeners, but awards people and decision-makers at companies much more influential than his.

But not entirely right, either. The story was the priority. If he didn't get that right, or if he fudged anything for the sake of making it sound more compelling, the entire house of cards would fall down around him. So Chase wasn't going to push the narrative any specific direction. He planned to follow where it led, and as of right now, it had led to the doorstep of a pediatrician whose taste in spouses skewed young and who'd had two wives turn up missing.

It was time to do some soothing and see if he couldn't underail this thing. "Sir, I'm gathering information and trying to cobble things together to tell the story of what happened. I don't have any preconceived notions about who did what, and I'm not trying to paint you in any particular light. If you would prefer," Chase leaned toward the recorder that sat between them on the coffee table and reached out a hand, "we can stop the interview?"

Dr. Wilson waved him off. "No, no. I'm here. Or I guess, more accurately, you're here. We might as well do it. Although, I can tell you that my lawyer would be a lot happier if I showed you out."

Chase had achieved the intended effect. He sat back in a relaxed posture, crossing his legs to mirror the doctor's own position and settling in for a low-stakes chat. "Can you tell me about your first wife, Beth?"

"I thought you wanted to talk about Valerie?"

"I'm trying to get the whole picture. There are a lot of things flying around, and I don't want an isolated occurrence to be the brush that paints you." *Geez, enough with the paint metaphors.*

"So you think talking about my other wife who disappeared is the route to go, then?"

"I certainly don't think you should try to avoid it. That looks even worse."

"Hm." It was more of a grunt than an enunciation. "She was the love of my life. It sounds cliche, but we were living the all-American dream. I'm the doctor. She's my gorgeous wife. Young family. Lovely social circle living in a big city. Birmingham was big for us anyway." Dr. Wilson looked past Chase as he reflected on the best parts of a long-ago life.

"Until?" Chase prompted.

"Until she had a surgery. Not even a major one. She had a

ganglion cyst on her wrist — they call it a book cyst — and it was bothering her, so she had it removed. Ashleigh was still real little. She asked for something for the pain. The doctor gave her a bottle of Lortab. I told to be careful with them, but it was the beginning of the end for her. We didn't know it then, of course. It was a long road."

"What do you mean 'the beginning of the end'?"

Dr. Wilson sighed, mournful, not impatient. "She couldn't kick it. When that first prescription ran out, she got another. When he wouldn't refill it a second time, she coaxed her OB/GYN into writing a prescription for her. That eventually ran out, so she went to her primary care doc. Back then, we didn't know there was an opioid epidemic in front of us. Pharma companies were pushing it, and a lot of docs were liberal about prescribing them. I thought a change of scenery would help, so I moved us back home. Here, to Jasper.

"For Beth, she covered up the problem for a long time. But Lortab gave way to other things. Her behavior got erratic. She'd go missing for days at a time. The kids noticed something was happening well before that. Kids are perceptive. I tried to get her to go to rehab."

Chase found himself getting impatient. He didn't want to get bogged down in the details. Everybody knew how this story went by now, if not the specifics. "So she never came back from one of her binges? Is that what happened?" He shouldn't suggest things in his phrasing. That was Interviewing 101, and he immediately regretted it.

"No, that's not what happened." Dr. Wilson stood up.

Fear leaped across Chase's chest that he was about to break off the conversation.

"I've got to go to the bathroom." The man strode out of the room. When he returned several minutes later, he was stoic, and his face appeared to have been freshly washed. "I've never told anyone this next part. Not even my lawyer. There was no need to. By the time she finally disappeared, the city police and sheriff had all been dealing with her for years. To spare us, they always brought her home instead of booking her. So when she'd been gone for seventy-two hours, I reported her missing. They did perfunctory searches of all the usual places where these people get messed up together. When she wasn't there and never turned up home or at the hospital, everybody assumed things had taken their natural course with these kinds of things. They didn't even do a proper investigation."

"But you knew different?"

He nodded his head and breathed in deeply through his nose. "It got so bad. The kids were out of sorts. I couldn't take it anymore."

Chase's stomach tightened. They were at some climactic moment, but he couldn't anticipate what it would be.

"I bought a car from some guy off Craigslist. Paid cash. When I got home, I parked it in the carport so nobody would see it. Then I gathered up some of Beth's clothes, not enough that anything would appear to be missing if anybody came looking. After the kids went to bed and Beth was as sober as I could ever expect her to be, I set the bag of clothes and a bag of cash in front of her. I told she could either get clean or get out and not come back. There were a lot of tears and a lot of anguish, but eventually she took the money. She wasn't herself by then. I think she thought there wasn't any coming back, that she was too far down the road."

"Did you ever hear from her after that?"

"A couple times. Asking for more money. I offered rehab and told her she couldn't come home unless she got clean. She tried it once, but left after a couple of days. Hardest thing I've ever done. I wanted my wife back. The kids wanted their mom. But after a while, she stopped calling."

"You know your kids are likely to hear this, right?"

"I do," he said grimly. "I'll tell them first. They can decide for themselves whether I was justified."

"If you had it to do over again, would you do anything different?"

The man couldn't have looked more sorrowful if the ghost of his wife were standing in front of him, waiting to hear the answer. "There are a thousand things I would change. Small things, mostly. Things that wouldn't matter to anyone but her and me. But the thing at the end — sending her away — I wouldn't change that. I had to protect the kids from what was left of their mother. It's the only thing I knew to do."

It was time to turn from the past to the present. "And Valerie? Is that what happened to her?"

"No. She's a saint."

The statement was definite. No room for question. Chase was having trouble finding his next question, something that hadn't happened to him in a while. Most everything that came to mind was either too overly broad or confrontational.

"I noticed you said that she *is* a saint. You think she's still alive, then?"

Dr. Wilson's face sagged as some of the confident front he'd been putting up yielded. "I hope she is. Hope is all I have left right now."

CHAPTER 30
AN OCCUPATIONAL HAZARD

CHASE

CHASE STEPPED OUT OF THE BLAZING AFTERNOON SUN and into The Warehouse. He opened his eyes wide, as if that might somehow affect the speed at which his pupils adjusted to the dimmer lighting. Seeing Sam seated at the booth where he'd first met her made a warmth spread in his belly, like tequila on an empty stomach, but without the side effect of making his nose hairs curl. He walked over and asked, "You mind if I join you?"

She looked up, apparently noticing him for the first time, and with the hand that had been wrapped around her glass of beer, gestured for him to sit. "Glad your time down here has taught you some manners."

He slid into the seat across from her. "If I recall correctly, I asked the first time, too."

She squinted at him. The squint of a person who had more than one drink in them and was trying to focus. "Maybe you did, and maybe you didn't. But you were awfully presumptuous about it."

Chase shrugged, then caught the bartender's eye and pointed at Sam's glass, getting a thumb up in return. A silence sat patiently between them while Chase waited on his drink to be poured. After Jake pushed it to the edge of the bar, Chase retrieved the amber beer and sat back at the table.

Chase pointed at a speaker and said, "What is it about country music that's so popular down here?"

"Stories. Country music tells stories, and the South is full of storytellers."

"Huh," Chase said.

"Look at Taylor Swift."

"She's not from down here. She's from PA, like me."

Sam shook her head. "No, but she started in country music. Her songs tell stories. Granted, it's mostly the same story over and over about some boy that broke her heart, but still." Sam took a pull of her beer and asked. "That what you came here for — talk about music?"

"I'm sorry about your brother. I texted a few times. But I didn't want to be pushy. Figured you'd hit me up when you were ready."

"Hit you up? Is that what the cool kids are saying these days?"

Chase rolled his eyes. "Is this your thing? You strip all the sincerity out of everything?"

"Oh, definitely. Defense mechanism. Buy yeah, I saw your messages. Thanks."

"Do you want to talk about it?"

Sam shook her head. "Definitely not. I want to *not* talk about it."

"I know I'm supposed to make some make some kind of transition from one conversation to the next, but I'm coming up blank."

"Get on with it," Sam said with feigned irritation.

"In that case, can we talk about Valerie Wilson?"

"Oh. I don't want to talk about one dead person, so you suggest another instead? Nice."

Chase's cheeks drained of some of their color. He stammered

his way to an apology before Sam's stern look cracked, and she fell apart laughing.

"That's not nice," he said.

While Sam kept laughing, Chase realized that their relationship felt much older than it was. Like someone he'd known for years and gotten really comfortable with. But clearly, he didn't know her all that well since he couldn't read her reactions at all. She reminded him of his friend Sarah from junior high and the first couple years of high school. They'd had no inhibitions around each other, which at that age resulted in a lot of silliness. Neither 'liked' the other, so there were no one-sided romantic feelings to get in the way of anything either. They were buddies in a way that could never fully survive into their middle teenage years. And it didn't. It wasn't anyone's fault. They just grew apart until one day there was an inexplicable awkwardness between them, breaking a spell and a bond.

"So you've solved the Valerie Wilson thing?"

"Hardly," Chase said, "But I don't think it was Dr. Wilson who ... disappeared her."

"Can you use *disappeared* like that?"

"No. Yes? English is fluid. Anyway, I don't know what her status is. It's kind of awkward."

"You're probably pretty far down on the list of people that's awkward for."

"No doubt," he said. "He seemed really broken up about it, though. Like in a genuine way. Not showy or anything like that. And did you know that his first wife was an opioid addict?" His brain felt like a squirrel in a field of acorns. He shouldn't have had that third cup of coffee.

"I didn't. Daddy was careful not to gossip about folks in front of us. And on the rare occasions when he did, we knew better than to ask questions or he'd get mad and say, 'You know better than to listen when I'm talking about somebody. It ain't none of your business about them.' Like it was our fault somehow."

"It seemed pretty messed up. Like she was stealing money and using it to pop pills."

"That's what he told you."

Chase crinkled his forehead. "Yeah, that's what I said — it's what he told me."

"You gonna take his word for that, Mr. Reporter, or do you want to corroborate that story?"

"I—"

Sam interrupted him before he could gather a response. "Do you know how many women go missing every year? In the U.S. alone?"

Chase closed his mouth and shook his head.

"More than a quarter million. Want to guess what percentage of murdered women are killed by their husband or boyfriend?"

He shook his head again.

"A third."

Her tone of voice said this was not the time to interject.

"So maybe before we take the good doctor's word for it about his wife's drug problem, we should keep on investigating."

Chase nodded for lack of anything better to do and finished his beer.

"You want another?" Sam asked.

"Sure."

She got up and went to the bar, returning a few minutes later with a beer for him and water for herself.

"Look," Sam said, following it up with a long silence.

Chase raised his eyebrows, asking an unspoken question.

Sam fidgeted and looked down at the tabletop where she'd splayed her fingers, either unsure what to do with her hands or because her slightly alcohol-impaired brain found some small amusement in it. In an unusually quiet voice, she said, "If something happens to me … I mean, it probably won't, but whatever … if it does, then it's been good getting to know you."

Chase smirked involuntarily. "Sam."

"What?" she said, still looking down.

"Look at me."

Slowly, almost painfully, she forced her eyes to meet his. "This was by far — and I mean this sincerely — by far the worst goodbye message I've heard since reading a junior high yearbook."

She punched him in the shoulder.

"I mean, you are really, really bad at this part of being a human."

"Shut up."

Her embarrassed smile made him want to give her a big bear hug, but that seemed like a bridge too far. Instead, he asked, "Why would something happen to you?"

"I was hoping you'd let that part go."

Chase shrugged. "Follow-up questions are an occupational hazard."

Sam looked like she was struggling to get started with whatever it was she had to say, or at least, was willing to say. Chase started to speak to provide a buffer that would let her ease into it. She held up a hand. "Hang tight," she said. He sat back in a more relaxed posture.

Over the next several minutes, Sam told him about her brother's killing and that it was accidental insofar as she was the one they'd intended to kill. Whoever *they* were. Sam had left out some pertinent details, like *who* and *why*.

"You think they'll come after you again?"

"Sure as the sun's gonna rise tomorrow morning."

"What are you going to do about it?"

Sam flashed a fierce smile that had no joy in it. "You ever read *To Kill a Mockingbird*?"

"Of course," Chase said. "Several times."

"You know that part where Atticus shoots the rabid dog?"

"I do."

"Why did he do that?"

The answer seemed obvious, which made Chase second guess himself. "Because it was dangerous?"

Sam nodded. "Because it was dangerous," she repeated. "When you've got a rabid dog on the loose, it ain't a matter of if it's gonna attack somebody, but when. So you gotta put that dog down. I should have put this one down already. And Daddy before me. But we let things lie, and now here we are."

The matter-of-fact nature of talking about killing somebody was something Chase couldn't get acclimated to. "Can I suggest an alternative?"

Sam raised an eyebrow in response. That's all he was going to get.

"You could leave. Set up a new life somewhere else. There's nothing tying you down here."

A fire smoldered in her eyes. "Buddy was the only precious thing in my whole life. They took him from me. I can't walk away from that."

After that, she looked past him. Or possibly through him. Either way, she wasn't looking *at* him anymore. He could probably have left the table without her noticing. Suddenly, the spell broke. "And Waffles," Sam said. "Buddy and Waffles."

A snort of laughter escaped Chase. He covered his mouth and waved apologetically. "I'm sorry. So sorry. I tried not to."

Sam grinned, giving away that she had counted on getting a reaction from him.

"Where are you and Waffles staying?"

"My aunt's house. But she threatened to kick us out and make us stay in the camper if the dog doesn't stop shedding hair everywhere."

"So, soon then?" he said, grinning.

"Yeah, probably. But that wouldn't be so bad either."

Having lived alone since getting out of college, he did know. Sometimes — most times — you didn't want other people having access to you at their leisure, even when you loved those people. The corollary to that, though, was that those same people you kept at arm's length weren't likely to come running when you beckoned them in a moment of need.

"I've kind of got a thing, too," Chase said.

"That thing is called a penis, and it's the root of most of the world's problems."

"That's … fair, but not what I'm talking about. Different thing." He reached into his back pocket, slipped out a folded white envelope, and slid it across the table.

Sam opened the envelope and pulled out the letter. A few seconds later, she looked over the top of it at Chase. "Who left this?"

He gave a quick shrug. "It was at the reception desk at the hotel. The guy there said he didn't see who dropped it off."

"That's not a lot to go on."

"I'm not asking you to do anything."

Sam waved the letter. "You can't show me something like this and expect me to stand by while you get murdered over something that's not really any of your business in the first place."

"Nobody's going to kill me," Chase said.

She pushed the letter back across the table. "There's some evidence to the contrary."

"It's nothing. Just somebody messing with me."

"You were concerned enough about it to show me."

He shoved the letter back into his pocket. "Forget about it. It's nothing.

"Chase," Sam said, pausing to make sure she had his full attention, "I'm not the only person like me."

CHAPTER 31
A SPRAY OF BULLETS

SAM

Sam swatted at unfazed gnats as she bedded in the chest-high grass. She grumbled quietly, "They really ought to mow this."

"Be glad they do not. Good cover," Rodrigo whispered.

"You think it's 'cause they want to help the pollinators have more flowers and whatnot?"

Rodrigo tilted his head and looked down at her as though she were one of the more curious things he'd seen. "I do not think that. Lazy, I think."

"And complacent," Sam agreed. "I thought the bugs were supposed to still be asleep until sun-up?"

Rodrigo shrugged in the darkness as he squatted near Sam. She nestled herself into her spot on her belly, propped up on her elbows. Once she'd gotten as comfortable as she was likely to get, she said to herself, "That'll do, pig." *Babe* had been one of hers—and Buddy's—favorite childhood movies. Sam pushed herself onto one side and reached back. Rodrigo slid into her hand the customized rifle she'd gotten from Shooter's crazy daddy. She flipped out the bipod legs and placed the rifle so that the end of the suppressed barrel barely cleared the overgrown grass.

Sam inhaled a long, slow breath, held it for a few seconds, then breathed out through her nose. Being a touch hyperactive, combined with a bit of nerves — *It's okay. I can admit to that.* — had her feeling somewhat jittery. That wouldn't do here, though. She pictured a box while breathing. A little dot ran along one side as she breathed in, made the corner when she held it and went on to the next corner. When the imaginary dot hit the next ninety-degree turn, she exhaled until it made the final angle and crawled toward the starting point. Several times through this exercise had her as stilled as she could get.

When she flipped on the switch for the thermal scope, the mostly dark screen indicated how much everything had cooled off overnight. Two bright human forms on either side of Bennett Clayton's oversized front entrance punctuated her field of view. One man's face was brighter than the other because he had the audacity to smoke at night. *Asking to get your ticket punched.* She envied him having a cigarette right now, though she would have the chance to light one up after this was over (hopefully), while he definitely would not.

Sam turned her head back toward Rodrigo. "Any others?"

"Si. Two walking around the house."

"You got 'em?"

"Si."

She returned her attention to her targets. Neither had moved substantially, though the smoker was now grinding out his cigarette butt on his boss' fancy tile. *I'm probably doing him a favor by putting a couple of rounds in him. Clayton would do it much slower.*

She practiced panning from left to right, establishing some muscle memory so she could feel exactly how much to move after firing the first round. Smoker first, then the non-smoker, who would need a second to register what happened. Even with the suppressor on the rifle, it would still make mechanical sounds that couldn't be avoided.

"Tell me when your guys round the corner to start walking

down the side of the house. Will you have enough time to get them both?"

"Will be close."

Sam took a second to think. She wanted to decrease the likelihood that one got away and alerted the inside of the house. She envisioned herself kicking at a fire ant mound and thousands of them pouring out to protect their home. That wouldn't be a good result for them. This was a guerrilla action, not a frontal assault. "Should we wait 'til they make another round so you can catch them on the approach instead of walking away?"

"Is better, yes."

So, they waited. Forever. The property was big but surely not that big. She blew at the gnats and mosquitoes, not wanting to make any kind of swift movements that might draw attention, especially with the sky was turning gray with the approaching sunrise.

Finally, Rodrigo nudged her foot. She opened her left eye without moving her face away from the scope. Two men were in view of the left side of the house. Urgently, but without hurrying, she steadied her aim, placing the green dot in the center of the smoker's head. Center mass would have been a more sound target, but if Clayton were on alert, they would likely be wearing kevlar vests.

"Go," she whispered. Sam released her breath slowly. With the pad of her index finger, she depressed the trigger. Immediately before her own rifle fired, she registered Rodrigo's first shot. A split second later, the smoker crumpled to the ground. Rodrigo's second shot. She swung the rifle to the right to find an empty space.

There was a burst of fire from an assault rifle. A spray of bullets thwumped the grass and trees to their right. Sam swore quietly but fiercely. Not that the quiet mattered anymore. Everyone in the house would have awoken to that sound.

Sam scanned to the right with her scope, finding the non-smoker running for the corner of the house, the only cover available to him. She and Rodrigo fired almost simultaneously, his shot coming right before hers. His bullet struck the man in the left shoulder, turning him a few degrees. Hers hit him in the side of the neck. The thermal scope showed the spray as the bullet exited out the front. The man's hand went to his throat as he stumbled to the ground and didn't get back up.

Sam sprung to her feet. "You get your two?"

Rodrigo nodded.

It was now light enough for her to see him clearly.

She said, "Alright, let's skedaddle." Not whispering now.

Sam slung her rifle cross-body over her shoulder. Rodrigo shoved his into the bag he'd brought, full of other potentially necessary munitions. Before they'd gone more than a couple of steps, a buzzing sound entered the equation. It originated from the house but grew quickly closer. Sam spotted a drone zooming toward them a dozen feet above the ground. She fumbled at her belt bag for her pistol, forgetting that she'd swung it around backward so she could lie on her belly earlier.

Rodrigo dropped his bag and yanked out a shotgun.

When the drone spotted them, its operator made it hover, leering down at them.

Assuming that Bennett was watching them, Sam gave the mechanical hummingbird the middle finger. Rodrigo followed the cue and blasted it out of the sky. They sprinted for the driveway, knowing it was only a matter of time before they were being pursued. They couldn't get caught on foot, or this would all end badly for them.

It was on rare occasions like this, where running was required, that she swore off smoking. She meant it in the moment, but it was always a fleeting commitment.

An engine roared to life in the distance, and tires squelched on gravel. Rodrigo yelled, "Rapido," as though Sam's lagging behind him was because she was piddling about. He jumped over the spike strip they'd laid across the gravel driveway earlier and ducked back into the woods. Sam followed and watched Rodrigo disappear behind the base of an ancient pine tree. When she rounded it, he was squatted down digging through the oversized duffel bag, his breathing heavy but controlled. She leaned over, hands on her knees. Sweat dripped from her face and hair. Her own breath came in heaves. Rodrigo handed her the shotgun he'd used earlier. She checked to make sure the safety was still off.

The vehicle drew closer, until there was a distinct popping sound, and it skidded to a stop. Rodrigo pivoted out from behind the tree and lobbed a frag grenade under the jeep. Several voices yelled simultaneously. Car doors opened. A thunderous explosion made her ears ring and the ground convulse. Nudged by Rodrigo, who now had an AR-15 in hand, she stepped out from behind the tree. Assuming there had only been four guys in the Jeep, none had made it out.

Because of the narrow place where Rodrigo had placed the spike strip, there was no room for any other vehicles to go around the mess they'd made. They wouldn't have any pursuers in the immediate future. Still, they ran to the truck.

CHAPTER 32

NO SPEEDING WHEN DOING CRIME

SAM

Sam's screen on her phone lit up a split second before it started ringing at her. She waggled it at Rodrigo, who averted his eyes from the roadway only briefly.

"Bennett Clayton," she said. "What do you reckon he wants?"

Rodrigo grunted.

"Think I'll let it go to voicemail."

He nodded. "Is best."

Sam double-clicked the button on the side of the phone, ending the incoming call. While they waited, Sam suggested, "You think you could drive a little faster? I'd rather they not catch up with us."

"No," he said authoritatively. "Jefe — your papá — say, 'No speeding when doing crime, and that's doubly true for the Mexican.' Yes? You remember?"

"Yeah, I remember," she said with a wry smile. *Daddy had a saying for every occasion.* Sometimes talking to him felt like a conversation made up only of expressions. It could be exasperating.

"You disagree?"

"You know I don't. Carry on." The phone chirped at her, and

a badge told her that a voice message was waiting for her. "That took a minute. He must've had a lot to say."

As tempting as it was to listen right away, she waited for the phone to transcribe the message. There was no need to listen to him squawk at her when she could read his words and catch his drift. When the transcript popped up, she skimmed through it, whistling at the opening lines of the message. "I hope he doesn't kiss his grandbabies with that mouth."

Rodrigo chanced a look her way and raised an eyebrow.

"He calls me a bunch of names, nothing I haven't been called before, but at least he was creative about how he strung some of them together. Then he hollers about, he 'thought we had an understanding.' Meaning he thought I'd do what he told me and leave him alone. But I distinctly remember telling him I was gonna kill everything associated with him on account of he killed Buddy. I haven't changed my mind about that. It's good that he's mad, though. Already making mistakes." She held up the phone as proof of what she was saying. "You can't go leaving recordings of threats like this. Says he's going to remove me and the rest from the face of the earth. What if something like that landed in the hands of the sheriff? He could find himself in a whole heap of trouble."

"You will not tell Tompkins, no?"

"Nah. I'm just saying. Don't ever put nothing in writing that you don't want read back to you in front of a judge and jury."

"Your daddy, he say that too."

"Yeah, yeah." She relaxed her neck and let her head lay against the headrest, closing her eyes for a minute. "I suppose you're wondering what's next."

Rodrigo waited patiently while driving. He'd been working with Sam long enough that he could tell when a response was necessary. She gathered herself to say something he wouldn't like. "Well, now … I've kicked a hornet's nest. A big one. So you gotta take your family and get out of town. No, not out of town.

Go to another state. Maybe even back to Mexico. I don't want anything happening to y'all on my account."

Without looking at her, Rodrigo said, "*We* kick nest. You and me. You do not do it alone."

The flood of adrenaline leaving her system must have knocked something loose. Sam's eyes welled with tears. Her constricted throat ached. "What about your family?" Her voice sounded weird to her. "They've got to go. And they need you."

"Gone. Maria y los ninos go to her mamá house." He waved a hand toward the west. "Far away."

She couldn't turn off the tears that slipped down her cheeks, despite wiping them away as quickly as they appeared. "Good. But you have to go too. There's no sense in you sticking around. They're going to try pretty darn hard to kill me, and they probably saw you too on that drone."

"No," he said definitively.

Sam was unaccustomed to Rodrigo contradicting her. "Now, list—"

"No," he interrupted. "You are comadre. Do you know 'comadre'?"

She swallowed her inclination to get her hackles raised about first being told no and then interrupted. "Like friend or whatever."

"More than that." Rodrigo stopped the truck in front of her aunt's house. Sam was reminded that she'd have to convince Teresa to skip town for a bit, too. *That'll probably go as well as this.* Rodrigo turned in his seat to face her. "In English is 'my children's other mother.' But means family we choose. I made promise to your papá. That is more important than blood. You understand?"

"Yeah," she said, her voice still croaky and thick. She immediately became self conscious of both that and her puffy eyes.

"Also," he said, his demeanor shifting. "I have much life insurance. They are not so bad off if I am dead."

Sam smiled. "Want me to arrange something?"

"Please, no. *They* may be better off, but not me. The priest says I will have much to atone for. Many years of purgatory."

Her eyes widened. "How much do you tell him?"

"Not so much."

"Alright, then." She nodded her head toward Aunt Teresa's house. "Now, I've gotta go talk her into leaving for a while. Wish me luck."

"You want I should stay out here?"

"Nah, we'll be alright."

With his thumb, Rodrigo pointed toward the back seat. "You need guns?"

"We're set."

When she opened the truck's door, he said, "Vaya con Dios, comadre."

As usual, the sincerity made her intensely uncomfortable. She hopped to the ground and shut the door. Through the opened window, she said, "Hasta luego, muchacho."

He shook his head slowly and put the truck into reverse. Sam ambled to the front door, finding it unlocked — *Add that to the list of things we have to talk about.* — and pushed it open. She was greeted by some of the best smells the world had to offer: bacon, eggs, and biscuits.

"Samantha Ray," Teresa's raised voice matched the tone of her splotchy, angered face, "if you think for one minute I am leaving this house, you have lost your ever-loving mind. And if you insist on arguing about it and let these eggs get cold, I'll tan your hide like you're still a child. Is that clear?"

Sam would never be confused for Sigourney Weaver, but she was still a helluva lot bigger than Teresa, and had been since she hit puberty. The thought of her aunt chasing her around the kitchen table, belt in hand, brought a smile to her lips. "Fine," she said, raising both hands in concession. "Alright."

"Good," Teresa said, patting her apron. Small clouds of flour poofed outward, courtesy of the scratch-made biscuits, which now sat golden and perfect on a platter on the table. "Glad that's settled. It *is* settled, isn't it?"

"Yes, ma'am."

Teresa gestured to the chair in front of Sam. "Sit. Let's eat."

Sam sat and immediately reached out toward the bowl of scrambled eggs.

"Excuse me?" Teresa chastised.

Sam frowned and retreated her arm. Teresa said a prayer of blessing over the food, but unlike unhinged Gaither Mann, she spoke her prayer aloud. When she was done, Sam sat tentatively, her belly growling at her. Teresa said, "Alright, dig in."

Waffles lay down beside Sam. Although she appeared relaxed, Waffles was a loaded spring ready to uncoil at the smallest morsel of food hitting the floor.

It didn't escape Teresa's attention. "If I catch you feeding that dog any of this bacon, I'll throw you both out. I can hardly abide having an animal in the house anyway. They ain't meant to live with people like that."

Sam smirked and leaned forward. "I seen you feed her while you're cooking."

Teresa raised her chin. "Well, I'm not going to let the poor creature starve either."

"Uh-huh, it's just us chickens here, Auntie. You can admit to liking her. Won't anybody know."

"She's tolerable," Teresa confessed. When she cut a biscuit open and took off the top, steam rose up and dissipated in the air. "Hand me the butter."

CHAPTER 33
SEVERAL MINUTES OF DOOMSCROLLING

CHASE

CHASE READ THE CRYPTIC EMAIL FROM HIS BOSS FOR the fourth time, but didn't feel any better about things as a result. It was more formal than usual, which of itself felt like cause for concern. Terry didn't normally include Chase's name at the outset of an email. This time, though, it looked almost like a letter:

> Chase,
>
> Please make yourself available at 9:00am ET on Saturday to discuss the status of your investigation into the Valerie Wilson disappearance (link). I will be looking for a detailed accounting of your progress, including witnesses you've interviewed, how close you are to identifying suspects, and a proposed timeline for wrapping up your stay in Alabama.
>
> Sincerely,
>
> Terry Jemison
>
> CEO, Squall Line Media

And since when did Terry put "CEO" in her signature line? What had been operating as a collective when he left (*How many days ago?*) seemed to have changed somewhat in the interim.

The bottom-right corner of his monitor said it was 8:57. He plugged his ear buds into his head and clicked the video-conference link embedded in the email. While waiting for the host to join the meeting, he clicked on the ring light attached to his monitor and tousled his hair.

Finally, after several minutes of doomscrolling political news on social media, the screen in front of him changed. His own image shrank while a black box appeared with Terry's name on it. A moment later, the black box converted to a live image of Terry.

"Hey, Terry," Chase greeted her with a smile and a wave, then felt dumb about waving. It's not like they were randomly running into each other on the streets of Philadelphia.

"Hi, Chase. Catch me up with your project," she said curtly.

So I guess we're jumping right into this. Terry's demeanor was off. Tense. He'd always described her to people as gregarious. She might have launched a "new media" company — far from her first entrepreneurial endeavor — but she had never carried herself like an insufferable tech bro.

"About six weeks ago, Valerie Wilson — second and much younger spouse of a pediatrician in Jasper, Alabama — vanished. Like, without a trace. Oh, and when she was a kid, she was one of his patients, so there might be a grooming angle to this. The police chief and sheriff aren't either one very helpful."

"That's to be expected."

"Right," Chase said. "They both spoke to me on the record, but neither really gave me anything noteworthy. Well, I mean, I guess it could be noteworthy eventually depending how this plays out, but for now, at least ..."

"Who else have you spoken with?"

Chase noticed that Terry was actually in the office, instead of working from home. She rarely came to the office in the mornings, preferring to get all the admin work done at home without interruptions, except for those provided by her several rambunctious dogs. She looked at something off screen for several seconds, and he heard some muttering in the background.

When Terry returned her attention to him, Chase asked, "Is there someone in the office with you?"

She appeared unprepared to answer this question. "Umm. Yes. It's … uhh … an intern … from Temple. They're here for a couple of weeks before fall semester starts up."

Well, that was a lie. Chase had no idea who was there, but it absolutely wasn't some random intern he'd never heard of.

Terry prompted, "Who else have you spoken with?"

"The doctor's daughter, who's college age and not super enthusiastic about a step-mom that's only a few years older than her and who babysat her as a kid. I've talked to some local folks for background. The doctor, of course."

"Have you made progress on identifying who's responsible for the disappearance?"

Everything about this meeting was weird. It was more like an interview. Terry's questions all felt rehearsed, as if she were reading them off a script. Even her diction was clipped and precise, and not at all conversational. They had never communicated like this in the past.

"Not really. At first, I thought it was Dr. Wilson, especially because his first wife — the kids' mom — seemed to have disappeared in a similar fashion. But after interviewing him, I don't think so. Apparently, she got messed up on opioids, so he kicked her out after a while. Didn't want it to affect the kids. The police chief corroborates that story. It could be a ransom thing, but if that's the case, it's been going on for a while, and that doesn't bode well for her."

Terry's attention flicked off-screen several more times while he'd been speaking, but Chase decided to carry on with his debrief instead of addressing it again. Maybe one of the other guys could tell him what was going on.

He continued. "There's something else, too. This county is

kind of known for producing hit men. Like, for a couple thousand bucks — or up to tens of thousands, depending on who you want bumped off — you can hire somebody to knock off," he shrugged, "whoever."

"Does that tie into the Wilson woman's disappearance?"

"I don't know yet," he answered somewhat sheepishly.

Terry sighed, then straightened her posture. "Well, it sounds to me like for all the time and money you've spent over the last month, you have very little to show for it."

Chase opened his mouth to speak. He hadn't even told her yet about the death threat. But he decided to hold it back.

"I can't let this go on indefinitely. I need a timeframe on when you expect to resolve this. And it *must* be resolved. I will not be one of those people who puts up a podcast that does nothing more than stir up questions without providing any answers."

Chase did his best to hide his confusion. When he'd left Philadelphia, their podcasting company had been a collegial business, almost a partnership. But this was definitely not that. This was every bit a scolding from a boss. What had changed?

He must have missed something during his introspection, because he tuned back in to Terry saying, "Is this frozen up? Chase, did you hear me?"

Glad to have an excuse, he said, "Yeah, it must have locked up for a minute. What'd you say?"

"I said, can you have this wrapped up with satisfactory answers in the next two weeks? Because I can't keep dumping money into this project."

"Lord willing and the creek don't rise, I can."

Terry opened her mouth to speak, but paused mid-thought, before saying, "What was that you said? What does that even mean?"

"Lord willing and the creek don't rise — it's an expression I picked up down here. It means, like, as long as something unexpected doesn't happen." He refrained from smirking, glad that someone else in this conversation was finally confused. Of course, he had no idea how he would figure everything out in two weeks. He wasn't much closer now to knowing who has behind Valerie Wilson's disappearance than he had been before stepping foot in Walker County.

"Is that *Creek* as in indigenous people, or *creek* as in a body of water?" Terry asked. "Because I'm not going to lie, one of those seems problematic."

"I … I don't … huh. That hadn't occurred to me before."

"Perhaps, you should spend less time picking up colloquialisms you don't fully comprehend and more time figuring out this case before I pull the plug on it." Terry looked past the monitor again at whoever was on the other side. "I have to go. I'm backed up to another meeting. Keep me posted."

Immediately, he received a pop-up that the host had ended the meeting. Chase closed the lid of his laptop. *That didn't go as expected.*

CHAPTER 34
TEXTING IN FULL SENTENCES

SAM

When Waffles growled, Sam kicked a foot out from under the covers and nudged her. Waffles wasn't laying on her side fussing at some imaginary vermin. She was on her belly, legs gathered under her, ready to pounce. Sam looked over the side of the bed at Waffles and saw the mohawk between her shoulder blades standing at high alert.

The sound of a shotgun tore through the house. Sam was on her feet almost as fast as the dog. She yanked open the nightstand drawer and grabbed the .40 Smith & Wesson that lived there. A lot of folks didn't like the Sigma series because it lacked a safety, but she didn't have a passel of kids running around, so not having a safety gave her one less thing to account for. She tucked both her T-shirt and the extra magazine into the waistband of her underwear, flinching slightly where the cold metal touched her skin.

After the initial shotgun blast, things had grown quiet. She didn't know whether that shot was someone shooting their way into the house (*a stupid thing to do*) or them trying to cut Teresa in half. Stuck in her room like this, there was no way to figure out what was going on outside. Except there was. She snatched her phone off the nightstand and typed a message. *"U ok?"*

Sam watched the gray dots impatiently while waiting for a response. If Aunt Teresa didn't insist on texting in full sentences with proper punctuation, this would go a lot quicker.

"I'm in my bedroom. I have the shotgun that was under the bed."

"U shoot earlier?"

"No."

"STAY PUT. I'll come get you."

"Like hell I will."

Sam swore under her breath. Teresa was going to get herself killed.

The handle on her door jiggled. A habit formed out of her Daddy not being able to keep his hands … and other bits … to himself. She couldn't stop it then, but at least a locked door gave her some warning. Sam raised the Smith & Wesson and put three rounds through the door at about chest height. Even through the ringing in her ears, she heard the heavy thud, followed by footsteps. One down. How many left? Just the second one? Probably not. More likely, they'd brought four. More than four grown men in a vehicle in the middle of the night would be odd. Two wouldn't be enough. Clayton would want to give his guys better odds than that.

Waffles whined. The loud blasts couldn't have felt good on her sensitive ears.

"It's okay, girl." Sam scratched the top of her head.

There was a scraping sound outside the door. A whimper trailed after it. She'd heard that sound before when one of Daddy's dogs got the worst end of a fight with a coyote. Daddy had stroked the dog's head several times and told her she was a good girl. Then he put his hands over the dog's eyes so it wouldn't have to see him putting her down.

Sam crossed the room, standing to the side of the door as she unlocked the handle. She flung it open and waited. Nothing happened. She peaked quickly around the corner, her eyes having recovered enough from the muzzle flashes that the sunspots had mostly faded.

The scraping sound was being made by the downed intruder, who was doing his best to drag himself down the hallway. It was too dark to tell where he'd been hit, but not so dark that she couldn't see he wasn't doing well. He'd left his shotgun where it fell. She crouched to pick it up. The man quit pulling himself forward. He was breathing too hard and getting too little progress for the work he has putting in. It wasn't worth the effort.

He craned his neck, trying to get a look at Sam. She didn't move to make it any easier on him. He rolled himself over with a gasp. The front of his shirt shimmered with the wetness of the blood that covered it. There was a close triangle of holes on his belly. "That might take a minute to kill you," she hissed, pointing her pistol toward his abdomen.

The man said nothing.

"How many are y'all?"

When she saw the word his lips were forming, she closed eyes and pulled the trigger. It's not that she didn't want to watch him die, but that the muzzle flash would send her rods and cones all spinning out of sorts again. Even through her eyelids, the flash was bright.

Sixteen minus four. Sam had twelve rounds left in the .40. And whoever was left likely knew they were down a number because the bang they'd heard was another pistol, not a shotgun. Maybe she'd have been smarter to put him down with his own weapon, but that hadn't occurred to her until after the fact.

When something cold touched the back of Sam's knee, she whirled around, nearly tripping over Waffles. Her eyes went to the bedroom door that she'd failed to pull closed behind herself. "You scared me to death," she scolded. The dog's tail drooped. "It's okay. That was my fault." Waffles pressed tight against her leg, and Sam felt her trembling. *Brave girl.*

Sam and Waffles walked down the hallway, pausing at each door — the spare bedroom, the laundry and linen closets, and the downstairs bathroom — to make sure the closed doors were latched. She'd always thought it strange that Teresa kept the doors to all the rooms shut. It made the house feel smaller. But it was helpful now. As creaky as those ancient hinges were, if anybody was hiding in one of those rooms, they'd lose any surprise factor the moment they went to make their exit. More likely, they were waiting to ambush her in the family room or the kitchen, or upstairs where her aunt's room was.

At the end of the hallway, Sam steeled herself. The kitchen opened up to both the right and left in front of her. And beyond the kitchen to the right was the dining room. The island in front of her could give her some cover, but it might provide cover for someone else, too. One wrong decision could bring this whole business to an abrupt and unpleasant end.

Sam thought through what her intruders would expect from her. The obvious approach would be to hug the right side of the kitchen and go into the dining room because she could more easily see both rooms without exposing her back. But that would open her up to fire from both rooms. Assuming there was more than one guy left.

Sam determined to scrape against the wall to her left long enough to duck behind the island. She poked her head out of the hallway and to her left. She flinched when it bumped into something. Someone.

One of the bad guys had been trying to peer around the same corner. They banged heads, both startled. They recovered simultaneously. Sam caught movement near her waist. The man was trying to swing his assault rifle around. She shoved her left hand out, pushing the barrel away from her. With her right, she pushed her pistol under his chin. Surprise was the last thing he registered before she pulled the trigger.

He made a mess. The hollow points she kept in the Smith &

Wesson were very good at mushrooming and destroying all the tissue they encountered. Teresa would be pissed, assuming she kept them both alive long enough for her aunt to be angry about the state of the kitchen. Sam turned her attention away from the newly dead man and crouched with her back to the island. Waffles sniffed at him a couple of times before joining Sam. *Eleven rounds left.*

CHAPTER 35

THE BEST ODDS

SAM

Sam crouch-walked to the edge of the island, looking every bit the duck version of Rambo, and peeked out. *I'd kill for some thermal goggles right now.* She lurched up and dashed into the dining room, hoping to catch any potential occupant unaware.

Behind her, Waffles growled and loosed a ferocious bark. Sam turned to a whooshing sound, a gun firing, and Waffles landing in a heap on top of a man crouched between the island and stove, opposite where she'd been. The dog's weight pushed the man to the ground on his back, his right leg bent awkwardly.

The man began sputtering and reaching for his neck. However badly Waffles had been hurt, it hadn't kept her from latching onto his throat and clamping her jaws. The man's legs writhed in panic. Sam rushed back into the kitchen, snatching a knife out of the block beside the stove top.

The man grabbed at Waffles' face, his fingers trying to find her eyes.

"Huh-uh," Sam said. The man noticed her for the first time as she knelt beside him, her knife held precariously close to his own eye. His hand retreated only as far as the dog's jaws. His breaths were shallow and ragged. "Waffles, let go." The golden retriever didn't budge. Sam set her pistol down and grabbed the scruff of the dog's neck to get her attention. "Let go, girl."

The dog loosened her grip and slid off him with a whine and fell to her side. Sam spied blood matting the fur on her chest. New rage seethed inside her.

She took Waffles' place and saddled herself on the intruder's torso, restricting his efforts to recover his breath. His chest heaved under her.

"Put your hands behind your head."

He took his hands away from his throat and slipped them under his head. Blood dribbled from places where Waffles' teeth had punctured the skin. She flicked her eyes to the right. The dog panted and whimpered.

"How many are left?"

The man shook his head.

"I can kill you now and go find out."

He shook his head again, and Sam thought his eyes glistened with tears. He croaked, "If I tell you, will you let me live?"

Sam pursed her lips. "Sure."

"You telling the truth?"

"Swear it on my Daddy's grave."

"Okay." He was uncertain, but decided to give himself the best odds. "Me and a guy upstairs."

"That it? Nobody outside?"

"Huh-uh."

"No one waiting in a car?"

He cleared his throat and shook his head.

"What did you drive?"

"Jeep Cherokee. Couple hundred yards up the road."

She saw the man glance down, noticing her bare legs for the first time. Sam scoffed, "Y'all can't help yourselves, can you? 'Bout to die, and you're still trying to get a peek."

"But you s—"

In a flash, Sam raised the knife high overhead and drove downward with both hands and a grunt. The man stuck up a hand to block the blow. He was too late. The knife tore through his palm, pinning it to his face, where it ripped through his eye and into his head. Sam's face almost touched his from effort her whole body had mustered. She whispered, "You shot my dog. I couldn't let that go."

She swiveled off the dead man and kneeled beside Waffles. The dog raised her head and whined. "How bad is it, girl?" She thought about turning her over so she could get a better idea of where she'd been shot, but decided better of it. She felt around on the dog's underside and her hand came away sticky. "Hang right." She petted the dog gently. "We'll make this quick, and I'll get you some help."

Sam picked up the pistol she'd set down a minute ago. She pulled the spare magazine out of the place in her underwear where it had remained stashed. With only one guy left, eleven rounds should be plenty, but sixteen was better.

She banked on the fourth guy staying put, presumably waiting to ambush her, and ran back to her bedroom for her phone. She texted Teresa, *"One left."*

Hurrying through the ground she'd covered, Sam crouched low in the dining room and family room. No sense dying because she trusted the word of a man who'd been sent here to kill her. She stayed wide of the stairwell, taking a circuitous route toward its base. She could either creep up or rush it, but neither was a good option. Both were likely to get her shot.

She hollered up the stairs. "You're the only one left. How about you come down so we can work something out?"

"I'm good, Cherry. Maybe you should come up here."

"Cherry, huh? It's been a minute since anybody called me that. I thought I made it clear how I felt about that particular nickname."

"I must've forgot," he said casually.

There were only about a dozen guys it could be. She raced through their names and voices in her head. "How do you see this working out?"

"Well, I got the high ground, so I thought I'd cut you down as you came up them stairs. Then I'd go get my sack of money from Mr. Clayton."

She slid to the wall and flipped a light switch that turned on the upstairs hall light. She saw a man from the shoulders up. He swore and backed up. Sam stepped back a pace too, keeping herself in shadow. "Jared Walker. I thought you were working for Drummond Coal?"

"Laid off."

"You still telling girls that the county's named after your people?"

"Nah," he said with a nervous laugh. "That played out after high school. Besides, I'm married now. Got a couple of babies."

Sam was about done playing for time and tried a new angle. "How much is Bennett paying you? I'll double it."

Jared took several seconds to answer. "Can't do it. Mr. Clay—"

The hinges of a door squeaked right before the door handle gouged a hole in the wall. A shotgun fired. Someone hit the floor. Casting all care aside, Sam screamed, "Teresa!" and pounded up the stairs. She nearly tripped over Jared's body when she landed in the hallway. A couple dozen pellets had ripped through the vital organs in his torso. He looked up at Sam as the life bled out of him. "I'll send some money for the babies," Sam said. It wasn't their fault their daddy was broke and made a poor life choice.

Teresa leaned against the door frame to her bedroom, rubbing her right shoulder.

"You okay?" Sam asked.

"I will be. Got a bit of a kick."

"Yeah, but that's not what I meant."

"I know what you meant. Just 'cause I'm not from your daddy's side of the family doesn't mean I've kept clear of all this."

"Sure. But fielding phone calls is a shade different than shooting a man down in your own home, right outside your bedroom."

Teresa nodded. "I'll come to terms with it. I can talk to Father Pettway about it if I need to."

Sam's eyes bugged. "You can what?"

"It's okay. He can't tell anybody except God, and He already knows."

Sam rubbed her eyes with the heels of her hands. This was too much.

Teresa's eyes flicked downward, noticing something for the first time. "Are you hurt? Why do you have blood all over you?"

Sam looked down reflexively, then swore fiercely. As she tore back down the stairs, she yelled over her shoulder. "Waffles. She got shot."

Teresa hurried after her. "Is she ..."

Sam ran through the house back to Waffles' side, flipping on lights as she went. The dog raised her head at the commotion. Her tail thumped the floor a couple of times, but she didn't attempt to get up.

"Thank God," Teresa muttered.

"Bring me a spare sheet," Sam instructed. Her aunt shrieked at the site of her blood-spattered kitchen. Sam stroked her dog as she waited. Teresa brought back a cream-colored sheet that was about to get wrecked. "Get on the other end, and unfold it a couple of times so we can put her on it. Okay. Now, I'm gonna lift her up a couple of inches. You slide it under her. Ready? Go." Sam grunted, and Waffles whined in pain. But a couple of seconds later, she was on the sheet.

Sam pointed. "Grab those corners, and help me get her to the truck. Then you call Dr. Hanks and tell him I'm coming."

Teresa glanced at the clock on the microwave. "You think he'll answer?"

"If you're persistent enough, he will. Tell him I'll pay whatever it takes to get him out of bed and to his clinic in the middle of the night."

CHAPTER 36
POPPING BY UNANNOUNCED

SAM

THE SUN HAD BROKEN OVER THE TREE LINE BY THE time Sam pulled up in front of Teresa's house, parking in the same spot she'd left several hours earlier. She backed the truck up to the front porch and turned off the engine. Before getting out, she gave Waffles a long look and gently patted her haunches. Between the length of bandage wrapped several times around her belly and the cone of shame that would keep her from messing with the wound, she was quite a sight. "You'll be alright, girl. Gotta take it easy for a few days." Still under the influence of anesthesia, the golden retriever snoozed heavily on the bench seat, and didn't stir even when Sam scratched her hind quarter.

Sam got out of the truck and walked around to the back of the house, where the shed stood unlocked. She took a couple of beach towels and tossed them over her shoulder, then pulled an old wagon to the side of the house, where she tumped it over and hosed out the remains of potting soil and long-dried bits of plant matter. Once she'd turned the wagon and towels into a makeshift gurney, she rolled it over to the passenger side of the truck.

At the sound of the truck, Teresa had stepped onto the front porch. Sam paused to listen to half of the conversation she was having on her cordless phone. *I didn't even know she still had a land line.*

"You should be ashamed — Ashamed! — setting out to do something like this on a Sunday. This is the Lord's day, Bennett. You're probably gonna get your family all gussied up and head to the church in a couple of hours, pretending like none of this happened and you ain't part of a killing. You got no cause to shed blood on the Sabbath." She stopped briefly to listen, but her volume increased several clicks when she interrupted Clayton. "Don't you *technically* me about what day is and isn't the Sabbath."

Despite how tired and emotionally drained she was, Sam smiled. *He probably hasn't been scolded like this since he was a child.*

Teresa wasn't done. "Let me tell you what you're gonna do. You're gonna come down here yourself. Don't you send your people without you being with them. I won't let a single one of them inside my house without you being here to reckon for yourself. And you're going to take these dead men away from here. For myself, I promise to do my level best to keep Samantha Ray from killing every single one of you on account of your men shot her dog. You hear me? Now, what time are you gonna be here?" Teresa looked at her watch. "That'll be fine. See you then."

The end of the call stood in stark contrast to the rest of it, like she was scheduling furniture movers to come over, not the removal of four bodies. She was a Southern lady down to her bones — even the most dire of circumstances didn't call for her to be unnecessarily rude.

Teresa leaned against the porch railing. "How's the pup?"

"Doc says she'll be alright. Got lucky. Bullet left a big gash on her belly, but it didn't go in. He had to give her some blood. She'll have an ugly scar, but she should come out okay."

Teresa nodded. "I guess her bikini-wearing days are over then."

"Nah, she should be proud of it. Shows she's a tough bitch that nobody oughta mess with."

"Like her momma."

Sam flashed a brief smile. "I gotta get her into the house before the anesthesia wears off. This probably won't feel good." She carted the wagon to the side of the truck, cradled the dog, and lowered her into it. Waffles snorted and whimpered in her sleep. "Sorry," Sam whispered.

She pulled the wagon toward the house and said, "I'll take her around to the back door. There's only the one step."

"I'll take her." Teresa pointed down the driveway. "You handle that."

Sam turned to see a brown Tahoe with a blue light bar on top driving their way. She muttered several unseemly things. Teresa took the wagon's handle from her, and Sam strode back to her truck and leaned against its side.

The Tahoe came to a stop, and the driver's door opened.

"Sheriff," Sam greeted.

"Samantha Ray."

"You're calling awfully early for a Sunday."

"What was that?" He pointed in the direction Teresa had gone.

"She's taking the dog in. Got in a hunting accident. Had to go see Dr. Hanks."

"I guess that explains the state you're in?"

Sam looked down at herself, having forgotten she was covered in blood. She nodded.

"Ain't nothing in season right now, Sam. What were you hunting?"

"Feral hogs. Teresa's been having a problem with them tearing up her garden."

The sheriff nodded. "I guess that explains the gunshots we got a call about."

Sam let him keep doing his job for now, so he could feel like he was in charge. She'd learned that it was important to let men in positions of authority retain their sense of power. When they felt impotent, they acted out. "I suppose it does."

"Wouldn't be any other reason for there to be gunshots, would there?"

"I can't imagine so." She guarded her responses now.

"Call came in a few hours ago from somebody who was driving by."

"You took your time checking on it."

"Yes, I did."

The radio in Sheriff Tompkins' vehicle started chattering, and he shut the door. "Everything alright out here?"

"We're alright," she answered, more-or-less truthfully.

Tompkins looked her in the eyes. "I've been hearing some things that are troubling me. I told you the last time I seen you that we couldn't have a war."

"And *I* told *you* there wouldn't be one. And there ain't. You can't go believing every nasty rumor you hear."

"You mind if I search the house?"

"It isn't her house," Teresa said loudly from across the yard as she walked toward them. "Besides, it's my understanding you need probable cause for a search."

"Well, Teresa, it's probably 'cause I think you got several of Mr. Clayton's men—"

"Whoa, whoa, whoa," Sam said. "So I'm *Samantha Ray* and she's *Teresa*? But he's *Mr. Clayton*? I think your misogyny is showing a little there, Sheriff."

"Now, Sam," Teresa said, "let's not antagonize the man. It's probably straining his capacities to be able to talk down to us feeble-minded women-folk."

The sheriff set his jaw. Sam could almost hear his molars

grinding against each other. He was accustomed to being treated with more deference than either woman was affording him, and since he was old enough to be Sam's father, it was particularly galling coming from her. But the thing about being in some-body's pocket is it undermines whatever authority you would otherwise bring to the situation. Sam had allowed him to question her earlier, but she was done placating the man.

Sam said, "Even if something happened in that house, it happened *in* the house, meaning that we were well within our rights to do whatever needed doing."

"Doesn't mean I'm not obligated to investigate it," Tompkins replied. "Like how I have to look into whose Jeep that is sitting by the road." He pointed. "Know anything about that?"

"No," Teresa said, "but I bet you ran the plates before you came down here."

"I did."

"And?"

"And," the sheriff sighed, "it's owned by some LLC."

Sam said, "Maybe you could call Lorraine after she gets out of church today and have them tow it for us. Don't want it junking up the neighborhood."

"Sounds like you don't expect the owner to come back for it."

"Couldn't say. Don't know nothing about it."

Sam pulled her phone out of her pocket and checked the time. "Sheriff, now that you've done your duties, it's about time you headed back to town. We got company coming."

"This early on a Sunday?"

Teresa shrugged. "We're popular girls. Next time, instead of popping by unannounced, you could give us a heads-up so we could have coffee and muffins ready for you. We can be real hospitable given some notice."

Tompkins gave her what he thought was a curious look as he

shuffled to the door of his patrol vehicle. "I thought we were friends, Teresa."

To Sam's ear, it sounded almost like pouting.

"We are friends, Jerry. But we ain't family. Now, you stay safe out there."

He grunted and hoisted himself into the Tahoe. Once he'd swung around and started heading back out, Sam said, "Well ... that was weird."

"I think you hurt his feelings. And if I can make a recommendation?"

"Uh-huh?"

"Maybe you could be less blunt with our next visitor? This situation could use some tact so things don't escalate further."

Sam grinned and held up three fingers in a boy-scout salute.

Teresa shook her head. "Girl, you're gonna get us killed."

CHAPTER 37

A SHARK DOING SHARK THINGS

SAM

WHEN CLAYTON BENNETT ARRIVED WITH HIS MEN TO collect the fallen cronies, they found Sam and Teresa waiting for them in rocking chairs on the front porch. A shotgun laid across Teresa's lap, the same one she'd used to put down the last of the invaders. Sam had noticed her favoring her right shoulder more in the hours since she'd fired it.

When Bennett's truck came to a stop, Sam was surprised that only two men got out with him. Maybe he was running low on henchmen after she and her folks had killed a bunch of them in the last couple of days.

Bennett strutted to the steps of the porch and stopped, waiting for an invitation. His close-cropped beard looked more gray than it had since Sam had last seen him only a week ago. But that was probably only her imagination.

He nodded toward the shotgun. "I thought I was here under a parley."

"You are, and you're my guest so long as you act right. But that don't mean I'm fool enough to let you turn this into a turkey shoot because I decided to naively believe your wolfish nature wouldn't get the best of you. You're a predator, Bennett.

You can't help the way you are, like a shark can't help but take a bite out of a beachgoer every now and then. He's just a shark doing shark things."

Clayton looked at her an extra couple of seconds after she'd finished, trying to decide whether or not to be offended. He produced a forced smile and said, "The sheriff called me a little while ago. He's worried about things getting out of hand."

Teresa stood up. "He need not concern himself with that. Sam and I are doing a fine job of keeping things in hand."

The corner of Sam's mouth twitched as she suppressed a grin. Her aunt's ability to be simultaneously subtle and insulting was a work of art. Sam hadn't mastered that skill set. To be fair, she hadn't put much effort into it. She generally preferred to inform people exactly where they stood with her, that way there were no surprises.

"Shall we get to it?" Teresa said as she walked to the front door, which had a substantial hole where there had once been a handle and deadbolt. "Don't mind the mess. We'll get that patched right up. Y'all come inside." She pulled the door open and stood aside, shotgun hitched under her other arm, pointed toward the ground. Clayton's two men followed him inside the house, and Sam trailed Teresa.

Once everyone was inside, Teresa pointed up the stairs. "One's up there. Follow me this way for the others." She led them through the family room and dining room. "There's one on either side of the island in the kitchen, and the last one is down that hall there."

Clayton gestured toward a coagulated pool of blood that didn't have a body attached to it. "What's that?"

Sam interjected. "One of your boys shot my dog."

"Sorry about that," Bennett said, seeming genuinely apologetic. Sure, he'd sent men to kill them in their beds during the night, but he hadn't meant for any animals to get hurt.

"If only it was that easy." Sam looked him dead in the eyes as she said it. She didn't want him to think he was off the hook just because he might feel bad for it. The list of things he had to atone for was growing. His feelings had no bearing on what was to come.

Clayton held her gaze for several seconds before telling his men, "Go get the tarps and bungees. Be careful to wrap them up good."

Teresa chimed in. "I don't need any more blood on the floors and walls than is already there. My girl's going to have a hard enough time as it is."

Clayton stayed in the house and supervised as one-by-one his men brought in tarps and carried bodies out. In the long minutes that transpired, no one spoke a word. As far as Sam was concerned, the time for talking had long passed. Everything that needed saying had already been spoken.

When the two men, both of whom were covered in pools of sweat as the day's heat had set in, retrieved the last body from the hallway leading to Sam's bedroom, the other three followed them out. Sam expected Clayton to head straight out to his truck without another word. They'd pick up where they left off until one killed the other. There was a comfort in the certainty of the situation. Although the timing of the end wasn't knowable, there was a predetermined finiteness to it.

Clayton paused before stepping off the porch, and Sam brought herself to a halt a couple of paces behind him. He turned on his heel and stepped back toward her. They were close enough that she could smell the coffee on his breath, smell that he hadn't showered that morning, had maybe even worked out. "You could've walked away," he hissed. "I told you that killing Buddy was an accident. It was supposed to be you."

His face was red with anger, but Sam didn't think this was the fury of indignation. This was fear. She stepped forward, closing the gap between them. He sneered down at her.

Sam said, "I already told you how this was going to end. There are no alternatives."

Clayton snatched the front of her shirt with both hands. "Listen here, little girl—"

Whatever else he was going to say was lost in the sound of a gunshot.

Clayton was confused. His grip slackened.

Sam backed away a step, revealing the .380 that she held up to his belly. The second he'd grabbed her, she'd reached around to the small of her back for it, but he'd been too caught up in the moment to notice.

Blood blossomed from the hole in Clayton's stomach and ran down his shirt. He stumbled backward two steps, falling from the porch and landing on his back.

Clayton's men ran forward from the truck, one with a shotgun, the other with a pistol. They glanced around wildly. Sam stepped off the front porch and stood beside Clayton, her handgun trained on the man with the shotgun. When Rodrigo emerged from one corner of Teresa's house and Jeb came around the other, the two men became jumpier still.

The man with the pistol dropped his gun. He nudged the other guy, who lowered his shotgun. Sam looked down at Clayton. He was grunting with pain, and his breathing sounded wet. When she'd shot him, the pistol had been pointing upward, so the bullet had probably hit a smattering of vital organs on its way through. "Don't you go anywhere. I'm gonna talk to these fellas for a minute." She addressed the two men in the front yard. "You know who I am?"

They both nodded.

"Y'all showed up here under a truce at my aunt's invitation. He," here she pointed toward the ground, "violated that when he laid hands on me, so I was well within my rights to do what I did. Anybody disagree with that?"

Both shook their heads.

Sam pulled a pack of cigarettes out of her back pocket, using the ritual of lighting it and taking the first drag to give herself a minute to figure out what came next.

"So here's the deal. Ole Bennett here ain't going back with you. He and I have business to attend to. You go back and tell Catherine what happened to her daddy. Tell her I don't have a grudge against her and her son, and if she'll let this be the end of it, we can all put this behind us." She looked down again and found Clayton's dark eyes squinting up at her. "Except you, obviously. I'm gonna feed you to the pigs." The man's hands clutched at the grass beside him as his body was racked with pain and not a little bit of fear. "Don't worry. I'll let you die first."

Sam looked back toward the men who waited to be dismissed. "Last thing before you go. I could use a couple more hands around here. So if you find yourselves in the position of needing a new employer, you come back after you're done. Understood?"

They nodded in unison.

"Alright then," she said and turned away.

The man toting the shotgun said, "He's got the truck key."

Sam squatted down beside Clayton and said, "Excuse me," as she reached into his pant's pocket. He grabbed her wrist, but the grip was weak and she broke it easily. Standing up again, she tossed the keys to the new driver.

"Thank you, ma'am."

After they drove off, Sam squatted beside Clayton again. His eyes followed her movements. "I can see you're hurting," she said softly. "I can let you suffer, or I can put an end to it. I'll leave that to you. But first, I have a question. Was it you who put Daddy's name in the Murder Tree? Did I do your bidding when I put him in the ground? Actually ... I'll tell you what." She stood up. "I'm not going to believe you either way, and it don't much matter. If you want this to end quicker, tell Rodrigo. Otherwise, you can lay here and bleed out." She walked away, not looking back. Not carrying with her any sense of triumph. No relief. No comfort.

She needed to go check on Waffles.

CHAPTER 38

THAT COMPLICATES THINGS

CHASE

Ever since the video conference that had wrecked his Saturday morning, Chase had been treading water, unable to find any way to move his investigation forward. Neither of the doctor's other kids would talk to him. He didn't have any additional reasons to hassle either the police chief or the sheriff. The local newspaper was stonewalling him. Not that he held that against them. Not really. They were a small operation hanging on for dear life, hoping that their hyper-local reporting and reputation in the community would keep them profitable enough to subsist on.

The combination of those things brought him to The Warehouse in the middle of a Tuesday because he had nowhere else to be. He was living in an episode of *Cheers*, but without the witty characters and laugh track. He hadn't previously considered how gloomy an existence it might be to spend your days at a bar because you had nothing demanding your attention.

Also, drinking made him too sullen and introspective. Not ideal when work was going poorly and he had no real personal life. As the alternate bartender — who did their job in an efficient but perfunctory way, but didn't engage with him like Jake did — slid another beer toward him, Chase's thoughts landed on the threatening letter he'd received ten days earlier. He'd not left town, but nothing untoward had happened to him … yet.

But what if it did?

If it did — if he turned up missing — what then? No one would probably notice for days. That was a depressing thought. He could be a bloating corpse discarded in the Alabama wilderness, and it might be the better part of a week before it occurred to anyone that he'd not texted them back or returned a phone call.

Chase took his hand off the already-perspiring glass of beer. Another one would not help. He had decided to cash out and go do … something as yet undecided, when a hand thumped him heavily on the back and a guy a few years younger than himself said, "Hey, partner," as he sat down beside Chase.

He didn't recognize the guy, though he looked vaguely familiar. The man held a finger up to the bartender. "Ghost Train El Rey, please."

Out of habit, Chase pulled his recorder out of his back pocket, laid it on the bar, and pressed the button with the red circle. You never knew where a conversation was going to lead.

Hoping that he hadn't met the guy before and wasn't about to embarrass himself, Chase stuck out a hand. "Chase Williams."

The man gripped his hand firmly, but not like he was trying to make a point of squishing it. "Nice to meet you, Chase Williams. You sound like you're a foreigner."

"Foreigner?" Chase said in surprise. "I'm from Philadelphia."

The man laughed and shrugged. "Same difference."

"You're from around here, then?"

"Walker County born and bred," the man answered with a satisfied smile.

Not knowing quite how to respond to that, Chase raised his beer glass in salute. "I didn't catch your name."

"Jeb," the man said.

"That short for anything?"

"Nah. The old man named me after the Civil War general."

While Chase didn't wasn't familiar the general that Jeb was referring to, the forearm tattoo of a Confederate flag being waved by a busty lady told Chase he did not ask which side the general was affiliated with.

"You that reporter asking everybody about Val?"

"I am. Did you know her?"

"Yeah, I did," Jeb said. He leaned in. "We had some good times in high school, if you know what I mean."

The bartender, who was walking by, said, "No they didn't. She was way out of his league."

Chase guffawed, caught by the surprise nature of the drive-by.

Jeb flushed. "Shut up, William. Like you'd know. You were too busy trying to give handies to the baseball team."

William continued tinkering with glasses without looking their way. "As I recall, you were on that baseball team. Are you ready to come out after all these years? It's fine if you are. I can walk you through it."

Jeb's embarrassment boiled into anger. He stood up and pushed his bar stool away. "I'm not—I didn't. Tell him, William, or so help m—"

"Oh, keep your pants on, Jeb. Or don't. I don't care." William looked directly at Chase for the first time since he'd come in. "He's *definitely* not gay. It's very important to him that you understand that." He winked and went to the kitchen.

"Never you mind about him. I knew Val." He dragged his barstool forward and sat back down.

"*Knew*. You say that in the past tense, like you don't think she's still alive. Or am I reading too much into that?"

Jeb wagged a finger at him. "You're quick. I'll have to mind what I say around you." But the glitter in the man's eyes said he wanted to talk, even brag, and wasn't there to be cautious with his words. "But to answer your question — no, she's dead. For sure."

"Just like that?"

"Just like that." Jeb took a long pull of his beer. "Let me tell you something. She's been gone, what, a couple months? You don't go missing that long in Walker County and then turn up on your doorstep one day. In fact, you don't turn up anywhere again."

"What do you mean? Like, you don't even think they'll find her body."

Jeb shook his head. "No way. Unless it's some amateur who did it. She's gone." He made a soft whooshing sound, reminiscent of a stiff breeze.

"At the risk of sounding ignorant, don't police find years-old remains of people in cold cases pretty regularly?"

"Not around here, they don't. There's a dozen ways to get rid of a body. Smith Lake's pretty deep, and they say there's catfish in there the size of Volkswagens. Catfish'll eat most anything. There's countless abandoned mine shafts you could drop a body in. It wouldn't never be found. Should I keep going?"

"Sure."

"There are a whole bunch of hollows that don't see people for years at a time. Plenty of buzzards and wild hogs that would scoop up the opportunity to dispose of a body. You ever see that one Guy Ritchie movie where the guy would feed people to his pigs? It's like that."

"You seem pretty knowledgeable on this topic," Chase said.

Jeb wore a coy expression. "A fella hears things."

"So, which of those things do you think happened to Valerie Wilson?"

Jeb finally sensed danger, though he still appeared to be enjoying having an audience to impress. "Can't rightly say."

"Can't or won't?"

"Is there a difference?" Jeb asked.

"Quite a sizable difference, the way I see it."

Jeb grunted and smirked, then drained his glass in an exceedingly large gulp that made Chase wonder how the man didn't get his Adam's apple turned upside down by taking a drink like that. Jeb put both palms on the edge of the bar and pushed back. "Guess I'll be heading off now." He pulled out a wad of bills and left a twenty on the bar.

Chase said, "That's a pretty big tip for one glass of beer. I didn't even think you liked the guy."

"Like's got nothing to do with it. He helps take care of his momma. Her health is failing, and I'm sure the government don't cover all of it."

Chase was trying to reconcile in real time two opposing perceptions of this guy. On the one hand, he had certainly wanted to give the impression that he was either involved in or at least knew a good bit about the disappearance and presumed death of Valerie Wilson. And on the other, he was being extraordinarily charitable to someone he'd known a long time and seemed to disapprove of. "Let me ask you a question. Did you come in here today to have a drink so you could have a valid reason to give him money? Or did you come in here to talk to me? Because I don't believe it was happenstance that you stopped by here today."

"Like I said," Jeb started walking toward the front door, "you're a quick fella, and I probably shoulda been more careful with you."

"What's your last name, Jeb? You didn't tell me earlier."

Jeb flashed a toothy grin. "Can't rightly say." He punched the door open and strode into the sunlight.

Chase put his hand on the recorder to turn it off as William emerged from the kitchen. He looked at the bill on the bar top and shook his head, bemused.

Chase asked, "What's his last name? He didn't say."

"Coleman."

Recognition flashed an alarming light in Chase's head. "Is he any relation to Sam Coleman?"

"Yep. She's his little sister."

Well, that complicates things.

CHAPTER 39

THE OPPORTUNITY IS LOST

CHASE

CHASE SWUNG OPEN THE DOOR TO THE CHERRY RED truck and hoisted himself up. "I have to admit, I was having a pretty miserable day until you asked me out on a date."

Sam rolled her eyes. "Not a date. Two people having dinner together. If anything, I pitied how miserable you must be eating bologna sandwiches or whatever every night for dinner."

"Is that what you think of me?"

"Absolutely." She let off the clutch and eased onto accelerator.

"I'll have you know I alternate between turkey and roast beef. Sometimes, when I'm feeling real fancy, I'll do both."

"Ooh. Look at you."

"Have you had barbecue since you've been here?"

"I had some at the airport in Charlotte while waiting on my connecting flight. Does that count?"

Sam cast some side-eye in his direction. "First of all. No. Airport barbecue doesn't count. And second, even if it did, North Carolina barbecue is not the same as Alabama barbecue. They don't have the right sauce."

"Isn't all barbecue the same — you just cook a pig for a really long time?"

"You, sir, are offensive."

While Chase was enjoying the banter, other things weighed heavily on him. Things he needed to talk to Sam about, mainly because her brother insinuating to him three days earlier that he was involved in the disappearance and possible death of Valerie Wilson. He didn't think he could keep up the chitchat much longer.

With his shifting demeanor, an unsettling lull slipped into the conversation with only Sam's choice of music to occupy the audio space. Chase noted that for the first time since he'd been around her, it wasn't country music she was listening to. He pointed at the radio. "What do you have going for us today?"

"A little Dirty South hip-hop."

"Really?" Chase smiled out of one side of his mouth as he said it.

"What? I can listen to rap."

"No doubt. It's ... not what I expected, is all."

"It's storytelling. Their stories are a little different from my people's. But stories are stories."

He hadn't considered it in those terms before. Maybe that was an oversight since he too was a storyteller by trade. Finally, he couldn't withhold his news anymore. "There are a couple of things I need to tell you."

"Same. Who gets to go first?"

"I think I probably should," Chase said. "It's kind of a big deal."

Sam pulled into a parking lot and brought the truck to a stop. "Let's get inside first."

"We shouldn't talk about it in front of other people."

"You do have something juicy, don't you?" Sam said with a great deal of interest. "I'll have them seat us in a room they usually reserve for parties. It'll be fine."

Over the next several minutes, as they got situated, Chase practiced the conversation in his head. How he would tell her the things he had to say, how she would respond. It was a useless exercise that never went as prescribed. But he'd done it his whole life and didn't know how to turn it off. It was made all the more obsolete because when he was debriefing conversations in his head *after* they'd occurred, that's when he thought of the most clever retorts. But it's not like you could tap someone on the shoulder five minutes later and deliver the line then. Experience had taught him that. He'd tried it in sixth grade with a girl who'd broken up with him, which had resulted in a bunch of snickering and whispers. Lesson learned. If you don't think of something clever in the moment, the opportunity is lost. Except that it lives in your mind indefinitely.

Once they were seated in the private room and their server had delivered sweet tea and enough cheese biscuits to feed half the county, Sam said, "You first."

"There are two things. One will matter more to you than the other. What do you want first?"

"The one I care about. That way, I can ignore the other one while I'm stuffing my face."

Chase smiled despite the jitters in his belly now that the time had come. "I was at the bar the other day — Tuesday — and this guy came in talking to me about Valerie Wilson. He was going out of his way not to say *too* much, but he also wanted me to know more than he was saying."

Sam nodded encouragingly.

"He was suggesting details about how to get rid of a body, different ways you could do it. Talking about how he didn't think she wasn't alive anymore because of how long she's been missing."

"Who was it?" She tried to make her voice sound merely curious, but there was an edge to it.

"Your brother."

"Jeb?"

Chase nodded.

"He told you his name?"

"Yes."

Sam shook her head and said definitively, "He didn't do it."

"He sure wanted me to think he did."

"It wasn't him."

"It wasn't Jeb that I was talking to, or it wasn't Jeb that abducted Valerie Wilson?"

"You may well have been talking to Jeb and he may have said whatever he said, but he had nothing to do with her disappearance." Sam had leaned forward as she spoke, not wanting to raise her voice that was strained with intensity.

"I'm not disputing you," Chase said, "but how can you be sure?"

The server came back for their order, and both Sam and Chase sat back in their seats, deescalating the conversation, if only temporarily. Sam ordered for both of them. "A pulled pork plate. A turkey plate, with the white sauce — we don't need the red sauce for that. Mac and cheese. And collards."

After the server left, Chase raised an eyebrow. "White barbecue sauce?"

"I'm about to change your life. It's a north Alabama thing. Used for chicken and turkey." The levity with which Sam said she was going to change his life didn't hang around. "What do you know about lions?"

Chase shrugged. He was largely indifferent about lions, but he'd watched *Tiger King* and his share of nature documentaries during the pandemic lock-down, like everyone else.

"When the patriarch of a pride of lions thinks that one of his sons is a threat, he either kills the threat or forces him to leave. Daddy was a lion. If either of the boys had stepped out on their own, they would've been a threat. And I'm not exaggerating when I tell you that he would have either brought them to heel or killed them. He'd have had a harder time with Buddy, but that doesn't mean he wouldn't have done it."

"That seems pretty harsh."

"It's a harsh life. There's no room for disloyalty within the family. Dissent is seen as weakness, and weakness is a death sentence."

"So there's no room for moonlighting or like entrepreneurship?"

"No," Sam said flatly.

Chase was aware that he may be crossing a line even as he stepped on it. "Didn't you kill your dad? How do you square that with your demand for loyalty within the family?"

"He was disloyal to me since I came into my womanhood. So the treachery didn't start with me, but it sure as hell ended there. The patriarch doesn't worry about the lionesses. He assumes they're in hand. But he should. They're the real hunters, and they can tear his throat out as readily as the males."

The coldness with which she said it ran a chill down Chase's spine.

Sam asked, "Now, what was the other thing you wanted to tell me?"

CHAPTER 40
ROOKIE MISTAKE

CHASE

THE SERVER RETURNED CARRYING PLATES PILED WITH barbecued meat and bowls of sides. Chase had no idea how they expected only two people to eat all the food that had been delivered. It could easily have fed twice that many. He waited until the server left before dropping his news. "I got fired," Chase said, then hedged. "Well, not fired exactly."

Sam took a bite of turkey and with a mouth full of it said, "Either you're fired or you're not."

The emails he'd received in the days since the video conference had provided some additional details about the situation, none of which were positive for him. "My boss sold the company, so—"

"So you're getting cashed out like you wanted?"

"Apparently not," Chase said darkly. "Regardless of lots of conversations about it being a joint venture and a partnership, when it came down to it, we didn't have anything in writing."

"Rookie mistake." Sam pointed at him with her fork.

With a bit of anger and no small amount of sarcasm, Chase said, "Thanks. Very helpful."

"Business agreements should always be in writing." Sam wagged that same fork. "Except for criminal conspiracies. Those should never be in writing. Learned that from Stringer Bell, but obviously. So what now?"

"The new owners are dropping the project, so I have to pack my bags and head home. And find a new job, I guess." He had never felt more dejected. The call earlier in the day had taken him to some dark places and brought back the dozens of conversations with his parents and the school counselor containing unsolicited advice about the precarious nature of the journalism industry and why he should major in something else at college. A decade later, he had nothing to show for the relentless hours he'd put in. Not even a job.

"So you want to hire me to go take care of your boss, then?"

Sam's words yanked him out of his despairing thoughts. "What? No? I didn—"

"It's fine. Plenty of people have done it. It's not a big deal. Most bosses kinda have it coming to them anyway. Hell, I killed my boss for free."

Chase held up both hands. "Please don't. I can't tell if you're joking."

Sam leaned forward and pushed Chase's hands down onto the table, patting them. She smiled gently. "You don't have a job now, so you think you probably can't afford it. Don't worry. I'll give you the friends and family discount."

"Please. Stop." Chase's face had morphed from depressed to appalled. "I can't tell if you're kidding, but it's not funny."

"Eh, it's kind of funny."

Chase's heartbeat resumed its normal rhythm once he was sure that Sam (probably) wasn't going to go up to Philadelphia to assassinate his boss (unless he paid her to). *I wonder what that even costs.* But he dared not ask, not wanting to stoke that fire again.

"So, what are you gonna do?" Sam asked.

"I guess I'm going to book a flight back home and look for a new job."

They ate in silence for a while. Chase's attention roved between the bustling restaurant and the Braves-Mets game on the television. Since both were the Phillies' division rivals, he'd sooner have to root for the heat death of the universe than either of those teams.

When Sam finished her plate of food, she pushed it to the side, leaning forward with unexpected intensity. "Hey, are you gonna leave out of here without ever uncovering what happened to Val, and no one's ever going to give her momma and daddy the comfort of knowing what happened to their baby girl?"

"I'm sure the police wi—"

"Oh, please." Sam glared at him. "You don't believe that. If the law were going to figure it out, they would've done it by now. They've probably been given several thousand reasons not to solve this one."

"I … uhh … Sam, I don't have any money. And as of a few hours ago, I don't have a job anymore. I don't have any options."

"Suppose you did?"

"Suppose I did what?"

"Had money," Sam said. "Would you carry on your investigation so you can turn it into a podcast?"

Chase wrinkled his brow, resenting the hypothetical. "Like, if I were independently wealthy and had money to burn? Or if I were a nepo baby? It's more likely I'd go live a meaningless life of luxury in Barbados or wherever, while people called me a colonizer behind my back, but sure, if I had money, I'd definitely have options."

"No, dummy." Sam rolled her eyes at him. "I'm looking to diversify my portfolio into more legitimate opportunities. Isn't that how you fancy people talk?"

Chase smiled briefly. "Yeah, I think you'd be right at home in Silicon Valley or Wall Street. But I thought you had … some other things going on."

"Nope. All wrapped up with a bow," Sam said cheerily.

"Just like that?"

"Well, it was a little more complicated, but the end result is the same."

"To be clear, several days ago, you were talking about avenging you brother, but now it's all taken care of?"

"Listen," Sam said. "I've done what I needed to do. There are a fair number of dead folks involved in that, including the person ultimately responsible for it. Most of those people were killed in self-defense. Nope. Is that right? Hang on. I gotta do some quick math." Sam looked up at the ceiling. "Yeah, fifty-five percent were self-defense, the rest were … preventative maintenance. Would you like more information? You always get a little squeamish about the details."

Chase decided quickly that as insatiable as his curiosity was, it was probably for the best that he not acquaint himself with certain details of Sam's life. It was exceedingly difficult to say no, because he had the distinct impression that she would tell him if he asked. With an irreconcilable combination of curiosity, revulsion, and regret, he said simply, "I'm good."

Sam smirked. She'd clearly expected he would decline. "Glad that's settled. Now, back to where I was going. You need a job. I have money. Let's make a deal."

She paused, giving Chase an opportunity to chime in. He sputtered, despite his experience with interview subjects dropping bombshells.

"How about I keep going? We'll form our own company. Fifty-fifty partners — in writing this time. I'll fund it obviously, because you're broke ass and busted. You do all the work. Make your podcast and put it out there. What d'you say?"

"I say—I don't know what I say. You just now threw it out there. How can you be so nonchalant about it?"

"I'm not being nonchalant," Sam said defensively. "I couldn't be more serious. Look, I'm not a super touchy-feely kind of person, but here's what I know about me. I have a pretty limited life expectancy. I might live to be an old lady, but if I stay in my current line of work, the odds aren't great. And I kind of like being not dead, so I'm working on changing that. And, I don't spend time with people I don't like and trust. I'm here with you. That means I like you and I trust you."

Chase squirmed with discomfort at the frankness of their conversation. He was accustomed to Sam being the one avoiding any form of intimacy or introspection.

"Because of that," Sam continued, "I'm willing to go into business with you. If you want to. Not that you have many options."

"Harsh," Chase said, "but fair. Okay. I'm definitely interested, but I think we have a conflict of interest."

"Jeb?"

He nodded.

Sam considered for several minutes. "We can ask our lawyer what he thinks. But I'm going to stay out of your end of it. You go wherever the story takes you, and come hell or high water, I won't stop you from publishing it. Fair?"

Chase smiled. "We have a lawyer?"

"Of course we have a lawyer. I guess *you* don't yet. But you will have. Then *we* will have a lawyer. I'll text him, and we can set up a meeting for Monday. Sound good?"

"Sure."

Taking stock of what was left of their dinner, Sam said, "You want some banana pudding?"

"Ugh," Chase moaned and put his hands on his belly. "They'll have to roll me out of here as it is."

"You don't have a separate dessert compartment?"

"Unfortunately, I do not."

"Fine. I'll get it to go, and you can eat it in your hotel room later after you punish yourself for over-eating by working out for two hours, or whatever it is you do to keep yourself looking like that. Oh, I have an idea for your next podcast subject too, by the way."

"What happened to staying in your own lane?"

Sam shrugged. "You do what you want with it. You remember that coal company who lost almost all their bigwigs in a plane crash last year?"

"Sort of?"

Sam said, "They're from Alabama. In fact, they have a bunch of coal mines in Walker County. But the rumors are some weird stuff happened out on that island. That's all." She flagged down the waitress who, a few minutes later, brought the carryout containers and set the check beside Chase. Sam snatched it up, and said, "Don't be presumption. I'm his sugar mama."

Chase buried his face in his hands. "Oh my gosh. I already regret everything."

CHAPTER 41
FIFTY-FIFTY SPLITS

SAM

Nick Davis' hand hovered over the form he'd printed out. "What's the name of this company?"

Sam looked at Chase expectantly, but his expression was mostly blank with sudden realization. She shook her head. "You didn't think about what you want to call your podcast company?"

"I knew I needed to think of it. I wrote a bunch of things down in a journal a long time ago when I used to daydream about starting my own company. But I don't have that with me, and — I don't know," he looked sheepish. "It didn't occur to me."

"I have a suggestion." Sam was ready for the moment. While she was nervous about it, due in no small part to being unaccustomed to working with a partner, she tucked the discomfort behind a facade of confidence.

"Yes?"

Nick waggled his pen impatiently.

Sam said, "Banshee Media."

Chase considered it for a minute. "Is it a little too … foreboding? I mean, aren't banshees harbingers of death?"

Sam didn't flinch at the criticism. She was prepared. "I'd say that for a podcast about a missing woman who's likely dead, with presumably more true crime podcast series to follow, it probably fits the bill."

Chase smiled. "You're the boss."

Sam said, "I'm not the boss. We are the bosses together. We have to decide this together."

"I'm good with the name. I like it."

Nick chimed in. "This is why I recommend against fifty-fifty splits, by the way. Someone ought to have the final say."

"I'm not changing my mind about this," Sam said. "What's your recommendation for breaking a tie?"

"Do it the old-fashioned way." Nick reached into his pocket, pulled out a coin, flipped it into the air, and let it land on his desk. "Tails wins."

"That's the best you got?" Sam said skeptically.

Nick answered. "It's fair and easily accessible. Almost fail-proof."

"Works for me," Chase said.

Sam nodded.

"Y'all are going with Banshee Media, LLC, then?" Nick asked.

Chase said, "Yes."

"I'll write it in, and we'll go ahead and fill everything out, but before submitting it to the state, I'll check to make sure there are no registered trademarks that will be a problem for you."

"Chase has way bigger problems to worry about that, anyway," Sam said.

He turned toward her in his chair. "What does that mean?"

She continued speaking to the lawyer. "Somebody left him a death threat at his hotel. I offered to let him stay with me, but he declined."

"Well," Nick said, "in light of your house getting burned to ashes and Teresa's being made into Helter Skelter, I'd say he probably made the right call."

Sam smiled because she was supposed to, but both events still weighed heavily on her with the family that was lost and those that could have been.

Chase said to Sam, "I thought we weren't going to tell anybody about that letter?"

"He's the lawyer, and now that he's *your* lawyer, we tell him." She pointed at Nick. "Give him the spiel."

In an exhaustively practiced monotone, Nick said, "I'm your lawyer. I'm the person, ideally the only person, you tell everything to — the good, the bad, and the ugly. Why? Because I can never tell anyone the things we talk about. Ever. With one exception. This is important, so please make sure you're listening." Nick paused and looked at Chase intently.

"I'm listening," he confirmed.

"You can *never* tell me that you're going to kill someone. Threats are bad, because they put me in an awkward ethical situation. But you can *always* tell me that you have killed someone. Got it?"

Sam laughed at the look on Chase's face.

He said, "I'm not going to kill anyone."

"Perfect," Nick nodded. "Now, if that changes, remember that you can only tell me after the fact. But beyond that, everything you say here goes to the grave with me. That's why I get to live a long and comfortable life, because all my clients understand this is a safe space."

"Have you ever had a client threaten you before?"

"Of course," Nick said. "I wouldn't say it's a regular occurrence, but it's not uncommon either."

"What do you do?"

"I'm going to give you the most lawyer answer — it depends. Most of them are hot under the collar about something. The prospect of jail time stresses people out, and by the time most folks get to my office, jail time is a certainty. My job is to mitigate the amount of time they have to serve. And most of those have already committed the unforgivable sin — tell him what it is, Sam."

"Never talk to the cops. Ever. No matter what."

Chase said, "But I thought the cops were—"

"Were your friends? Are there to help? Would understand if you explained?" Nick waved his hand at the nonsense he'd heard a thousand times.

"But you talk to the cops," Chase accused Sam.

Sam put a hand to her chest. "I have a different arrangement with them than the other schmucks who wind up here. Besides, I've never been arrested."

Nick spoke directly to Chase. "I have told her that one day, she will get burned by them. Someone will pay them more, or they will tire of her sass, which I'm sure you'll agree, can be exceedingly tiresome."

"I am a delight," Sam protested. "But let's get back to business. I've got better things to do than sit around playing grab-ass all day with you two. After I leave, y'all go see Stan about setting up the new bank accounts, however that needs to be done, and getting them funded. Chase, you'll need to figure out your operating expenses and how much to pay yourself." Directing her attention back to Nick, she said, "Move around whatever money you need from my personal accounts to fund it. You need anything else?"

Nick held up the form they'd started the meeting with. "Who's the owner on your end — you or the holding company?"

"Me, until we figure out how to buy out Jeb from the holding company. I don't want him thinking he can worm his way into anything else I'm doing.

"Last thing. Chase, tell Nick and Stan what your salary is. Make sure it's enough to get you out of that awful motel you've been staying at." Sam stood up and strode toward the door, leaving the men where they were sitting.

"But I don't know how long I'll be here."

"Short-term rentals — they're a thing. Look it up."

Chase asked her back, "Who's Stan?"

She kept walking, feeling no compulsion to answer the question that someone else could handle.

CHAPTER 42
UNKNOWN CALLER

SAM

As Teresa scraped the remains of her lunch into the sink, a wet nose booped her on the leg. "No, you can't have people food. You're fat enough as it is."

"Do not make that poor girl feel bad about her body. Come here, Waffles. Don't listen to your auntie talk to you that way. You're not fat. You're like eighty percent hair." The dog hurried to Sam, her tail wagging wildly. Sam said softly, "You are a little fat, but it's okay."

Teresa rolled her eyes, then asked, "Isn't she supposed to still be wearing that thing around her head that keeps her from biting?"

"The cone of shame?!" Sam feigned shock. "First, you destroy her self-esteem, now this? Close your poor, dumb ears, Waffles. You don't have to tolerate this kind of abuse." Sam scrutched under the dog's ears and received in response a guttural and deeply contended sound. "But actually you kind of do, because no one else will take in a couple of strays like us."

"Speaking of you being homeless, what are you gonna do about the house?"

"Dunno yet. I don't really have to decide until they finish

clearing the lot. But I was thinking about putting one of those tiny houses on it."

"Hmm," Teresa responded.

"You have thoughts about that, do you?"

"I didn't say anything."

"Don't gaslight me. *Hmm* means I disagree with you, but I'm too passive aggressive to say anything, unless you ask me my opinion, and then you will have brought it upon yourself. Sound about right?"

"No, it does not." Teresa managed to make herself sound indignant. "*Hmm* means I am making a sound so you'll know I heard you."

"If you say so. Let's try this a different way. Dearest Aunt Teresa, do you have an opinion about whether I should put a tiny house, or maybe even a trailer, on the property that I own?"

"Since you asked," Teresa said, "I thought it would be nice if you rebuilt the house pretty much like it was and didn't turn the place into a trailer park."

"Well," Sam had a gleam in her eye, "I hadn't even thought of converting the land into an RV park, but with the river running through it, people would love it."

"Don't you dare."

Sam's phone rang in her belt pack that was lying on the dining room table. She excused herself from the conversation and went to answer it. When she saw the screen displayed "Unknown Caller," she nearly clicked off the ringer, but on a whim, answered it. "Yes?"

"This is the broker."

"Why are you calling me directly? That's not how this works. And how did you get my number?" Anger flooded her system. Sam walked through the kitchen and back to her bedroom. The protocols were in place for a reason, to protect everyone involved. She considered hanging up to make him go through the proper channels. This would set a dangerous precedent.

There was a long pause on the other end. Perhaps he was considering whether to tell her. She decided to encourage him. "I'm not going any further until you tell me who gave you my number."

Still, he took a minute to answer. "The client."

"Huh." More than likely, that meant the client was local and probably knew her. That wasn't necessarily a common occurrence, but it wasn't rare either. At a minimum, it was something to be mindful of.

"Are you sufficiently satisfied to hear more?"

"Yeah. What's the timeframe we're working with?"

"Soon, but not urgent."

"The target?"

"A reporter. Not really a reporter — a podcaster."

A wave of chills crawled over Sam's entire body. All she could manage was "Uh-huh."

"His name is Chase Williams. He's from Philad—"

"Stop." Sam had recovered herself somewhat, though her palms and armpits were pouring bucketfuls of sweat.

"What?" The broker on the other end sounded testy.

"He's off limits."

"What does that mean?"

Sam turned her snarkiness up a notch. "I think there's only one way to interpret that. But since you're being dense about it, it means that you need to drop it and tell your client you can't accommodate them."

"Look, lady, either you want the job or you don't. If not, I'll move on to the next number on my list."

The earlier chills melted under a surge of heat. "If anything happens to him, you're the next number on *my* list. Got it?"

"I'll take that as a no," he said flippantly, and the line went dead.

She pulled the phone away from her ear and stared at it in disbelief.

"Problem?" Teresa asked, leaning against the door frame with her arms crossed.

"Problem," Sam said. "Somebody's taken out a contract on Chase."

"Your new boyfriend who's been sticking his nose into everybody's business? Imagine that. So you decided threatening the broker was a good idea?"

Sam shrugged. "It just kinda happened. I gotta call Chase."

"You could always tell him to find his way back to wherever it is he's from." Teresa pushed away from the door frame with her shoulder and moseyed down the hallway toward the kitchen.

Sam punched at the phone. Her hands shook, an uncommon experience for her. When it started ringing on the other end, she put it back to her ear. It rang half a dozen times, Sam becoming increasingly anxious with each one. Chase's voice broke through, but only to give her instructions about leaving a message. She made an effort to keep her voice level. No need to freak him out. "Chase, call me. Immediately. And be careful. I'm serious."

After hanging up, she sent a text message, too. "*CALL ME*".

Sam paced a circuit through the kitchen and dining room until Teresa shooed her out. "You're acting nervous as a whore in church."

Sam stopped and turned to her. "You can't say that anymore."

"Look who's woke all of a sudden," Teresa said, not hiding contempt in her voice. "Killing folks is fine, but slut-shaming is off limits — is that about the sum of it?"

Sam rolled her eyes and pulled her pack of cigarettes out of the front pocket of her plaid button-down. She smacked the pack against her palm a couple of times before pulling a cigarette out and setting it between her lips.

"If you think you're gonna smoke that in this house, you have lost your mind."

Sam turned on her heel without a word and strode toward the front door.

From behind her, Teresa hollered, "Or can I not say that either because it's offensive to crazy people?"

"Boomers," Sam muttered. The moment the front door closed behind her, Sam lit up. After a couple of drags, the edge fell off her jitters, though the bulk remained. At least she could think clearly enough now. She popped her head back in the door. "Going for a drive. Can you feed Waffles in a bit?" She didn't wait for the answer.

Sam hopped out of the truck as she ripped the key out of the ignition. In the motel lobby, the clerk couldn't be bothered to get off TikTok to attend to Sam, who pulled the phone out of the girl's hand and set it face down on the counter.

"Excuse you!"

"I need to see one of the folks who's staying here — Chase Williams — but I don't know what room he's in."

"I can't tell you that." The clerk appeared to relish the opportunity to be unhelpful to the person who'd invaded her personal bubble. "If he wanted you to know, you'd know."

Sam reined in the temper that was trying to get the best of her. "Do you at least know who I'm talking about?"

"I seen him. I'd let him take me to the break room and teach me a few things if he wanted to."

Yeah, I'm sure your particular brand of meth-mouth is exactly what he's into. "Look, I need to see him. Something's happened that I need to tell him about."

The clerk's shrug meant, *Not my problem.*

Sam knew how to handle this. She unzipped the belt bag at her waist, only momentarily considering allowing her thumb to rest on the .380 it held. Instead, she pulled out four one-hundred-dollar bills and laid them on the counter, keeping her hand over the top of them.

The clerk showed interest for the first time. "I may be able to help."

"That's what I figured."

"He lit out with some big guy — real big — a little bit ago. That's all I got."

"Nothing else you can tell me, even if I sweeten the pot here?"

She shook her head.

"How about letting me in his room?"

"Can't," the clerk said dejectedly. "I'll get fired. I gotta have this job."

Sam palmed the bills and walked away.

"Hey!" the clerk yelled behind her and followed it up with some trite insults.

CHAPTER 43
UNCOMFORTABLY EXPOSED

CHASE

CHASE FELT LIKE THEY HAD BEEN DRIVING FOR HALF an eternity. He'd noticed years ago that when uncertain of his destination, drives always seemed to take far longer than the amount of time they actually occupied. By contrast, return trips seemed to go far quicker. It's one of the things that led him to believe in the principle of the relativity of time. *Not that physicists thought personal experience had anything to do with the flow of time, but still. Why should gravity have a higher claim to causing time to be relative than our own subjective experience?*

He looked down at his phone. It had been a long time since the upper right corner had shown anything other than no service. It also showed that it was still recording. A whole lot of nothing so far, and the quality wouldn't be great even if it picked up anything usable, but it's all he could manage for now. He set it face down on the bench seat between himself and the driver.

Shooter peeked over at him and must have read his mind. "Never has been any cell service out here in the sticks. We're on the edge of the Bankhead National Forest. It's about a couple hundred thousand acres, and most of it is a dead space for cell phones. Not enough people for the cell companies to make money. And besides that, the mining companies weren't real big on that kind of infrastructure either.

"I remember when Daddy used to leave out to go deer hunting, Momma would say, 'What am I supposed to do if something happens while you're out, and I can't reach you?' He'd say, 'Same thing as you did before we had these infernal things in the first place.' Then he'd walk out into the dark. I bet I heard some form of that same conversation a couple dozen times."

Having no way to communicate with anyone other than Shooter left Chase feeling uncomfortably exposed. He probably should have realized sooner that going off into the boonies with someone he hardly knew (however nice he appeared to be), especially while he had a death threat looming, wasn't super smart.

"You spend a lot of time in your own head, don't you?" Shooter said.

"Yes? I suppose." Chase was caught off guard by the question and was unimpressed by his answer. "Doesn't everybody?"

"I don't expect so. Tell me this — are you one of those people who always has a conversation going in your head? Like your brain is chattering away all day long?"

Chase hadn't ever thought of it in those terms, but more significantly, he hadn't considered that everyone else may not have that experience. "Yes. You?"

Shooter pointed to his temple. "Quiet. Not always, like not now when we're conversating. But say I was making this drive by myself. It'd be pretty peaceful."

Chase let that percolate for a minute before he said, "Whoa. That sounds spectacular."

The big man grinned. "It ain't bad."

Chase was watching the heat shimmer off the asphalt, creating small roving oases when Shooter slowed the truck and flicked on the turn signal, even though they hadn't seen another vehicle in at least five miles. The tall grasses growing up between the tire ruts suggested this path wasn't frequently traveled.

His belly clenched a bit more. Not only did he have no way to reach anyone, but also, almost no one ever made their way out to where Shooter was taking him.

"May be hard to believe, but you take a shovel and clear off about a half inch of dirt and detritus, and you'll find the remains of an old road under us. No telling how many thousands upon thousands of tons of coal got carried out of here. Sometimes, I wonder if it ain't why there's so many broken people in these parts."

"What do you mean?" This conversation kept taking peculiar turns.

"We ripped the heart out of the earth and sold it to the highest bidder. For a while, times was good. But then the coal ran out — or at least, the mining companies figured cheaper ways or places to get to it — and everything went to hell. More than half the people in these counties were broke with nothing but black lungs and a paltry pension to show for it. It's like how that old-timey musician fella sold his soul to the devil to teach him to play the guitar. It was all well and good until Lucifer came to collect."

"You believe that?"

As the truck bounced along, Shooter said, "Which part, the story about him selling his soul or the devil being real?"

"Either? Both?"

"I don't have any way of knowing about that guy selling his soul or not. But I suppose people have done it for less. And as for the devil, you can't see the things I've seen — and heard tell of even more — without hoping there's something out there driving people to such wickedness. I'd hate to think they came to it of their own accord."

As Shooter finished his sentence, he brought the vehicle to a stop. The path they were on didn't end so much as it changed.

In front of Chase and Shooter stood a concrete slab plastered to the face of a mountain. A barred mouth was set into the concrete. The mouth was wide enough that, if the set of bars were removed from the entry, a pickup truck could pass through it comfortably.

Getting out of the truck, Chase grabbed his phone and slipped it into the front pocket of his button-down. Shooter reached into the bed of his truck and pulled out a backpack. Chase was reminded again of the man's extraordinary stature and his own foolishness in being here. The backpack would have been normal-sized on Chase, but strapped to Shooter, it appeared to be a somewhat smaller version of itself, like it had shrunk in the dryer.

"What's in the bag?"

Shooter reached around and patted the bottom of the pack. "Headlamps, respirators — probably won't need those though — some water, and extra batteries. Always extra batteries. You lose your light down there ..." He gestured with his chin toward the darkness beyond the gate and shook his head without finishing the sentence. Chase filled in the gap with imaginings of fumbling around in the dark until you eventually gave up and many, many days later, you died. You ran out of water first, though. And the battery on your watch had long since given out. So hours and days meant nothing. The passage of time was marked only by your descent into madness.

"Don't think about it," Shooter suggested. "You'll freak yourself out."

No kidding.

Shooter walked to the padlocked gate without carrying bolt cutters or a key. Chase followed beside him, but trailing somewhat. When they reached the bars, he saw that the lock wasn't actually clasped. Chase did a double-take. "They don't lock it?!"

"No point in it. The people who really want in will break the lock. The folks who are curious but aren't truly committed to going in will be discouraged by the appearance of it being locked and will convince themselves that unfortunately, they can't get in. It's not a bad system." Shooter took the padlock and pocketed it. "We don't want to take a chance on some jackass coming along and locking it on us while we're in there."

Chase continued to discover new fears he hadn't even known existed. Sure, they might survive the mine, but someone could still lock them in. They wouldn't die in the darkness; instead, it would happen with their faces pressed to the bars, breathing fresh air.

Shooter pushed open the door. "Ready?"

CHAPTER 44
PITCHING THINGS DOWN HOLES

CHASE

CHASE ENTERED THE UNDERGROUND PRISON WHILE wondering what caused mines to collapse. Shooter strapped a headlamp to himself, adjusting the light to sit snugly on his forehead, and handed one to Chase.

"How far back does this go?" Chase asked.

"'Back' isn't the real question. Down is the question you should be asking. How far down does a coal mine go?" Shooter began walking as he asked a different question rather than answering Chase's.

Chase figured Aaron Sorkin had never envisioned this sort of walk-and-talk in any of his shows. His were all in much tidier spaces like the White House lawn or a cable news studio. "Alright, how far *down* does it go?"

Shooter allowed the question to linger for a while like a rank smell as they walked further into the enveloping darkness, soon having to turn on their headlamps. The beams of light showed that many hundreds of people appeared to have frequented the abandoned mineshaft. Graffiti abounded, from scribbled names to intricate art. Char marks from the remains of small fires littered the floor alongside empty cans and broken bottles. Apparently, the place was no small secret. Among all of it, modified rail tracks led into the gloom, though following them with his light, Chase saw that they led to an impermeable blackness.

That blackness eventually revealed itself to be a rectangular hole. But *hole* did the chasm an injustice. Chase steeled himself to approach close enough to peer over the edge and found that its depths were seemingly endless. He looked toward Shooter, careful not to blast him in the face with the LED light. Chase repeated his question. "So how far down does it go?"

"What's the tallest building you've ever seen?"

Chase thought for a minute, trying to figure out whether it was one of the buildings in Chicago or New York City, then remembered that the new World Trade Center was symbolically 1776 feet tall. "Probably One World Trade Center."

Shooter nodded. "About that deep."

Chase recalled standing near the base of the tower while craning his head and squinting at the sky. The building was impossibly tall, dwarfing everything around it. "No way," he said. The idea that you could dig that far into the earth mystified him. Going up was one thing, but going down was another. A shiver ran down his spine.

Shooter sauntered over to an unbroken bottle, picked it up, and came back. He held it out over the abyss and let go.

In his head, Chase counted, *One one-thousand, two one-thousand, … ten on—*

The tinkling sound of shattering glass reached up to them. "Whoa," Chase muttered. He didn't bother working out the math of how far something free-falls in ten seconds. He'd always been more a humanities guy than a math or science nerd. "There's no way I'm going down there."

Shooter moved to stand beside him. "Couldn't if you wanted to. No, that's not true. You could get down. It'd take you about the same amount of time as it took that bottle. Probably the same result, too."

Chase instinctively stepped back.

Shooter smiled at the effect. "When the company announced that it was closing the mine, the fellas working the mine took exception to being out of work with no notice. So when the last man was out, they cut all the cables to the elevator and let it drop to the bottom of the shaft. Wanna guess how long it took to get to the bottom?"

"About ten seconds?"

"Yup. And it was followed by all the office furniture and computers and filing cabinets that were on site. When the company brass saw the riot on their hands, they skedaddled real quick. Didn't want to find themselves in a pinch. Anyway, that was fifteen or twenty years ago, and it's all still down there. Maybe some archaeologist will come across this place in a couple hundred years, figure out a way to the bottom, and think they hit the mother lode."

"Pun intended?" Chase asked.

"Ha. Nope. Didn't even think of it."

"So this is it, then?"

"Yeah, pretty much," Shooter said. "Unless you wanna see the burned-out shell of the office building. After they got tired of pitching things down holes, they moved on to more fiery entertainment. Ain't much left, though. Just a pile of bricks, really."

Finally, Chase couldn't help but ask a question that had been gnawing at him from the outset. "Why did you bring me out here?"

The big man shrugged. "Thought you'd be interested to see it. Was I wrong?"

"No, not at all. It's ... it seems kind of random, is all."

"I figured it's not many folks gets a chance to visit one of these places, and what with the work you're doing, I thought it might be pertinent."

Now, we're getting somewhere. "How's that?"

"You're looking for a missing person, ain't you?" Shooter

nodded toward the elevator shaft. "There's more than a couple of missing persons at the bottom of a coal mine. And there's any number of old mines around here."

"Am I gonna be one of them?"

Shooter appeared to be surprised by the question. "Not unless you fall in." Understanding settled on him. "You thought I brought you out here to kill you, is that it?"

"It crossed my mind."

"But you came anyway? That doesn't seem very smart. No offense intended."

"It didn't cross my mind 'til we were already in the truck."

Shooter grunted.

"I got a death threat the other day. A letter," Chase offered.

"You think I sent it?"

"Not really."

"Based on what?"

Chase said, "I'm a pretty good judge of character. Usually."

Shooter cocked his head and stared down at Chase. "That something you're willing to stake your life on?"

"I suppose I already have."

Shooter nodded in agreement. "I guess your intuition served you fine this time. I ain't got no bad intentions for you. But it seems to me trusting your gut to that degree is a recipe for getting your ticket punched pretty early on."

Chase couldn't argue with that.

"If it makes you feel any better, I don't shoot anything that doesn't have antlers. Even that I don't much care for. They do make for some fine eating, though. But so's you don't have to take my word for it, let's get back toward the sunshine, so you can breathe a little easier." Shooter turned and started walking toward the gate contained within the small point of light that indicated Chase's freedom.

"You think something like that is what happened to Valerie Wilson?"

"Hard to say." He walked without adding more for a while, then said, "It's my understanding that the folks in that line of work all have their own preferences for making sure folks don't end up found when they're not supposed to. And in a place like this, there's about as many means of doing it as you have the imagination to conceive of."

Chase shuddered, a physical response to the stress that he felt bleeding off as they neared the mine's exit. Once Shooter got him back into town, he expected to spend several hours decompressing at The Warehouse.

CHAPTER 45
CHECKING YOUR REARVIEW

CHASE

As they made their way back toward civilization — *Not close enough to pick up any cell service*, Chase noted, as he tapped his screen again — Shooter asked, "What kind of music do you like?"

"I'll answer your question if you answer one of mine first."

"Alright," Shooter said without looking his way.

"Why do you keep checking your rearview mirror every few seconds?"

"You noticed that, huh?"

"Yup." Chase fidgeted with his seatbelt, noticing for the first time that Shooter had to use one of those seatbelt extenders on account of his girth. He'd read an article once about how frequently those failed during crashes. A younger Chase would have mentioned that to Shooter. Older Chase recognized it was better than no seatbelt at all.

"There's a truck back there. It's been back there a minute, maintaining exactly the same distance from us."

Chase said, "Maybe it happens to be going the same direction as us?"

"Maybe so," Shooter conceded. "But I'm fairly certain that same truck followed us most of the way out of town until it had a pretty good idea of where we were going, and now it's picking us up on the way back."

"How certain is 'fairly certain'?"

With his eyes on the mirror, Shooter dropped his sunny disposition and said quietly, "It's the same one."

"Why would he do that?" Chase tried to hide the quaver in his voice.

"Couldn't rightly say. Unless you'd like me to pull over so we can ask him?" Shooter looked at Chase with raised eyebrows.

"I'm good." Chase's phone vibrated and made several different noises in quick succession. It showed him a couple of voicemails and numerous increasingly offensive text messages from Sam. "Sam's been trying to reach me. She seems pissed."

"That's gonna have to wait," Shooter said, his voice tense.

Chase turned in his seat and looked behind them. The truck was no longer trailing at a safe distance, but bearing down on them. Its engine made a guttural throbbing noise as its driver pressed the accelerator. Chase noticed that the chrome bumper held a Confederate flag license plate with the words, "The South will rise again." *Classy.*

Chase felt Shooter going faster, though his old beast of a truck was made more for hauling heavy things than outrunning other vehicles.

When the approaching truck got within a few feet of Shooter's truck, it jumped wildly over into the lane for oncoming traffic and began pulling alongside them. With less windshield glare because of the angle, Chase got a good look at the other driver. "Hey! I know that guy." He didn't have time to tell Shooter it was a guy named Jeb that he met at the bar.

Jeb slammed the nose of his truck into the side of Shooter's bed, forcing the truck sideways. In the quickest fraction of a second, they were perpendicular to the road. Shooter's door crunched against the other truck. But only briefly.

Things shifted. Chase was looking up. Shooter was above him. They were rolling. Chase lost track of time and space.

When Chase came to, he was being dragged by the armpits away from the truck that was crumpled and upside-down and leaking from several places in the tall grass. His first thought was that Jeb must not want to kill him — he assumed it was Jeb who was now wearing a ski mask for some reason — or he could have left Chase in the truck and set it alight. Chase peered into the cab but didn't see Shooter.

Jeb dropped Chase, whose head bounced off the hard ground beside the shoulder of the road. Translucent shapes sprung to life in his vision, overlaying the world around him. "Shooter?" he asked. Jeb didn't respond. Chase pushed himself up, supporting himself with both arms splayed out and behind him as the scene became a tilt-a-whirl.

He closed one eye to see if it would help. It didn't, but neither did it make things worse. Not far from the truck, near the base of a tree, lay a great bulk that Chase discerned to be Shooter. Knowing he couldn't walk there, Chase rolled onto his hands and knees to crawl.

"Stay put," Jeb said.

Chase swung his head around toward Jeb's voice. He stood in the road, pointing a pistol down at Chase. *The death threat must not have been a scare tactic.* Chase tried to clear his head of the dizziness. The rise in the road that crested several yards behind Jeb looked like it was rolling. Nausea overwhelmed him, and he was sick on the ground. *Concussed.* He'd had a concussion before playing football when he went to tackle an all-state running back and took a knee to the helmet. Coach called it a dinger and stuck him back in a few plays later. He didn't remember being in the game after that, but the film showed he'd been there.

Jeb used his gun to gesture toward Shooter. "He's still breathing. I checked him before I got you."

Chase thought it odd that Jeb bothered to tell him how

Shooter was doing. If he was going to kill him, why did it matter that he know Shooter was okay? Or at least, not dead yet.

"9-1-1?" Chase asked.

Jeb shook his head. "That's not how this is gonna go. I got a job to do."

He could have done that job about a half-dozen different times by now. And much more cleanly than executing Chase on the side of the road. Sam must have been a bad influence because even with his brain lightly scrambled, Chase was thinking about all the ways Jeb could have done this more effectively than he was now. Probably best not to suggest them now, though. His mind turned to figuring out ways to delay.

"Why are you wearing a mask? It doesn't matter if I know who you are if you're going to kill me. Besides, I already saw you. We met at the bar the other day."

Jeb's attention had strayed toward Shooter, but this last statement brought Chase back into his focus, seeming to startle Jeb that he was known. "You aren't the only one here, are you? I didn't mean to hurt Shooter."

"What did you think was going to happen when you wrecked us?" Sensing the concern Jeb had for the other guy, Chase swapped from sarcasm to sincerity. "Go check on him if you're worried about him. Where am I gonna go?"

Jeb shook his head first. "Gotta take care of you first."

"Who hired you?"

"None of your business."

"To the contrary," Chase said, "I don't think there's anything that's ever been more my business — knowing who wants me dead so badly they're willing to hire it out." *Besides that, getting into other people's business* is *my business. Literally.* But he didn't think that would help his cause any.

Both Chase's and Jeb's attention were torn away from each other by the sound of an engine and a flash of cherry red and chrome flashing over the rise in the roadway.

CHAPTER 46
CHOOSING SURVIVAL

CHASE

As the cherry truck barreled over the hill, it kept all four tires on the asphalt, but barely. Rather than hitting the brakes hard, like you would expect of a driver who encountered someone standing in the road, Sam accelerated and veered to the left to hit the masked Jeb head on. He never had a chance to dodge the truck. Or maybe he did, but he froze.

Sam's crinkly blond hair blew out behind her from the wind blowing in through her open window. Chase was reminded of Cruella DeVil chasing after the dalmatians in the old Disney cartoon.

Sam's truck smashed into Jeb with a thud. The front tire bounced as it ran him over. Chase rolled away in time to avoid seeing the back tire strike him.

Tires skidded to a stop. A door opened and closed. Chase sprang to his feet, the adrenaline negating the worst of the dizziness for the time being.

As Sam ran toward Chase, pistol in hand, she yelled, "You okay?"

He nodded. Physically, he would be okay. But as he stared at the broken and obviously dead body of the man who had intended to kill him, he was uncertain whether he'd be entirely okay after this.

When Sam got to the body, she squatted down beside it. She grabbed the ski mask from the bottom and pulled it up over the man's face. She stumbled backward in an awkward crab walk. An involuntary "Oh" escaped her, and all the color drained from her face.

This was not a reaction Chase expected from the woman who he knew to have killed several people and suspected to have killed even more.

She rose to her feet, wobbled, and hurried to the side of the road, where she hunched over. She supported herself by propping her hands on her knees.

"What's wrong?" Chase asked.

Sam didn't answer, didn't even acknowledge him. Instead, she kept looking like she was going to puke.

"It's her brother," Shooter said, as he ambled up to Chase.

"Oh."

Shooter winced and reached for his right side.

"What's wrong?" he asked for the second time in as many minutes.

"Busted some ribs, I believe." His breaths were deliberate and slow.

Sam still hadn't moved.

"I think I came out the window," Shooter said. "Wouldn't have thought that was possible. Lucky I missed that tree, or my innards would be squashed."

Chase looked over to where Shooter had been lying. There was a fair bit of luck involved in either of them walking around right now.

"Better go check on her," Shooter suggested to Chase.

"What do I say?"

The larger man shrugged. "Dunno. There may be nothing to say."

With all the caution of a person approaching a mountain lion, Chase walked up to Sam. Having no words to offer, he laid a hand on her back. For a minute longer, she stayed bent over, but when she stood her eyes were dry. Chase had expected tears. *Maybe that comes later, or maybe not at all.* His own relationship to crying was all messed up. One of those sad Sarah McLachlan puppy commercials could bring tears to his eyes, but the deaths of his grandparents, nothing.

Sam said, "I didn't know it was Jeb."

"I know."

"I didn't see his truck. All I saw was a guy standing in the road holding a gun on you."

"It's not your fault."

Sam's head jerked as she looked at him more directly, even contemptuously. "Fault? Who's talking about fault?"

"I … uhh … I'm …" Chase stammered for a bit, thoroughly confused. "I guess I'm confused here. I'm saying it's not your fault that you killed your brother. You couldn't have known it was him."

"Yeah, I heard you the first time. And I'm saying, this isn't about fault. Fault's got nothing to do with it. I just would've liked to have known it was Jeb I was running over."

"Because you wouldn't have done it if you'd known?"

She tilted her head and squinted at Chase. "I'm not sure we're on the same page here. I made the choice I made. I wouldn't unmake it now, if I could. What I'm saying to you, and what you can't seem grasp, is when you kill the last person in your immediate family, generally a person wants to know ahead of time they're doing that. It's kind of heavy."

Chase gaped at her. "You would have chosen me over your own brother?"

Sam looked past him and yelled, "Shooter, did you do something to him? Why's he being so dense?"

Shooter raised both hands palms up.

She returned her gaze to him. "You're reading things into what I said. I killed the person who was holding a gun on you because they were about to execute you and then turn you into a missing person. If I had known that person was Jeb, it wouldn't have changed what I did. But it might have changed how I did it. He should've known that he died because he went against the family. Went against me. There's a hierarchy, and he stepped out. He knew that. And if he's willing to undermine me, to disrespect me like that, then he'd be willing to stick a knife in me. If he had the guts to try. So no, I'm not choosing you over him. I'm choosing survival. But also, I would have chosen your life over his, regardless."

Chase nodded, though he was sure he didn't fully understand.

Shooter put a hand on his shoulder. "That's beautiful, Sam. Almost philosophical in a way."

'A man's gotta have a code.' The infamous line from an iconic character in *The Wire* sprang to Chase's mind. *This contract killer from rural Alabama may have more in common with a shotgun-toting Baltimore gangster than anyone would have guessed.*

Sam asked, "What do you think we ought to do about my brother?"

The question was undoubtedly directed toward Shooter, who looked around the scene, taking everything in. "Let's not over-think this. He was in a wreck, right? Sometimes vehicles catch on fire when they wreck." He shrugged at the end of his proposal.

"Okay," Sam said flatly. "Can you two get him into his truck?"

Dread coursed through every vein and capillary in Chase's body. The only dead people he'd seen until now had been in caskets. The idea of handling a dead body and perpetrating a crime — *more than one, probably* — made him shudder.

"You alright?" Sam asked, a smirk on her lips despite the grim circumstances.

"I don't think so."

"I got you," Shooter said, turning toward Jeb.

"Wait," Chase said. "Your ribs. You shouldn't be lifting anything heavy."

"It'll only hurt for a few minutes."

"Unless one of them punctures a lung."

Sam sighed. "Look, you can either tell him all the reasons he can't do it, or you can help him. One of those goes a lot further than the other."

By the time Chase caught up to him, Shooter already had his hands under Jeb's armpits and had pulled him upright. "Grab his legs." With a fair amount of huffing, they shuffled over to Jeb's truck. "We gotta set him in the driver's seat." Fortunately, Jeb had been in enough of a hurry that he left his door hanging open. On Shooter's insistence, Chase handed Jeb off to him so that he was cradling the dead man as he shifted him into the truck.

Chase walked back to Sam, readying himself to ask a question that was bothering him. She was leaning against the side of her truck, looking somewhat forlorn. "You're not here by happenstance, are you?"

She looked him in the eye. "Nope." All sense of lostness that was there a moment ago had dissipated. Defiance replaced it. She knew what his follow-up question would be, and she was going to make him ask it.

"How did you know I was here?"

"You remember that day you told me about getting the death threat? You left your phone on the table when you went to the bathroom instead of taking it with you. So I helped myself to it and shared your Find Me thing with my phone in case I needed it." She shrugged. "Today, I needed it because you didn't answer my calls or texts."

"Sam, you can't do that. You totally violated my privacy." His ears were hot and red. He swooned with dizziness again.

"If you're expecting me to apologize, you're barking up the wrong tree. You'd be worm fodder by now if I hadn't done it."

She wasn't wrong, but that didn't make it right.

Shooter sauntered up, pretending to be blissfully unaware of their argument. "You two need to hit the road before somebody comes along."

"You're not coming?" Chase asked.

"Can't. The man got in a wreck with something." He pointed at his truck, which was turned over on its side. "And that puppy there ain't going anywhere." He addressed Sam next. "I'll call the police and handle the rest of it after you go."

"Alright. I guess that'll give this one," nodding her head at Chase, "plenty of time to scold me for saving his ass while I wait on the sheriff to call and deliver the news."

CHAPTER 47

COMPLYING WITH PROTOCOLS

SAM

WHEN SAM STRODE INTO THE OFFICE, NICK DAVIS looked down at this watch. "Fancy seeing you here unannounced and without an appointment, like I've got nothing better to do."

Sam sighed. He was only pestering her. He wouldn't turn her away. She grabbed a stack of hundred-dollar bills out of her belt pack and tossed it onto the desk. "Here. Top off my retainer."

"Hear me out, here. If you want," Nick said, "we could set a standing appointment every week."

"I'm good. I like our current arrangement."

Nick sighed. "Glad it works for one of us. Sit down. Tell me what's on your mind."

Sam plopped into a chair. "Did you hear about Jeb?"

"No. Should I have? Did he get arrested again?" Nick checked his phone. "I told the jail to call me when they book one of my folks."

"Not arrested," Sam said. "Dead. Got killed in a car accident yesterday."

Nick raised an eyebrow at her. "Did he?"

"Did he what?"

"Die in an *accident*?"

"Yes, it was a car wreck, like I said."

"Those aren't the same thing. But the only reason I ask is that you don't seem all that broken up over it." It was a sentence, but he made it sound like a question.

"I'll work on that."

Nick tapped his desk several times while he weighed whether he wanted to pursue the topic any further. With his next statement, Sam knew that he'd moved on. "You just kind of sprang this on me. It'll take me a bit to review the paperwork and see where this leaves ownership of everything and all that."

"That's not why I'm here."

"Ah." Nick leaned back in his chair as he said, "How about I quit being presumptuous and let you tell me, then?"

For one of the few times in her adult life, she followed the social cues and gave him a polite smile. Nick furrowed his brows in momentary confusion. He let that moment pass, too. Sam's smile evolved into a smirk. She'd been irreverent so long that people were now confused when she complied with protocols.

"I need a favor."

Nick cleared his throat. "Is this the kind of favor that's going to make me exceedingly uncomfortable?"

"Not if you don't ask too many questions, it won't."

"Let's hear it."

Sam unzipped her belt pack and pulled out a piece of paper with a phone number written on it. She sat forward and laid it on the desk with a pat. Nick swiveled in his chair so that he could reach it without too much effort. He held it out at nearly arm's length, at what must have been the sweet spot with his glasses. "What do you want me to do with this?"

"I need the name and address that it belongs to."

"You don't think it's a burner?"

Sam shook her head. "I think this guy is less meticulous than he ought to be."

"I assume you've googled it?"

"You mean, have I used my phone or laptop to do a search on something that could be traceable back to me even if I used the 'private' setting? No, actually, I have not done that. I try not to be stupid in that way."

Nick adjusted his position in his seat. "Fine. Fair. I deserved that, I guess."

"Well?"

"Yes, I have a guy who can do that."

"I expect it might be difficult to track down," Sam said with some concern.

"You can also expect then that he will charge you accordingly." He looked at his watch. "Tomorrow okay?"

"I would prefer it today."

"Today it is, then. Anything else?"

"You wanna go make funeral arrangements with Teresa?"

"I'd rather not," he said.

"That makes two of us," Sam sighed, pushing herself out of the chair. "I may go across the square first to get good and lubricated, then make Jake drive me home."

"Sounds edifying."

She showed him the bird and then showed herself out of the office.

Sam set the cigarette between her lips and reached for her lighter. She didn't normally smoke inside, but this wasn't her apartment, and it wasn't somewhere she was likely to return to. The metal made a satisfying scratching sound as it scrubbed against the flint, creating a spark and a small flame. There were other kinds of lighters, but she enjoyed the tiny ritual of this one. Humans had been making fire the same way for as far back as time could find them. She didn't feel any need to abandon it now, though her surgical gloves made spinning the wheel a clunkier operation.

With the nearly inaudible crackle of paper and tobacco, she breathed in. The grating sensation that had been gnawing at the edges of her nerve endings dulled somewhat. As much as she thought of herself as an independent woman, she'd never been able to kick her dependency on this. Maybe she would give it up. She loved smoking but hated being a smoker. But she had nothing to really to replace it with. It's not like she would ever take up vaping. *Gross.*

A key scraped the lock. The deadbolt turned. Connor Randolph walked through the door with an armful of groceries, which he promptly dropped as he let out a little shriek upon spotting Sam. She held a cigarette in one hand and a pistol in the other. The gun looked much larger than it actually was because of the suppressor she'd attached. She didn't like to use a suppressor. It affected the gun's accuracy and natural balance, but being in an apartment meant loud noises wouldn't likely go unnoticed.

Randolph gaped at her with the door wide open behind him and food scattered around his feet.

"Shut the door, Connor."

He complied silently and robotically, then turned to face her. She took a drag and blew the smoke out slowly, tilting her head to take him in. Fear and discomfort rolled off him like breakers in a storm.

"I'm allergic to cigarette smoke," he said.

She recognized the voice from the couple of phone calls they'd had together. "How allergic?"

"I get hives." It came out as a whine.

Sam loathed whiny men. Of all the unbecoming traits a guy could exhibit, that topped the list. "I can live with that."

Randolph tried an alternative approach. He puffed out his

chest and pushed his shoulders back. He made his voice sound more baritone when he said, "Do you know who I am?"

Sam stood up. "Course I know who are. For one thing, I already used your name. For another, I'm not here by accident. I'm here so we can reach an understanding, because apparently, I failed to make myself clear before."

"Before?"

So he doesn't recognize me. Good. "Yes, before. You don't remember our last conversation?"

He shook his head.

"Pick up your groceries, and put the cold ones away. I don't want them to spoil on account of me."

"Thank you," he said. "Food prices are so high these days. I heard the other day they're up forty per—"

"Connor," she interrupted, "I'm not here to chatter with you like we're a couple of old hens. Put the stuff away."

"You're not going to kill me? Because the food doesn't really matter, if you're going to kill me."

"As yet undecided." She wagged the pistol in the direction of the kitchen.

Randolph cobbled together the items that had spilled out of their bags and toted everything to the small island.

"Hold it," Sam said.

Randolph froze, like a child playing freeze-tag. She had really made an impression on him. Sam tossed her cigarette butt into the sink and shooed him away from the island. She opened and closed the drawers. "Gotta make sure you're not gonna whip out a gun and draw down on me." Then she checked the refrigerator and freezer. It would be foolish to store a gun in either, but that doesn't mean someone wouldn't do it.

Sam turned around to find that she must have been searching in all the wrong places. Randolph held a gun on her. His hand wasn't visibly trembling, but he appeared uncomfortable with the turn of events that he'd initiated.

CHAPTER 48
UNBECOMING TRAITS

SAM

Sam sighed. "I wish you hadn't done that. Like, really wish."

A cloud of confusion passed over his face. "Why?"

"I was planning for us to have a pleasant chat, and then I would leave, and you would still be alive."

He complained, "How was I supposed to know that?"

"You're still alive, aren't you? I didn't turn out your lights the moment you crossed that threshold. But that might be my fault. I didn't make my intentions clear, and you're probably not used to being on this end of things. You're the guy handle the phone calls."

"Wha—how do you know what I do?"

"I'll answer that, but first, let me do something. Do you mind?"

"I guess not?"

"Thank you," Sam said, then called out, "Rodrigo."

"Si."

Randolph's head whipped hard to the right toward the hallway he'd had his back to. He saw a menacing Hispanic man who had a shotgun leveled at his chest.

Sam used the opportunity to relieve the broker of his handgun. He didn't resist. "Rodrigo, don't kill him."

"You sure, jefe?"

"I'm sure. Connor and I have some things to discuss. And afterward, we can all go our separate ways and live happily ever after." She turned her attention to Randolph. "Can you get on board with that?"

He nodded.

"Good. Let's go sit and make ourselves comfy. You first."

Randolph trudged to the sofa and plopped down on a worn cushion, what must have been his usual place. The other two cushions looked almost new. He rarely had company, she guessed. She sat in a recliner perpendicular to him, laying a pistol on each armrest. Rodrigo dragged over a chair from the kitchen table, sitting down and setting his shotgun across his lap, but keeping his right hand near the trigger guard. The broker may or may not have known it, but he couldn't so much as cough unexpectedly without Rodrigo turning him into a tangle of guts and lead.

"Do you know who I am?" Sam asked with genuine curiosity.

"No. Should I?"

"Give me your phone."

He hesitated.

"Not your everyday phone. The one you use for business calls."

Randolph reached into his pocket slowly. "It's the same one."

Sam swore under her breath. "You're a menace. You know that? A hazard to everybody you do business with. How are you still alive?"

He leaned forward to hand it over with the demeanor of a puppy that had been swatted for tearing up its owner's shirt.

"Unlock it first," Sam instructed.

Randolph tapped the screen several times before handing the phone over. Sam clicked the green phone icon with a blue glove-covered finger and scrolled down to the calls from two days earlier. Aside from seeing MOM several times, most of the other entries had descriptions instead of names. When she came to HITMAN, HILLBILLY, GIRL, WALKER CO., ALA. (HOT?), she pushed the information icon, and saw her number come up. She gave the phone back to Randolph. "How about now?"

"Oh," he said. "I did think you sounded familiar."

"Is it my hillbilly twang, Connor?"

"I didn't mean anything by it."

"Of course not," she said. "So am I hot, Connor, or do I disappoint in that department?"

He blushed but didn't respond.

"It's okay. You can answer." Sam pinched her forearm. "I got thick skin."

"Not really, no," he said. "But you're not ugly."

"High praise, Connor. But at least you're honest. It's useful not being particularly pretty. People don't pay as much mind to you."

"Maybe if you used some makeup?"

"I'm not looking for tips."

"Sorry. I'm nervous," he said.

Sam sat forward, resting her elbows on her knees. It was a risk, positioning herself where she couldn't as quickly grab one of the guns if she needed to. But she trusted Rodrigo. He looked calm as a copperhead, but he could strike just as quick. "I'm not gonna lie. I'd be nervous in your shoes, too. Do you remember our last conversation?"

"I do."

"You remember I told you the reporter was off limits and I was very clear about it?"

Actual tears filled the corners of his eyes. *He remembers.* "The client, she was very insistent. I tried to tell her."

"So you called somebody else, didn't you?"

"Yes."

"That person's dead now. Do you know that?"

"No."

"I killed 'em."

Randolph shook visibly and stared at the floor. He may have been in the business of arranging deaths, but he wasn't accustomed to being confronted with it.

"Connor." He looked up. "That other person you called was my brother. And now he's dead on account of it. I'm not bragging about killing him. I'm telling you so you can appreciate the importance of answering this next question."

The tears spilled over. He understood the gravity of his situation.

"Who is your client?"

"I don't know. I'm sorry." He clasped his hands in a pleading gesture and whispered, "I don't know."

She believed him that he didn't have a name. The client's name wasn't all that pertinent to the work, just the name of the mark and the transfer of funds. "Tell me what you do know."

"Okay. Okay." He was almost hyperventilating now. "She was a girl. Not like a kid. An adult but young, okay."

Sam skimmed through the recent calls list again, quickly finding what she was looking for. She rolled her eyes hard enough to strain something. CLIENT, SOUNDS SEXY, WALKER CO., ALA. She showed him the phone. "This her?"

"Yes," he said in a clipped voice.

Sam slid the broker's phone into her back pocket. She'd have to call Nick later and have his guy do some more techno magic, though she had a pretty good inclination of where this would lead. "Look at me," Sam said. "You sure that's all you know about her?"

"I'm sure. I'm sure. Please," he pleaded.

When Sam stood up, Rodrigo did the same. She tucked her

own pistol into the holster in the small of her back and kept his in her left hand. She stepped forward and crouched down in front of the broker. "Are your neighbors home at this time of day?"

"What time is it?" His voice was hardly more than a whisper.

"A little after lunchtime." She spoke as gently as though she were coaxing an animal to come out of hiding.

"Work. They're all at work."

Sam noticed Rodrigo had stealthily positioned himself so that she wasn't in the firing line between him and Randolph. This was the tricky part where things could go sideways, quick as a hiccup.

"Connor, I'm not gonna lie. This next bit is gonna be hard."

"Why?"

"I want you to scooch back and try to relax." She put her hand on his knee and pushed with some pressure. He slid backward and sank into the sofa. "Good. Now, we're going to do this as easy as we can. Close your eyes."

His eyes widened, and he tried to sit forward. "No, no, no no."

Sam planted her palm on his chest.

"You said, 'happily ever after.' That's what you said."

Sam stood up, looming over him. "You're a liability, Connor. You're like to get me caught or killed, and I can't have that."

He kicked out at her. Instead of backing away, Sam leaned forward, her knees against the edge of the sofa, somewhat straddling Randolph and pinning his legs. It was a precarious position, and she wouldn't have attempted it if she were alone. "Now, close your eyes." All the gentleness was gone from her voice.

As Randolph closed his eyes, tears slid down his cheeks.

"Give me your hand."

He lifted his right hand off the couch. She placed his gun in it and wrapped both of her gloved hands around his. He resisted somewhat as she turned the gun toward his chest.

He started to ask, "Can I ca—"

Sam used his finger to pull the trigger twice, then jumped back to let his arm and the gun fall in the most natural way. Randolph's eyes flew open.

Watching him die was the worst part. Always. But it was necessary. A few seconds later, she mouthed to Rodrigo, "Let's go." Her ears rang for a while afterward.

CHAPTER 49

NOT THAT KIND OF GIRL

SAM

SAM AND CHASE ROCKED ALONGSIDE EACH OTHER IN chairs on Teresa's front porch. With the evening finally cooling below eighty degrees and the humidity being appreciably lower, sitting outdoors was tolerable again, so long as you had enough mosquito repellent. When Chase crushed his second empty beer can, Sam said, "We gotta switch to water for a while."

"Oh?" Chase's eyebrows emphasized the question.

"Yeah, we've got decisions to make."

"Sam," he said, "don't you think it's a little early in the relationship to be talking about this kind of commitment?"

"Shoot, not that kind of decision. I want nothing to do with your man-parts. Besides, you already committed. I got the paperwork to prove it."

"Alright then. Maybe you can tell me what we have to decide."

"Actually, it's more of a *you* thing than a *we* thing." Sam watched him and wrinkled her lips. She was pretty sure this was the right way to go about it, because it wasn't really her decision to make. "If I could tell you who tried to have you killed, would you want me to?"

He looked at her for several long seconds before leaning

forward in his chair and rubbing the scruff of his chin and jaw. She'd seen him do this before when he was considering something.

"Is this a hypothetical, or do you know who it was?"

"It's not a hypothetical."

Chase cleared his throat, stood, and walked to the porch railing. Seeing an opportunity, Waffles stood up, stretched each of her legs in turn, and hurried to Chase. He scratched behind her ears and patted her on the side. Even though he stood up again, the dog stayed nearby in case he had a change of heart.

"Do I want to know?"

"I couldn't possibly answer that for you. You probably ought to consider what you're going to do about it if you find out."

Chase watched the bats swoop down for unseen bugs before answering. "I guess it depends on who it was."

Sam nodded. "That makes sense. I can tell you this — I think it's probably going to make a real sizable puzzle piece fall into place for your podcast you're working on."

Chase turned to face Sam, seeing if she was messing with him. "You've kind of baited me into it now, haven't you?"

"You were always going to ask. And I was always going to tell you. This keeps you from hem-hawing about it anymore."

"Fine. But for the record, I wasn't hem-hawing. I have no idea what hem-hawing even is. But I might have been dilly-dallying."

Sam stared at him from her rocking chair, her posture hardly having changed since they first came outside after stuffing themselves with the red beans and rice that Teresa had made. But with Conecuh sausage instead of andouille, because Teresa said Conecuh sausage is about a thousand times better. There was a chocolate pecan pie waiting for them. First though, Sam had needed to clear the air with this and fill it with cigarette smoke — *so it's not all that clear* — before moving on to first dessert. Second dessert would be when she had half a slice before bed. If either of her brothers were still here, one of them would say, "A moment on the lips, a lifetime on the hips." And she would hit them. They'd been doing some version of that for most of their lives. It hadn't entirely settled in that they were both gone. Being orphaned was one thing, but being without her brothers — however awful they were most of the time — felt a lot like standing naked in front of the entire world. She'd had a security blanket, but it got stripped away from her.

"Well?"

Sam blinked. "Sorry. Got lost in some thoughts. Ashleigh Wilson."

"Huh."

"What does *huh* mean?"

Chase said, "I thought she wanted to jump in bed with me, not murder me."

"A woman can want both things."

"Really, though?"

Sam nodded.

"That feels kind of weird that somebody I talked to and was friendly with tried to unalive me."

Sam considered that. "You get used to it. I'd venture to guess that most of the people who ever had it out for me were folks I was friendly with at one time or another."

The sun dropped below the horizon, smearing the sky with pinks and oranges that deepened to purples and blues. Sam watched clouds morph from one thing to another while giving Chase time to come to terms with things. She'd heard once that bears were the only other creatures known to sit in a scenic place and take in nature's offerings.

But Chase only got so much time. "What are you going to do about it?"

He shrugged. "What do you think I should do?"

"You're a reporter, aren't you? You have a podcast — scratch that. *We* have a podcast you're working on. What's more compelling than interviewing the girl who tried to put you under the ground and getting a confession from her? All those true-crime moms out there will eat that up."

"To be clear, you want to use me as bait so we get more downloads?"

"Of course I do. Tell me the part where that's a bad idea."

"How about the part where she might kill me?"

Sam waved the idea away. "She ain't gonna do it herself. She's not that kind of girl. But if I'm wrong, I'll finish out the pod for you. How's that?"

"That sounds fair, I guess," he smiled. "Sucks for me, obviously, and the podcast would have a very different atmosphere with you behind the mic. But I can see the appeal."

"You mean I don't have the dulcet tones of Chase Williams?" Sam said in a mocking baritone.

Chase shrugged again. He wasn't going to comment on her sounding like Southern white trash. *Smart man.*

"There is one hitch in this plan," Sam said.

"I'd be surprised if there weren't."

"We can't go trying to get a confession from a suspected killer without involving the police, or they'll skin us alive. I'm not normally one to suggest cooperation with the authorities …"

"Or anyone else," Chase suggested.

Sam ignored the snarky aside. "… but this is too high profile for us to exclude them. I think we'd both get arrested on trumped-up charges of interference with an investigation or obstruction of justice or some such."

"You think you should talk to your lawyer about how to handle it?"

Sam corrected him. "*We* should talk to *our* lawyer, yes. We'll go tomorrow."

"Don't we need to set up an appointment and see if he's available?"

"Nah, he doesn't mind if I pop in."

Chase tilted his head. "That doesn't sound like any lawyer I've ever met."

"One last thing," Sam said. "We're gonna go in there and eat Teresa's chocolate pecan pie, and you're going to rave about it like it's the best thing you've ever eaten in your life because it probably will be, but also because if you don't, her feelings will be hurt."

"What if I don't like it?"

Sam stood and opened the front door, ushering Chase in. "You will."

Chase paused at the threshold. "It felt like there was an unspoken 'or else' in there."

"There definitely was."

CHAPTER 50

THE FLIRTY FACADE

CHASE

Leaning back after turning on the recorder, Chase said, "I'm glad you agreed to sit down with me again. There have been a lot of developments since our last conversation, so I wanted to come back around to you." It sounded so practiced when he said it. It was, obviously. He found it difficult to sound natural when he was being intentional about it.

"Glad to," Ashleigh said, putting a hand on his leg and leaving it there. "I thought I made it clear that I'm available to get together whenever you like."

Chase gave her a small smile in acknowledgment, but didn't want to encourage the flirty facade. In reviewing his notes and the audio from the last session, it definitely seemed to contribute to how things had soured. "If I recall correctly, we left on bad terms. So I appreciate you giving this another shot."

"Of course," she said. "So, did you talk to my dad? I've been walking on eggshells around here ever since we kind of put it together that my mom and Val both disappeared without a trace."

"I did, actually. And I'm not gonna lie—"

"Here it comes — is this the big reveal?" Ashleigh grabbed a throw pillow and put it in her lap.

"I'm afraid not. What I was gonna say is, I don't think it was your dad. I don't think he … you know, did anything." He watched her face carefully to see what it would reveal. She should have been relieved that he didn't think her dad had disappeared her mother and Valerie. Instead, he sat across from someone with the acting skills of a third grader in a school play, but whose face twitched with the motions of figuring out the right expression for the moment.

Or had he been unclear? "I'm not sure what happened to your mom, but if you haven't talked to your dad about it, you probably should. And as for your step — sorry, Valerie — I don't think he was involved with that either."

"So, what, you have one conversation with a guy and you think you know him? You think you know what he's capable of?"

"Definitely not. I only know what people choose to tell me. And there may or may not be any truth in that."

"What's that supposed to mean?"

Chase called an audible. He understood what he was supposed to do. Every good interviewer went into a session with certain objectives and a plan to achieve them, but his gut was telling him that tiptoeing through this conversation in search of an opening wasn't going to get him any results. "Let's say somebody didn't like me going around asking all these questions, and they decide they'd be way better off if I was dead. What do you think the chances are they'd come right out and tell me that?"

"Not very good."

"I agree. But you know what they might do? They might send me a note telling me to get lost. Or go a step further and send me a death threat. Anonymously, of course."

He had kept his voice casual and hypothetical, but Ashleigh grew still and tense regardless, her every nerve tight as a guitar string.

"Maybe they drop that death threat off at my hotel. They're

careful, but not careful enough. Do you know why it's so hard to get away with murder these days?"

She shook her head.

"Everything is tracking us. All the time." Chase patted his shirt pocket. "Your phone. Your car. Traffic cameras. And let's not forget security cameras in businesses. They're so cheap now. Everybody has them. Even that cheap rat-trap of a motel I was staying at." He paused to see if she had anything to say. When she didn't, he decided to separate the truth from fiction. "I know you're the one who left a death threat for me." He didn't.

"Is that right?"

"I checked the footage from the cameras." He hadn't.

"I didn't drop it off!" Her 'gotcha' moment that he was pretty sure she didn't mean to say out loud. Ashleigh flinched, then swore. She dropped the pillow from her lap and stood up, not with a plan but to have something to do. "It was a joke. It's not a big deal."

Chase didn't stand, though he didn't love having to look up at her. "I can't believe that. Not after somebody tried to kill me. Got awfully close, too."

Ashleigh leaned over to the coffee table and pushed the bottom to stop the recorder. She turned, standing directly in front of him. "You can't prove anything." Ashleigh slid herself onto his lap, straddling her legs around his hips and pushing herself snug against him. "But maybe we can come to another understanding anyway." She leaned in close and reached for the top button of his shirt.

Chase stood hastily and dumped Ashleigh in a heap on the floor. "Sorry," he muttered as he clumsily stepped around her, his flight response kicking into high gear and adrenaline surging. Ashleigh jumped to her feet, rubbing the back of her head where she'd hit it on the table. Her cheeks flushed with embarrassment and fury.

Ashleigh hurried to a side table and yanked open a drawer, pulling out a handgun. She whirled and pointed it at Chase. "I didn't really think it would come to this."

His legs went numb and wobbly.

"It won't be hard to make it look life self-defense. I've seen *Gone Girl*."

The front door burst open in the next room, and a half-dozen people stormed through the house, firearms at the ready. Ashleigh turned from Chase to face the intruders. As soon as Ashleigh spotted Chief Richards, she tossed the gun onto the couch and ran to him. She threw her arms around his neck and buried her face against his shoulder. "Thank God you're here. He tried to rape me," she sobbed.

The police chief pried her off of him, gently holding onto her wrist. "Look at me," he said. She met his gaze. "We heard everything." She swung her head back toward Chase. He beamed at her with a broad smile. It was easier to do without the threat of immediate danger.

Chief Richards gently bent Ashleigh's wrist behind her back and clasped a handcuff around it. He motioned to one of the other officers to bring her other arm around. She didn't resist, though she cringed at the sound of the gears tightening. But mostly she stared blankly at the wall in apparent shock and disbelief.

Sam sauntered from the cluster of police officers to where Chase stood apart from the commotion. He didn't understand how an outlaw could be so nonchalant in the presence of so many people who would, in other circumstances, be arresting her.

One of the officers who stood in front of Ashleigh pulled a small card out of his pocket and read, "You have the right to remain silent. Anything you say can and will be used against you in a court of law. You have the right to an attorney. If you cannot afford an attorney, one will be provided for you. Do you understand the rights I have read to you?" He paused for a response, but receiving none, he read a last line. "With these rights in mind, do you wish to speak to me?"

Ashleigh said, "Blow me."

Sam leaned toward Chase and muttered, "Anybody who's not a rich white girl would probably catch a beating for that."

"I can't believe they let you be here."

Sam shrugged. "The whole thing was my idea. They owed me. Besides, I'm a delight, remember?"

Chief Richards turned Ashleigh to face him. The aging police chief said in a soothing voice, "Ash, I've known you your whole life, and I have no idea how I'm going to tell Dr. Wilson about all this, but everything will be a lot easier if you'll tell me what you did with Val. I don't think you did it yourself. You had help or hired someone. We'll find out eventually, but it'll be easier if you tell me early on."

Ashleigh's eyes wandered toward Chase and Sam. Tears sat on the verge of falling. Given her demonstrated lack of acting skills, Chase guessed them to be genuine. Ashleigh had initially cast into doubt everything he believed about his ability to read people. He saw Sam catch Ashleigh's attention and give an almost imperceptible shake of her head. Ashleigh looked down at her feet and said nothing.

An officer walked up to Chase, and all his nerves went back on alert. They were going to be pretty well frayed by the end of the day. "I need the mic."

"Oh, yeah. Okay." He touched the top button of his shirt, recalling his jumpy reaction when Ashleigh had done the same thing a few minutes earlier. He unbuttoned the top two buttons and pulled the tape off his chest, letting the mic fall to his other hand at his waist. He pulled out the transmitter and handed the device to the officer. "How'd I do?" he asked.

"You didn't get the confession we were looking for, but we can work with it." He walked away with no further comment.

"Don't be needy," Sam said, nudging him in the ribs. "It's not a good look."

As a trio of officers led Ashleigh out of the house, Chase let his shoulders slump and said, "I'm gonna need a drink."

CHAPTER 51
NOT BY A LONG SHOT

CHASE

CHASE AND SAM SLID INTO OPPOSITE SIDES OF THE same booth at The Warehouse, where she'd begrudgingly met him six weeks earlier. He had no idea then what he was getting himself into. And he was fairly sure he still didn't know entirely.

He pushed his beer aside for the moment. "I've got a bone to pick with you."

Sam sat back, nonplussed. "Get in line, boss."

"You said I wouldn't be in any danger. She wouldn't do anything herself."

"Yeah," Sam grinned. "Turns out I was wrong about that. Girl had more gumption than I thought. Kind of proud of her, actually."

Chase's jaw fell open. "What is wrong with you?"

"Think about it. That's going to be amazing for the podcast. Would have been even better if she'd shot you though. No offense."

Chase shook his head at her. "Unbelievable." He probably shouldn't have expected some kind of apology, not from Sam.

"Did you get it all on tape?" she asked.

"Yeah. She turned off the recorder at one point, but I had my phone going in my shirt pocket as backup. The sound quality isn't great, but it'll do."

"What happened there in the middle? The sound on the mic got all scratchy."

Chase blushed. "She … uhh …" His voice trailed off, and he gestured, showing how Ashleigh had been sitting on his lap.

"She mounted you like a wild stallion? Is that what you're trying to say? And why are we playing charades?"

"I was going to be more delicate about it."

"Well, if you're going to be the one talking about it to total strangers on the internet, you best get more comfortable saying it out loud than you are now."

She was right. "I will, but I'm not usually part of the story."

"The reporter is always part of the story. They're just the unspoken part that decides what gets told and how."

Sam still continued to surprise him with bits of wisdom that she threw out effortlessly. But something gnawed at him. There was no good way to go about asking her, either. As much because the question itself was uncomfortable to ask, but also because he was genuinely afraid of the answer.

Chase pulled his beer back in front of him and drew lines in the condensation on the glass. Sam watched him obviously delay.

"Sam."

"Chase."

"I have to ask you something."

"Shoot."

He breathed in deeply and exhaled slowly. Ever since he'd come to understand the realities of this little corner of coal country, he was afraid of what the consequences might be of asking one question too many. Yet, here he was about to do that with perhaps the most dangerous person in the whole county, who was also his friend. Right? They were friends? At minimum, they were business partners. And he had to be able to ask her tough questions. Right?

"After the police arrested Ashleigh and read her rights to her, they asked her about who helped her with Valerie Wilson, who she hired."

"I was there. I heard it."

"You caught her attention and shook your head no." It came across more like an accusation than he wanted. But it was an accusation. Or at least, the accusation was coming next.

"True. Are we going to do this piecemeal, or are you going to strap on a pair and ask whatever it is you're trying to get to?"

He'd more than half expected a denial. "Why?"

"Are you recording this conversation?"

"No," Chase answered. "Should I be?"

"Don't matter to me. My answer ain't gonna change either way."

Sam leaned in, looking him intently in the face. "We've talked about this before. The cops aren't on your side. Ever. No matter what. Whether you're wearing cuffs or not. You never, ever talk to the cops. Ever. Do you understand?"

He nodded, but there was a lot more to unpack there.

Sam wasn't done. "And for that girl, if she did have someone help her — especially if she had hired help — talking would be a fatal mistake. It doesn't matter what kind of deal they promise her. She would never make it so far as to see the result. Talking to the cops is a real quick way for her to wind up on the wrong side of the grave." Even after she finished her sentence, she stared at him. "Ask. Ask the next question."

Chase wasn't entirely sure he wanted to ask the next question. In fact, he was entirely sure he didn't want to ask the next question. There were several potential outcomes, and most of them were bad. She could lie to him. She could tell him a truth that he didn't want to hear. Or she could tell him the truth that he wanted to hear, but he wouldn't know if he could believe her.

"Listen," she said. "You remember that last scene from *The Godfather* where Michael tells Kay, this one time she can ask him about his business? And then he lies to her?"

Chase nodded.

She pointed back and forth between the two of them. "This isn't like that. You ask me what you want, and I'll answer your questions, even if you'll find the answers disagreeable. But then you have to live with it."

There was another, and unspoken, half of that last sentence. *You have to live with it because if you tell anyone, especially the cops, then you'll get dropped down a mine shaft where no one will ever find you.* Sam wouldn't say it. She didn't have to.

"Did Ashleigh hire you to kill Valerie Wilson?"

"No."

"Okay."

"We good now?"

"Sure," Chase said. But that wasn't the same as believing it.

For most people, an awkward silence would accumulate that would become increasingly difficult to topple, but not for Sam. She immediately moved on to the next thing. "Good, so what's next?"

"I need to go back to Philadelphia and start organizing all the interviews and figuring out how to tell this story. Then, I have to hire a producer. There's more research to do, probably more interviews too."

"Oh," Sam said. "I kind of thought this was the end of the line and you put it all together now and — poof — you're done."

Chase shook his head. "Not by a long shot. There is *so much* left to do. But this is Friday, so they won't hold the arraignment until Monday. I'll probably fly out a couple of days after that. Should give me plenty of time to get all my affairs in order here."

"You mean like to check out of your hotel?"

"Don't forget I have to return a rental car too!"

"So, just like that, you're outta here, huh?"

He sensed some hurt behind the question. "I'll be back. Like a lot. You're probably going to get tired of my expense reports for flights from Birmingham to Philly."

"Not me. I'm not dealing with the paperwork. It's the accountant you'll have to answer to. And I'll gladly pay if you're going to make us gobs of money on this thing."

Chase held up both hands. "I make no promises."

"You best be making some promises," she said with a smile. "There are white women everywhere dying to hear this story. They just don't know it yet."

CHAPTER 52

THE QUEEN OF WALKER COUNTY

SAM

AFTER ENDURING A MISERABLE THANKSGIVING, MADE only worse by Auburn beating Alabama in the Iron Bowl, it didn't take Sam and Teresa long to decide they had to get out of town for Christmas. They were even quicker to decide on Florida. Everyone Sam knew lived within a fifty-mile radius of her, except the one outlier in Philadelphia. So they landed on weathering the holiday season on the beach. Rodrigo could run the dry cleaners and laundromats for a few weeks.

Aside from escaping reminders everywhere of holidays past, she needed to recharge, figure out what was next. Being a legitimate business owner was all well and good, but it didn't occupy all of her time. It probably could have if she had wanted to work at one of the locations, but she knew she'd be a pretty terrible employee. She'd never in her life worked a nine-to-five and she wouldn't start now.

She stepped out of the back door of the beach house and skipped down the worn wooden steps right onto the sand. The tangy scent of the gulf was still new enough to register every time she walked outside. Like the smell of a thunderstorm in summer, it's something she hoped she never forgot to notice.

Sam spied the chairs and umbrella that Teresa had set up

already. Waffles pounced on something that washed up with a wave, then sniffed at it. Satisfied that it was sufficiently disgusting, she flopped herself down and rolled in it. It would serve her right if it were a jellyfish. Sam groaned. She'd be giving the dog another bath tonight.

Waffles popped up and shook sand in all directions, then shimmied down to the water to lap up a bellyful. Sam trotted the rest of the way, yelling, "Waffles, no! No!" And being ignored. When the dog finally noticed Sam, she wagged her whole hind end in joy before being distracted by seagulls that needed chasing.

Sam sat in the chair beside Teresa. "You can't let her drink the ocean water. She'll get sick."

"Gulf."

Sam squinted in the bright sunlight. "What?"

"This is the Gulf of Mexico, not the ocean."

"Don't get all sassy and technical with me, like you're some local."

"Technically right is still right," Teresa said.

Sam reached over and pinched her arm.

"Ouch! Leave me alone, girl. I'm reading."

Sam dug in the bag beside her chair for her earbuds. Her fingers bumped against the .380 that was zipped into the side pocket. It seemed wildly out of place considering the setting, but she wouldn't let herself get caught unable to attend to a situation, despite having no reason to think one might arise.

Finding the case, she pulled it out and popped in the earpieces. She scrolled through her phone until she found the link Chase had sent her. The first episode of the podcast was out. He had refused to tell her the title or show her the artwork. He wanted it to be a surprise. So when she clicked the link, and the podcast app opened and populated, she immediately smiled. He had done it perfectly — The Queen of Walker County.

Sam listened to his familiar and comfortable voice start

telling her a story she knew intimately, as she grabbed the mallet and a length of PVC-pipe-turned-rod-holder. She walked toward the tideline and pounded the rod holder in the sand.

Realizing she hadn't seen Waffles in a minute, she glanced around and spied her hunkered in the shade of Teresa's chair for a quick siesta. Sam grabbed her fishing rod, baited the hooks with sand fleas, and cast it as far past the surf as she could get it. She slipped the rod into place and pulled out a cigarette and lighter from her belt pack opting for a quick smoke while she listened to Chase set the stage for the disappearance of Valerie Wilson and waited for a fish to take her offering.

When she'd finished her cigarette and the rod gave no indication of having caught anything, Sam retreated to her chair, uncertain that she had the patience for saltwater fishing. She much preferred casting and reeling and casting again. Her mind began to drift.

Ashleigh and Valerie may have been the ill-fated queens of Chase's podcast. They were certainly homecoming queens and beauty queens. But when it came to the things that really mattered, Sam was the undisputed queen of Walker County …

… unless she moved the Florida. The beach was nice, and she hadn't decided what to do with the insurance money from the burned down house yet. She could buy a beach house. It didn't have to be this beach. The tourists would be an atrocity nine months out of the year. There were other beaches in more out-of-the-way places.

A fish grabbed her line and made a run for deeper water. "Oh, no you don't." Chase droned on in her ears, telling the beginnings of his story. Sam hopped out of her chair and shuffled through the sand toward the rod holder.

To her left, Waffles barfed up saltwater and breakfast. The other beachgoers cast scathing looks her way. She gave them the middle finger and enjoyed the appalled reactions of the young mothers trying to cover the eyes of their small children. "A little help here?" she called to Teresa.

"Can't. Reading a book about that girl from the coal company plane crash last year."

Sam said, "That sounds more like *won't* than *can't*."

"Fine then, won't. Not my dog, not my fish."

Sam decided that if she did move to the beach, Teresa had to have her own place. A little one. And not on the water. Maybe she'd still have to work at Dairy Queen, too. That would serve her right.

AUTHOR'S NOTE

For many reasons, *A Good Way to Wind Up Dead* was a difficult book to write, but most of those reasons had little to do with the book itself. This novel took longer to write than any of the prior five novels. That was due in significant part to the second half of 2023 and the entirety 2024 being the busiest periods of my law practice that I've ever experienced. Obviously, that's good in many ways, but when it comes to having the time and mental energy to write a novel, there are certainly some tradeoffs.

As for the novel itself, it was born out of a short story I wrote a few years earlier, *The Murder Tree*, about a family of hitmen in Walker County, Alabama. That should sound familiar by now. Many of the people who read *The Murder Tree* requested more story in that world, and it's one that I too wanted to revisit. I just didn't know when that would be.

After I finished writing *Watch Party*, I was in search of my next novel. With no shortage of ideas in my idea spreadsheet (yes, I understand how nerdy that is), I wrote the beginnings of three different novels to see which one grabbed hold of me. Two of those were fantasy novels set in the same universe as my prior fantasy novels. The third was *A Good Way to Wind Up Dead*.

When I first contemplated *A Good Way to Wind Up Dead*, I knew that it would start minutes after the short story ended, with Sam having just killed her father. But this is not the story I expected to tell. In fact, *A Good Way to Wind Up Dead* ended up as the merging of the ideas for two different novels involving Sam. Chase wasn't supposed to come along until the second book. But my muse and these characters had other things in mind.

I gave in fairly early and allowed the story ideas to meld into one novel in which Sam would be fighting for her life while developing a new friendship and figuring out what she wanted her life to be. Meanwhile, Chase tromped in, unwittingly kicking hornets' nests and upending the accepted order of things.

One of the bigger things that plagued me throughout the writing of *A Good Way to Wind Up Dead* – which was similarly true in *Watch Party* – was that there were two things I didn't know until well into the story. One, whether the missing woman was dead or alive. Two, who was ultimately behind causing her disappearance.

But these things have a way of sorting themselves out. My experience has been that I just keep writing and moving the story toward its resolution point, and as I get to know the characters better, they enable the story to unfold and work out all the kinks. In order to foster that process, I have a spreadsheet for everything along the way, which helps me prevent the kinks from becoming knots.

I hope you enjoyed reading *A Good Way to Wind Up Dead* as much as I enjoyed writing it.

J. W. Judge
December 22, 2024

ABOUT THE AUTHOR

J. W. Judge lives in Birmingham, Alabama, also known as The Magic City. In his day job, he is a lawyer, practicing commercial defense litigation.

A Good Way to Wind Up Dead is his sixth novel. His first three novels are all part of the dark fantasy series The Zauberi Chronicles: *Vulcan Rising* (Book 1), *Seeking Sanctuary* (Book 2), and *Forging Bonds* (Book 3). His fourth novel is a dark fairy tale, *Casual Business with Fairies*. His fifth novel *Watch Party* is a suspense novel where "*Lost* meets Agatha Christie."

If you enjoyed *A Good Way to Wind Up Dead*, sign up for Judge's newsletter for information about other stories he's working on. You can also follow him on social media for updates, developments, and news about other projects. If you'd like to reach out to him by email, please do so at jwj@ jwjudge.com.

Please help others find and enjoy *A Good Way to Wind Up Dead* by leaving a rating and review on Goodreads or your preferred retailer, or by sharing about it on your own social media.

WORKS BY J. W. JUDGE

Fiction

Watch Party

Casual Business with Fairies

Vulcan Rising (The Zauberi Chronicles, Book 1)

Seeking Sanctuary (The Zauberi Chronicles, Book 2)

Forging Bonds (The Zauberi Chronicles, Book 3)

The Murder Tree (A Short Story)

Non-Fiction

Write Your Novel One Day at a Time: How to Write a Novel While Having a Career, a Family, and a Life